Journey to Moscow

The Adventures of Olivia Ozanne

Wendy Robertson

Room To Write

Published in Great Britain
by Room to Write

ISBN 9781495243844 (Trade Paperback)

Published by Room To Write
http://roomtowritepublishing.wordpress.com/

FOR …

…Debora Robertson who loved her time in Russia and revealed to me the unique fascinations of 1990s Moscow. I have to say, though, that she - unlike Caitlin Ozanne - is the perfect daughter.

AND FOR…

…the Room *To Write* team - Gillian Wales and Avril Joy – whose belief and enthusiasm sustained me as I wrote this highly personal story that leapt into my imagination and onto the page as I reflected on my stay in Moscow in those historic days in 1991. In those days the Soviet Union was on the cusp of radical change. We have truly lived through historic times. Now, as the role of Russian evolves even further I hope readers will find entertainment and insight as they take the journey to Moscow with Olivia Ozanne.

CONTENTS

ONE

The key turns in the lock. The big man flicks a finger towards the door, smiling very slightly. 'Ignore it, dear lady. It is only the Aunties. They will invade. It is necessary to tolerate them.' His deep voice is threaded with laughter; his eyes reflect the distant blue - sapphire on the surface - of the Black Sea. His silver grey hair flows down over his shoulders. His white skin brings to my mind horizons glittering with permafrost.

I wriggle my bottom into the chair which has resisted me, its hard carcass moulded to other bodies: other generations.

He moves languidly across the room to the far wall crowded with wide shelves improvised from highly polished wood. Brass-bound keyholes here and there disclose the wardrobe-door origins of these shelves. The shelves filling the wall are crammed with books and battered silver tableware, heaped with old-fashioned ring-files spilling papers, boxes locked against time and eyes; small samovars made for decoration only; pudding-faced clay figures of fish-sellers, and gamblers sitting around a crude clay table. In a clear space of its own stands a yellow horse, whose mane is curled like some little girl's, recently in rag-curlers.

The man's slender hands hover over a white porcelain decanter. He lifts it to fill two fragile cups so full that the liquid bellies up from the rim. Now he walks towards me, elbows out, his eyes on the alcohol as it glitters in the lamplight. 'We will drink,' he says.

I lift the white porcelain cup. 'Bottoms up,' I say. Now an inferno envelops my tongue and inside my mouth the soft flesh feels flayed.

He throws his drink into his throat with an audible gurgle, takes a breath, and then laughs. '*Bottoms up*! What kind of toast is that? Hah! The English obsession with the rear end.'

Now the handle of the door, worn to naked wood in parts, turns gently. Our eyes turn towards it. Silence fills the air like soft gauze and then I jump as an unseen hand rattles the door handle.

The man, whose name is Volodya, shakes his head and thick strands of silver hair leap in the lamplight. 'That is the Grey Auntie, she is a bad lady,' he says. 'We must ignore her. All the time she rattles at my door.' He pours himself another drink. 'It gets very bad between two o'clock and four o'clock in the morning and in the afternoons also.'

I try the liquid fire again and sit back in the

lumpy chair.

'You are thinking how can I stand all this, Mrs. English- Woman Olivia Ozanne? The Brown Auntie and the Grey Auntie in attendance always? In this minuscule flat.' He lingers over his 'I's, his tongue flicking out like that of a snake. His skin is marble white, netted with creases that look like they're marked with a fine lead pencil.

I shake my head. I had noticed seen these Aunties as we came in from the lift. They were lurking on the long corridor which edges the three rooms, linking them together into a single apartment. Each of these old women is small. Neither of them reaches my shoulder in height. And there is indeed a 'brown' one and a 'grey' one, dressed respectively, right down to their over-large felt boots, in brown or grey. One wears a grey beret-type hat from which escapes lank coils of dyed black hair. The other covers her sleek grey hair with a brown scarf, worn bandana style round her fine-boned skull. The eyes of the Brown Auntie are needle sharp, watchful as a squirrel's, but the other old woman, the Grey Auntie, has vacant blue eyes, slightly red at the edges.

The man is talking again. 'I was in England once. Do you know that, Olivia?' He sits on the single hard chair beside the long table that serves as a desk, dining-table, and extra bookshelf all in one.

'You told me you've been in England. You told me that in the cafe´.'

The invitation to the cafe´ had come after a casual conversation about my choice of roses at the crowded flower stall beside the Oktoberskaya station. We stood drinking the thick bitter coffee while standing up in the open air, beside the chest-height circular table. He told me his name was Volodya and I complemented him then on his accent, which is very good. He uses slightly dated colloquialisms. .'It is raining *kets* end *dawgs*'), displaying an extensive old-fashioned vocabulary. My compliment is phoney. In fact his accent is a strange hybrid. I have to suppress a shudder at the equal lacing of American slang and the transatlantic nasal undertones.

Should I be thinking think *over*tones now this long war seems at last to be melting? I read pieces now in *The Guardian* about how we are the children of the Cold War, me and my generation. One day I threw a dish of mashed swede at Kendrick – you know, my husband – for outlining, for the fiftieth time, a scenario where my much dreamed of Russia instigates the final Armageddon and we all frizzle in the final meltdown.

Volodya continues to murmur. 'As I say, Olivia,

6

I was in England once. And in America. And I have had the excellent English people teaching me here in Moscow.' He moves across to the window and peers at the ant-eye windows of the block opposite which is, I know, the mirror-image of the one in which we stand. 'Hah! Space! Over there in England, in America, you have *space*. When I was in England I swam in space like a fish, in echoing voids between rooms, between people. Kilometres of space between men and men, women and women. These very close quarters here, where I share my little flat with two old women must seem jolly strange to you?' He throws himself into a complaining chair and stretches out his long legs, crossing one leg over the other, the much-mended toe of his leather shoe hovering only two inches from my own.

Now don't get me wrong. I am no fool. This man could murder me. Slit my throat, say. Or spike my drink and roll me into the canal, with a little assistance from the Brown Auntie. Perhaps even the Grey Auntie also, because this man is not young, sixty if he's a day, and slender as a wand.

Well, to tell you the truth I'm no lightweight myself. I can hear the ponderous echo of Kendrick's voice, telling me to *cut out the starch*, to *take some exercise*, to *watch where* I go and *not speak to strangers*. However it is a fact that apart from this tall man and the dotty monochrome aunties, not a soul in this world knows that I'm here in this flat - three floors up in this grey apartment block, in the heart of what that dithery actor called *the Evil Empire*. Or was that the second-hand car salesman?

My daughter Caitlin has actually met some of those world leaders. I reflect on this and she scolds me. 'Really, Mother, they're hardly the giants of good and evil that inspire one's childlike sense of power in the world, you know!' I suppose she would know. But she will insist on lecturing me. All the time. She's more than a little like her father Kendrick to be honest. I suppose if she's like Kendrick she must be like my mother, as Kendrick and my mother two are so alike. Now that's a thought.

Caitlin goes on at me. 'They're not the flesh-eating giant at the top of the beanstalk, Mother. They're just somebody's uncle or factory manager, or head teacher, or caretaker. Plumped up. Jumped up—'

'Except for Stalin of course,' I interrupt quite gently. She really does not like being stopped in full flow.

'Now there you do have a figure for your nightmares, Mother. A gigantic evil creature who has

8

left dark stains on the Russian soul.'

She has a way with words, Caitlin. Always did. I'm so pleased that she's making a living out of it. She's never looked back since she wrote about the little green parrot with the bright eye. She was five, then.

She goes on about him a lot. Stalin. 'That man even left his evil stains on the landscape, Ma. Just look at those obscene vertical villages. Villages! And the Ring Road.'

It's true. That road is truly monstrous, a behemoth of a road system, cutting right through the heart, the centre of this city. To build it they must have cleared out the avenues and streets that reassured individuals of the human scale of things. The roads are huge. Scampering across them, you feel like ants.

She goes on. 'No by-your-leave here like at home, Ma. No planning permission! Clear out the old roads. Just like the agricultural planning that left millions of dead. And then there were thos untidy writers and artists and politicians. They ended up in asylums for thinking wrong thoughts.'

Stalin, she asserts, tidied people away into the wilderness; he tidies away people or places that did not fit in with his vision. He had this great respect for the sanitising property of blood.

9

'God save me from tidy people.' Caitlin says this often, with feeling.

I'm a bit of a tidy-Betty myself, but I don't take this personally - even though that is how it is meant. Caitlin's small apartment here in Moscow is kept elegantly, scrupulously clean by Katya, the housekeeper with whom Caitlin carries on her own icily smiling Cold War.

Oddly enough Caitlin's room at home, even when she was tiny, was always volcanically untidy. I struggled with this in polite despair. And then at the age of eight she forbade me entry to her room, so, with some relief I took her at her word and never ventured inside again. When Kendrick and I parted I left that room as it was for the house clearance people. (I was at a conference in Heidelberg at the time, so I didn't see their faces as they opened her door.)

Kendrick declared that it was just another example of my incompetence, my irresponsibility. If I could speak Russian I would tell poor long-suffering Katya about eight year old girl's room.

So you can see that Caitlin's loathing of compulsively tidy people is a statement from the heart.

I have to believe Caitlin about all that Stalin stuff. She's the expert: respected all over Europe for her expertise; quoted in other people's articles, as well as writing her own. Books too, these days. She did a signing, once, at Hatchards on Piccadilly. She looked so beautiful among her crowd of eager readers that I dare not approach her, so I fled, my own copy (dutifully bought), clutched in my hand.

*

So, here in this Volodya's flat Caitlin is still very much on my mind. I parted company with my daughter, at ten o'clock this morning, by the plump, glittering towers of the Kremlin. She protested very loudly and clearly at my desire to go off on my own. But she knows I've always been proud of finding my way round cities. Think of Amsterdam!

So Caitlin didn't get her way, didn't keep me tethered at her side like some three-year-old. (I've counted kids' heads myself in a dozen foreign cities, in the days when you didn't need a diploma to take kids on a trip. But I don't want my head counted. Not at my age. No thank you.)

Now in Voldya's room, in this battered apartment that he shares with two batty old ladies, I look at his clock: a quaint nineteenth-century confection, quashed beside a broken-backed file which is spilling paper.

Oh dear, It's coming up to three o'clock. Caitlin'll be waiting for me now beside those plump glittering Kremlin towers. Piotr, her driver, will be beside her, smooth in his leather jerkin, tapping his hand lightly on the steering wheel, keeping time with pirated western pop music on his black-market stereo. Caitlin says all the drivers are KGB or ex-KGB. 'Nice enough guys though,' she says.

Here in the flat I stand up, smoothing down my skirt. 'I have to go, Volodya. I am an hour late for an appointment with—'

'Your daughter, the very clever person. I read her articles, Olivia. I hear her once, when they interview her on the BBC World Service. She has good knowledge but, I think, no deep heart.' He unwinds himself from his chair. 'We will continue the conversation,' he says with quiet certainty. 'I will see you at the flower stall. Noon tomorrow. Now, we will get you a taxi.' He leads me purposefully through the dusty streets. In Gertsener Street we have to clamber by a great drain, half the height of a man, which is lying above the ground. 'What's this?' I gasp, breathing in very deeply to squeeze by.

He shrugs. 'A bureaucrat would say the utilities pipe was to be buried, dug into the ground. Then there would be no money to pay for the diggers. Or perhaps, in the bureaucrat's notebook, on his American computer, he has a note to say that this job is done and paid for, the pipes have been buried deep in the ground and covered with a smooth pavement. So it must be, though in reality we clamber over it every day.'

He strikes out into the humming traffic and puts up a hand. A car, not visibly a taxi, draws to a stop. A young man with the face of a Botticelli angel grins up at me from his window. He is wearing an unlikely electric blue tracksuit.

'The Kremlin!' I say in an over-loud teacher's voice. I developed that voice when, as a girl, too young to cope, I had to corral leather-clad cigarette-smoking fifteen-year-olds in my art class. Once time a boy painted a picture all black. Every square inch of it. 'What is it?' I said. 'Black,' he said.

The Botticelli boy is staring at me. His pupils are dilated. I lift my head and speak even louder. 'I wish to go to the Kremlin.'

The boy laughs loudly, leans over and thrusts the door open. Volodya stands back for a second, hesitates, and then jumps in beside me. 'I will come with you. Deliver you to your daughter's hands.'

I push at him. 'No, there's no need. I'm not a parcel.'

He folds his arms and avoids my gaze. 'I will come. I will come.'

The car shudders forward as the driver clanks the car into gear. We set off on an erratic journey through the streets, the driver talking away in this language which is supposed to express melancholy, but which always to me seems to have a soldier's laughter as an undertone. He is gesticulating as he talks, first one hand off the wheel, then the other. Sometimes both. I'm getting tense now. Volodya starts talking to the driver in a clipped voice that seethes with irritation.

We drive round a corner into a street whose eighteenth-century houses seemed to have escaped Stalin's housewifely architectural attentions. An old woman is wandering into the centre of the road. The driver turns the wheel.

'Christ!' I yelp, finally clutching Volodya's arm. 'He's aiming the car at her. Get me out of this car. Get me out!' The car swerves past the old woman, missing her by inches. Suddenly Volodya is talking very loudly and quickly indeed and the driver is laughing. I listen to the blast and counter-blast of barter.

Now Volodya is shouting. Very loud.

The car shrieks to a stop. I reach for the door handle. Volodya puts his hand on mine. 'Do you have two dollars, Olivia?'

'I have roubles.'

'No, dollars. It must be *dollars*. This madman tells me he will only stop the car for hard money. Hard currency. I told him you would have some. Dollars.'

I nod, and scrabble in my bag, thrusting the notes into his hand. He pays the driver who laughs uproariously, his eyes sparkling with glee. We scramble out of the car and watch it roar away. I breathe out. 'That's the first time I've had to bribe a taxi-driver to stop. This city is full of firsts.'

'He's a crazy man,' he says softly. 'Drunk perhaps. Or something. He takes something today. Perhaps drugs. Your daughter writes a good piece about it in her paper. Drugs. Taxi drivers and the Mafia. Good copy, I think they call it. Much good copy in Moscow these days, huh? We all consume each other.' He puts his arm through mine, an almost feminine, comforting gesture. 'Now, in ten minutes we walk to the Kremlin from here.'

Of course when I get there Caitlin is not speaking to me. You would think she'd grown out of that. She was about three years old when she first treated me to that special form of punishment. Something had not suited her one day when we were pottering about in a big store: I was walking too slowly, or had not answered an urgent query. She turned her back on me in silence and would not respond to any plea to move. The punishment was amplified when she later lost herself twice, and had to be rescued from the same security man, to whom she was talking very earnestly, not a tear in sight. I could hear her saying 'I am not very happy. . . .' The second time I collected her he gave me what my mother would have called *an old-fashioned look*.

Now, she is here beside me in the back of the car, sitting bold and upright, rattling away at that portable machine of hers: a nice toy. And she sighs without speaking, exhibiting a very public restraint, just a little more patient now than when she was three. My own mother used to do this thing, this patient sigh. I learned very early to fear it, to run and hide, or face the wall so I could pretend that I couldn't see her striding towards me, bent on her very adult vengeance. She once made me sit in a bath of cold water for two hours, for placing my fork on the wrong side of my plate.

Now, to dilute Caitlin's restrained and silent anger, I focus on her driver Piotr's glossy brown locks as they snake down over his brown leather collar.

A whole generation of time has galloped by since yesterday, when Piotr drove me to Caitlin's flat from

16

the airport. My first, hungry sight of Moscow was from the dusty windows of this Volvo. The murky landscape was infused with that dun shade that clothes and bedding get when the original colours have leeched into each other. You know, when you bung your whites in with your coloureds for a year or so? It's such a temptation with these modern machines, don't you think? The all-in daily wash.

My mother used to put her washing in neat piles: whites, coloureds and darks, each bubbled through their own water: washed, swished, wrung, rinsed and finally wrung again and hung.

I've never done that for many years. I see that here in Moscow Caitlin's housekeeper Katya does the washing just like my mother, despite the constraints of Caitlin's tiny apartment and the sophistication of Caitlin's all-singing, all-dancing, catalogue-bought German washing machine. Katya's whites are frosty white all right: Siberian white.

Outside the car window the dust is swirling, moving and re-piling itself with anarchistic fervour. The car bounces across holes in the road. Flat-back trucks trundle by. Piotr steerd round some deep ruts. 'And here, Madam Ozanne is a particularly large crack!' He does not say much in English but he does have terms for road conditions and shopping off to a tee.

A shining Mercedes limousine draws past to our right, trailing behind a small black car follows like a glossy black bridesmaid. Caitlin lifts her eyes from her laptop and peers out with a journalist's curiosity. 'Dutch Ambassador,' she says briefly.

We move onto the centre lane and follow the Merc. Caitlin she tells me that a year or so back, - even less - this wouldn't have been allowed. The centre track was strictly for the official limos. I relax at her softer tone and watch as she puts her machine away. 'Who was he, mother?' she says. 'That man who came with you to the Kremlin?' she says.

How carefully she has restrained herself, holding back that burning question to this point! I admire that quality with some reluctance. Likes things under control, does Caitlin.

'Just a man that I met,' I say, with what I hope is the right tone of disinterested humility.

She explodes at this. 'You don't *just meet* a man here, mother. Nothing happens *'just by accident'* in Moscow in 1991.'

'Well it *did*. I was trying to buy some roses for you and he helped me.'

She turns her head, peering round me. 'Roses? Where did they get to?'

'I left them at his apartment.'

'His *apartment?*' The beautiful voice which usually reverberates with such intelligent restraint is growling with suppressed rage. 'You went to his apartment? Ma! What did I tell you? Be careful! Don't you get into one of your scrapes here. Me For God's sake. Promise?'

I shrug now and become the mother again, retrieving this hurtling role-reversal. 'I can't think what you're talking about, Caitlin. I know nothing about *scrapes.*'

'What about Amsterdam? And Vienna?'

I peer out of the window. 'Too much imagination, darling,' I say very crisply. 'That was always your problem. Even in infant school. That nice Miss Smithson said so, remember? That day you wet your knickers and she had to bring you home?'

I can feel rather than hear her draw a very sharp breath beside me.

'Now where is that market you were telling me about?' I relish the smoothness of my tone.

We go first to Caitlin's office so she can shoot her deathless prose down the line. I meet Elizabeth, Caitlin's assistant who speaks perfect English and has a closed but rather sweet face. She's sitting with a pile of Western papers, cutting out news clippings. She shakes my hand very warmly, bringing her face closer than an English woman would with a stranger. She smiles her pleasure at meeting the mother of the esteemed Caitlin Ozanne. Then Caitlin introduces me to Roger Slett-Smith who's here on some kind of post-university work experience. He has a bright, eager face, sharp with watchfulness and ambition, only superficially softened by the John Lennon glasses.

The telephone rings and Caitlin picks it up. She embarks on a stream of talk and makes this waving gesture to Piotr her driver.

He pulls on his black leather gloves and beams across at me. 'Now, the market, Mrs. Ozanne.'

Now, as he said, we go on to the market. He is to be my shopping adviser and bag carrier. Unofficially Piotr is my minder; I listened as he was briefed in rapid Russian by Caitlin to make sure I do not escape again. From her severe tone she was obviously telling him to put on my reins if I am any trouble. Or handcuffs.

If Piotr is ex-KGB, as Caitlin claims, he probably has handcuffs in his pocket anyway. Very convenient. They say handcuffs are quite popular now, back at home in Palatine Close, the neat little cul-de-sac where I finally washed up after the debacle with Kendrick. Sex games they call them these days.

Harmless fun, apparently.

The market herein Moscow is large, but crowded. I find myself dodging between heaps of glistening fruit. There seem to be few shortages here. I think briefly about all those queues of people with hungry, haunted faces - the ones I've been looking at on television at hone for months now.

Janey, my big friend, my bosom buddy, tried her best to persuade me not to come. She looked at me over her owl-like glasses. 'You're looking at three weeks' starvation rather than three weeks' holiday. Olly! You must be mad.'

She was lolling back on my beat-up chaise-longue, glass in hand, pontificating in her usual West country drawl. I was sitting in the peacock cane chair, the only other piece of furniture in my very tidy room. Kendrick had filched the rest of our stuff to set up home with his primary school teacher. (Don't get me wrong. I've nothing against primary school teachers. I was one myself once, a long, long time ago.)

Anyway, in the years since I divorced Kendrick I've never been tempted to replace any of those old pieces, any more than I've been tempted by another husband. Other *men*, yes. Currently I am involved with Lee Compton, a man I used to work with. Lee is quite charming over dinner and satisfyingly energetic in bed.

Fitness is his thing. We had an intriguing time in Vienna once, when we had that run-in with those fascists in the Judenplatz. His fitness came in handy there. But I know I wouldn't have Lee in the house permanently. I rather like my life to be uncluttered. It makes anything seem possible.

Here in the Moscow market, the traders are well wrapped up against the cold, their faces an international poem, evoking in turn countries as far apart as China and Finland.

Some of them tout for business in English. 'Here, madam, very tasty!' The trader knows I am English, of course. My own face, for a fleeting second, is part of the international poem and not difficult to read.

Now other traders encourage us to taste peaches and plums, tomatoes and watermelons. At one stall, wild mushrooms, biscuit-coloured and random shaped, strut their dementia from two large boxes. As I say, it seems there is no shortage in this market.

Piotr busies himself questioning the traders closely on the regional origin of the fruit: Chernobyl is still casting its long shadow here in Moscow. We consult Caitlin's carefully typed list, and buy big beef tomatoes, earthy misshapen carrots, two pounds of plums and four shiny purple aubergines. Then, on a quick impulse, I fill my arms with stately white and pink gladioli with speckled trumpets.

I pay in roubles, the price is ridiculously cheap to me. Piotr shakes his head. 'One week's wages for a worker,' he says, holding up the laden basket.

Then we make our way to the Butcher's Market: an echoing tiled cathedral of a building, dripping with blood; a symphony in peeling paint. Here, there are customers, male and female, in hats and smooth coats, handing over hard currency, dollars and pounds stirling - for slabs of meat. I view these people closely for my notebook later. Caitlin has told me that the only people in Moscow with hard currency are the Black Market men and the foreigners. She would have known which were which in here, but I can't really tell.

The butchers in bloody aprons work at long counters built of cracked marble slabs which have seen better days. There is no refrigeration. These burly men stand shoulder to shoulder, pushing their meat at us.

Obeying the instruction on Caitlin's typed note, we buy a lump of red meat (veal of questionable cut), and a chicken with very long legs. As Piotr stuffs the roughly packed parcel into the second basket I am revolted by the smell of decaying blood and decide to return to my long abandoned vegetarianism for the duration of my stay.

Finally we reach the Dairy Hall. Here again we are greeted with the same peeling green paint, the battered marble slabs and the cracked tiles: all magnificent once: art *nouveau* that has seen better days.

The women in the Dairy Hall have broad faces: a peasant look as old as the marble itself .They are muffled with the over-layered clothes of those accustomed to poverty or living close to its very edge. They remind me of those women at home, the bag-ladies in the centres of English towns, who move slowly like tortoises, carrying their homes on their backs. I once saw one stand, with her legs apart peeing in the street.

One of these market women reties her headscarf and serves us a single delicate slice of cheese, then another, then another. All the cheeses are mild, almost indistinct: very pleasant on the tongue. Then with swollen hands and purple sausage fingers she pushes forward screw-topped jars of cream and sour cream. We buy the latter, as instructed by the presence of Caitlin, made manifest in the typed list.

We make our way back to the car, passing a line of people who stand, blind eyed, with single items to sell. A man holds up a pair of shoes - brogues with uppers gleaming like conkers and worn soles. A young boy pulls a fur cap out of his capacious anorak and thrusts it under my nose. A woman holds out two cheap plastic dolls, the kind I was given for Christmas in the Fifties. But these dolls are new, with an Asiatic cast to their features.

And then, at the very end of the line an old woman holds up a red silk dress heavy with twinkling bugle beads, made garish by the contrast with her own clothes, which are an unrelieved brown.

I am just handing over packages to Piotr, who is stowing the shopping in the boot of the Volvo with a domesticated neatness when the hair on the back of my head prickles.

I turn around. *Unrelieved brown.* The woman holding the red silk dress is the Brown Auntie, the old woman I passed in the hall this morning, at the apartment of the man called Volodya.

I race back to the entrance to the Dairy Hall. Piotr sets off after me. I am determined talk to the Brown Auntie. I will buy the dress, find out just where I spent my morning, and find out more about the man called Volodya.

But when I get there the old woman has gone. Her place has been taken by yet another young man who offers me a black telephone with, Piotr now tells me, documentation to prove it was used in the Lubianka prison in the Sixties.

*

Caitlin is giving a dinner party tonight, so Piotr has
instructions to leave me at the Tretyakov Gallery for
an hour, to keep me out of the way while he takes the
groceries back to Katya and her friend Linia from
Turkestan. They are to concoct a feast, following
another set of Caitlin'styped instructions to the very
letter.

On the way to the gallery Piotr takes me to see
the fallen statues of Lenin, Stalin and other Soviet
heroes. Children are clambering over huge stone
heads, stepping on noses or on the sharp edge of lips,
chiselled competently in times of Soviet realist
certainty, totalitarian confidence. I'm so glad that my
mate Janey's not here. She'd have said something like
'so are the mighty fallen', as though it were a brand
new observation.

Fallen and viewed sideways, Lenin's face still
exudes his solid serenity, his forceful placidity, his
engineered, glacial potency. I squint down at him to
make my view hazy, and for a second I can see
Kendrick's face, hear his voice saying icily, 'Olivia *do*
slow down! You have this house like a raging inferno
with your schemes and pranks.'

Well, I expect Kendrick has a nice calm life now
with his primary teacher doll wife and her doll

26

children, in their doll's house in their toy-town street. The wildest thing those two will ever do is make violent and very short-lived love on my own black leather sofa, Kendrick jabbing into her as though she were just another leather cushion.

Come to think of it, it was the only thing that turned him on: that leather sofa. He'd have made love to King Kong, to Darth Vader, to Mrs. Thatcher, on its leather lap, and believed himself in heaven.

Like all anal-retentive bureaucrats Kendrick likes things neatly in their pigeonholes. And the black leather sofa was his pigeonhole for sex. I couldn't bear to sit on it during the day. Its very creaks made me shudder. The scent of it made me hear the echo his wild neighing laugh as he reached his climax and the rasp of the leather as he rolled away. One time when he was mid-neigh I moved my shoulder and he clattered right off the sofa and indulged in one of his more entertaining bouts of post-coital rage.

When I was young I used to like leather, but since I married Kendrick I've never worn a leather jacket, even when they were the height of fashion. Once I was sick on the spot when I found myself beside a rack of leather coats in Peter Jones, and that particular aroma hit my nose. The girl assistants were very kind to me in a frosty way, but I've never been back to that shop from that day to this. You wouldn't, would you?

When Kendrick left me, he said I'd never been responsive to his . . . he paused then . . . *needs*. Well the future doll-wife had been responsive all right, in the washroom attached to his office where he had a leather chair for that especial purpose. And down murky back lanes on the leather back-seat of his Mercedes. It seems that somewhere on that leather they had managed to make babies. Perhaps she wore leather knickers for the occasion.

I wonder if those children are anything like my daughter. Caitlin favours her father after all.

When we finally arrive at the Tretyakov, Piotr shepherds me like a fussy nurse through the large glass doors, shows me how to leave my cloak in the extensive cloakroom. Then he pays the very cheap entrance fee to the special exhibition called *Twilight of the Czars*.

Last night I was treated to a lecture from Caitlin about the mould-breaking nature of this exhibition, the first time Russians themselves had been allowed to see this bit of their own history. One impact of *glasnost* is getting to know your own history I suppose.

When you think of it the same thing happens to us every time documents pour out of our government after the thirty-year deadline. Our leading clique keeps things from us too, protecting themselves and their forebears.

What about those spies! How long did it take us to find out that in the Fifties and Sixties very eminent, top-drawer people, individuals who were very much *one of us*, were spying for the Russians. Playing boys' games in more ways than one, I suppose.

One could argue that it's not possible to see the truth of this country or any other that I've visited; especially on these jaunts when there's nobody with me to reflect on what I see, or correct my inevitable misapprehensions.

But I like that, don't you see? It's very good to be the stranger and be alone. When you're alone you see the surface of things and this surface can be wild and improbable and very surreal. And on that surface you can invent your own mystery, your own kind of truth. This is not the truth of guidebooks but . . .

When I try to explain all this to my Caitlin, her eyes darken and her lips twist with visible pain at my misguided cupidity.

I can still see her face that time she came to rescue me from that hospital in Amsterdam. And didn't she scowl that old frustrated scowl (a shade of the child Caitlin) when, a day later, I insisted on going on to my seminar to meet my speaking commitment? I only just prevented her from coming with me on the train right to the college for my lecture. That would have blighted my experience, stopped me playing the part of respected writer and set me up, to her satisfaction, as 'the mother of that star journalist', Caitlin Ozanne.'

Here at the Tretyakov it seems that all the visitors except me are Russian. This intricate and intriguing debris of Imperial life is being pored over by workers in overalls and cleaners in aprons, as well as students, neatly dressed teachers and clerks.

It says something about me, my own country, that I even notice such a thing here. At home, museums remain the abode of the earnest, the culturally ambitious, and the educated, with white rather than blue collars on their shirts.

Me, I've always loved museums; always sensing the objects manically blurting their story to me across the years. I count it as the greatest success of my teaching career that I made just a handful of children experience the way in which material objects will tell you their story.

That is, if you listen.

Here at the Tretyakov a hum of interest and appreciation is buzzing its way through the galleries.

An old man peers closer and closer at a display case until his nose is on the glass. A female attendant comes and speaks to him sharply. He draws back, cringing, his demeanour faintly tinged with an unforgotten fear. A parent is rattling away at two children of junior school age – like the first class I ever taught on teaching practice: full-faced, bright-eyed and still prepared to believe.

An old woman with a wool scarf tied round her head is crying. And now I'm overwhelmed with love for them all and tears come to my own eyes.

I blow my nose and focus on the pictures and the items themselves that are, if anything, mundane: family photographs; women and children of outstanding beauty, all in white; a glamorous boy-child clasped in the arms of a sailor.

I look at the furrowed planes of the sailor's face. Is this the one who ran away when things started to hot up? Or is it the one who was arrested for defending his young charge, then casually - very finally - shot.

The language beneath the pictures has no meaning for me. This is what it must be like this to be dyslexic: a crucial code denied to you, so that you're driven to look around and make use of other clues. I admit that one can make very profound mistakes in this way. On the other hand perhaps I see greater truths.

Except for the forbidding images of their very last days these members of the Imperial Family, including the mother and father, have the blank beauty of children: they are all playing soldiers, playing sailors, playing houses, playing picnics, playing churches, with the world around them exploding and humble, dark people creeping in from the edge.

The father is too familiar to the English eye: cousin to our own King George, whom my mother used to call *the Old King*. This one might be his twin. I read, once, of the guilt felt in upper echelons in England, at letting this shining family slump into their own blood in some far distant cellar. I read in another place as well that their cook and the doctor were shot with them. How grand is that? Having a cook and a doctor in jail with you to the end. Although perhaps they were friends by then? *Comrades?*

A hand touches my elbow. I come out of my fog and swing round suddenly full of fear. 'Volodya! How . . . ?'

He is smiling down at me with delight. 'You mention the exhibition. I pray to myself you are still here. And I run.'

I shake my head. 'But you just left me.'

32

'There was something I wished to say, but ...'
Now his hand is on my elbow and he is guiding me down the stairs. He retrieves my coat from the cloakroom and, after watching me button it up, he tucks a scrap of paper in my pocket. 'My number. I knew I'd left you without my telephone number. There are no telephone books in Moscow. If you need someone's number, they have to give it to you. Some time, I think, you will need mine.'

He puts his arm through mine, then, and marches me out into the September sunshine.

'Where are we going?'

'To the park.' His arm is half hugging, half guiding me. We dart across the dual carriageway, dodging flat-back trucks and dusty cars. The grandiose colonnade of Gorky Park rises before us and attenuated old-fashioned pop music drifts out tinnily towards us from the loudspeakers.

I allow myself to be dragged into the park, and walk slowly with Volodya down the paths, through the cyclists and past the football game. The edges of the path are furry, tufted and carelessly kept: a bed of tall, rangy marigolds is under attack from a hundred red admiral butterflies.

Finally we arrive at a little arena with a circle of seats before a battered piece of staging.

Volodya stands still and I turn and lean my back against an advertising hoarding. He puts a hand either side of my head and kisses me, closed mouthed. His lips are soft as a peeled grape and he smells of some kind of cologne: an old-fashioned smell which reminds me of my father. His lips wander across to my cheekbones and I am suddenly embarrassed.

The last time I *necked* with someone like this in public I was fourteen. That time all around us younger children were playing with hula-hoops; through a nearby window I could hear Jimmy Young, full cheeked and as yet unreconstructed, singing *Unchained Melody*.

Now I struggle out from under the circle of this man's arms. Easy Meat. That's what I am. I move to make clear space between us. 'What is it Volodya?'

He leans up against the wall beside me and lights a cigarette. 'I came to tell you I was looking forward to seeing you tomorrow at the flower stall.' He puts the cigarette to his lips. 'But I came also to tell you that if you do come to the flower stall, it will be *bed*, Olivia Ozanne. Bed, bed and more bed. Love.' He narrows his eyes to see me better through the veil of smoke and I laugh.

I cannot stop smiling as we walk back along the paths. I smile all the way back out of the park and laugh into Piotr's face.

Piotr hands me into the Volvo, having growled menacingly at Volodya who is grinning through the ornate iron gates of the museum. 'Who is that Russian, madam?' he spits out the word *Russian* like an expletive.

'He thinks he's Humphrey Bogart, Piotr. Don't worry about him.'

Piotr pushes the protesting Volvo into gear and presses his horn hard to clear a way into the second of the four lanes on this side of the great ring-road.

I sit back and wonder about this road before Stalin got his claws into it; whether the Imperial carriage passed this way with its cargo of immaculate moths in fluttering white. I also wonder just what Piotr will report back to Caitlin. But I suppose for Piotr, spying is an informed instinct impossible to stifle. We will see.

And still, still, I smile, as the car bumps over the holes in the road and swerves to miss a prostrate body - a Vodka drunk perhaps - lying in the middle of the road.

TWO

I am sitting on my bed in my capsule of a room, staring at my image in the mirror, wondering what it is the man called Volodya sees. Sharp face. Rough hair. Elegant nose. Crooked teeth and strong jaw. Hardly beautiful. Never, ever beautiful.

Once, at college, my best friend and I were in love with the same man: a muscular Australian who had turned up one night at one of the rare college dances. He squired us both around for months. No *sleeping-with*, you understand. You didn't *sleep-with* in those days. Well, *we* didn't.

One night we were sitting toasting bread on the coal fire in my friend's college room. The Australian sat back and surveyed us fondly, his beautiful blue eyes moving from one to the other. 'I love you both,' he had said grandly. 'You, Julia, for your body, and you, Olivia, for your brains.'

Later, having been liberated by Germaine Geer, I was to reflect how crassly sexist this was, how politically out-of- the-window. But at the time I was entranced. I saw the Australian's point of view. Didn't I love Julia myself, for her narrow-faced radiance, her glossy hair in its abundant pony tail? Hadn't she somehow made me breathe out, after an over-earnest childhood endured in a home cold with my mother's despair? Brains were easy, compared with the touch-paper delight of Julia's personality.

Now here in the elegant narrow constriction of Caitlin's Moscow flat (standard for most foreign journalists) I breathe in the cooking smells that are creeping under my bedroom door: an enticing mixture of coriander and dill, purple basil and turmeric.

Out there, voices are raised in dispute. I can hear Caitlin being firm but fair, like a good mother, and the dispute fades. I feel sympathy for the maid Katya who has to come to terms with the fact that cleaning and occasional cooking for a Westerner pays infinitely better than being a teacher of small children, the job for which she had been rigorously trained in the Soviet fashion.

We have both been teachers. We have that in common, Katya and I. But I don't think she really knows that.

When I got in from my museum jaunt Katya had shoo'd me out of the tiny kitchen as though I were a small child, cross at me for peering into her oven. Caitlin, annoyed at being upstaged by her staff, actually grasped my arm and steered me out of the

37

kitchen, and told me, in the voice of a good mother, to *go and put my feet up*, rest before the party.

I hear Caitlin running her bath and feel glad for Katya and her friend Linia, glad that they can have a breathing space now, without their employer crowding them, souring their sauces.

I have to admit that I don't like Caitlin, don't really like her at all - any more than I liked my mother.

It was a great relief for me when I realised that - though we were genetically alike, the architecture of our flesh and bones sharing similar structures - I did not have to be like my mother. That there was no need to panic about the tests of endurance and cruelty that she set me. As an adult I can forgive her, rationalise her actions through the abstraction of academic study of the pathology of childhood. This has helped me to see that her cruelties were unforced if not actually unintentional.

The tragedy is that I cannot forgive her is that enduring that childhood has stopped me properly loving my own daughter. And even as a baby Caitlin knew this.

Still, I have to remind myself that without Caitlin I wouldn't be here in this Russia, which is already filling my senses, as I knew it would. For so long I have wanted to be here in this strange country:

a country which has been with me all of my life, alongside my world, like a half-seen winter shadow.

I suppose I know as much about Russia as anybody else of my generation: the intricate stories of Chekov, grand historical sweeps of Tolstoy and the black worldview of Dostoyevsky were the richest of food for my starved childhood imagination. 'Idiot' was an epithet my mother frequently spat at me, so I leapt on Dostoyevsky's story of that name with frantic relief. My mother's repeated wartime fantasy with the notion of *'Russkis with snow on their boots standing fast in Stalingrad'* has echoed and reechoed in my mind for nearly half a century, reduced now: distilled to a joke.

And then there has been 'Uncle Joe' Stalin. Then, alongside *The Female Eunuch*, live the literary images of the romantic Lara, of the Gulags, of the varied nightmares of Siberian exile and torture in the Lubianka portrayed in popular fiction. It's as though it's been possible for the adventure fantasy to neutralise the visions of cruelty and allow us to absorb a sense of this country into our souls.

Then, with the Fifties and Sixties came the Cold War: the build-up of bile, the paranoid fear of infiltration and engulfment, which was somehow healed in my young mind by Marxist ideals and notions of peace and love. Then, when I was still consciously political, like many young people then, I toyed with the notion of Marxism as a grand scheme for justice and equality, only to abandon it as the Soviet Russians marched into Budapest. I feel sure that the Russians were devastated at my defection.

But we knew we were safe, didn't we? Wasn't Russia this great hulking backward continent, after all? Like the idiot-son? Then one day we were catapulted out of our provincial patronage, into the shock of equality as Sputnik twinkled in our skies, intensifying the balance of fear and respect which was the high-octane fuel of the Cold War.

'Mother! Bathroom's clear.' Caitlin's face pops round the door like an elegant, stray balloon. Her eyes bulge slightly as she notes my naked state. 'Really, Mother! Remember how small this flat is! You might have a modicum of decency.'

I pull my dressing gown up over my chest, and meet her gaze calmly, even bravely. *Modicum of decency.* That was one of Kendrick's favourite phrases. He started to use it on me like a spare flail only a few months after we were married. It only took him those few months to realise that I wasn't the mild little primary teacher he had proposed to in the cinema one night, after watching Paul Newman flashing his big blue eyes in a forgotten film called *On the Terrace*. I see now that Mr. Newman's selling a rather pretentious brand of pickle in his old age. How glamour dies.

There is a red spot on each of Caitlin's beautiful cheeks. 'It's the staff, Mother! Katya might come in any second. I told you I stored the spare plates under that bed. It would embarrass her, finding you like this.'

I stand up and pull on my gown, tying it tightly round my waist. 'I hear you,' I say, picking up my toilet bag and towel. I peer out of the window, down at the littered square which stands at the centre of the rearing blocks of flats built specially for foreigners in the 1970s, and the tram terminus beyond. 'How you can live here without a scrap of green defeats me.'

'Oh, Mother!' Caitlin says. 'You can be such a trial.' She vanishes, her rage expressed in the tight click of my bedroom door behind her.

The table is crowded, the dining-room so small that Katya and Linia, demure in black with frilly white aprons, have to squeeze by to serve from their heavy platters.

I am wedged between Charles Conrad, a burly British newspaperman (for whom I am learning Caitlin probably carries a bit of a torch), and a man called Jan, a willowy type from the Dutch Embassy who I think probably sleeps with this same Charles Conrad.

The talk starts with Caitlin's news of of her projected thousand-mile trip to the city of Perm, to visit men described as the last political prisoners. This soon dissolves into gossip about an Italian diplomat who is tangled up with the daughter of a lieutenant in the burgeoning Russian Mafia. Charles Conrad talks about the Gulf War, which he covered for his paper. He stayed in Amman. '. . . never did reach Baghdad, unfortunately.'

'Then someone tells yet again the story of how, during the recent coup, the American Ambassador's wife took great stacks of pizza to the protesters on the barricades And there were some so-called *inside stories* of Mr. Yeltsin's prodigious appetite for vodka.

Caitlin stays silent at this stage of the discussion. To her eternal rage, she'd been on home leave during that crucial week of the coup. She was in London promoting her new book on the implications of *glasnost.* So she missed the whole show. The girl opposite me, the German wife of a Turkish diplomat leans forward, her chiselled face, keen in the candlelight, her pale eyes meeting mine. 'I believe you write children's stories, Mrs. Ozanne?' she says politely. '

Yes,' I say, 'I do.' There is nothing else one can say, is there? My voice falters into a sudden pool of silence. The others have stopped refighting the coup.

Charles Conrad stirs beside me. 'Children's writer? Should we know you Mrs. Ozanne? Do you write under your own name?'

This is such a common question. At this point I usually make a sarcastic apology for not being Beatrix Potter or J.K. Rowling. But Caitlin throws me a glance and I swallow it. I smile sweetly. 'Yes I *do* write under my own name and no, probably you don't know me.' I say. 'Children's books are—'

'Are you published?' Charles butts in, with a journalist's desire to get at the value-level of a story.

From the top of the table Caitlin is leaning forwards. 'Is it your tenth or your eleventh book, you're on with, Mother?' I admire the affecting layer of pride she has painted on her face. Or is it genuine? She is so hard to read.

'My thirteenth book, and yes, Charles, they are indeed published. By Walton Books in England—'

'And America and the rest of Europe,' puts in Caitlin, almost too eagerly.

Charles looks at me thoughtfully for a moment. 'And are you enjoying your visit to Moscow, Mrs. Ozanne?'

'It is amazing, wonderful,' I say. 'I've dreamed of coming here many years. It's strange, exotic, mundane by turns and . . .' My voice tails away. Looking round the table I see I have done the wrong thing. Such enthusiasm can be so *provincial*.

Charles raises a finely arched brow. 'Interesting,' he says. Then his glance flickers away from me to the Dutchman on my other side. 'Now, Janni, how did the meeting with the Americans go?'

The conversations around the table – half work, half play– begin again and the room buzzes with relief at having dealt, politely enough, with the rather embarrassingly enthusiastic stranger.

I sit back, duly dismissed and relieved to be out of that scorching spotlight. Katya leans across me to collect my plate and I catch her scent, an old-fashioned odour of soap and dust. 'Madame?' she says softly.

I know I have more in common with her than with any of these news-hungry high-fliers around Caitlin's table. I want to tell her that I, too, was once a teacher like her. But Katya and I cannot surmount the impenetrable language barrier. We tend to smile and nod a lot. And I feel embarrassed when Caitlin has one of her paddies and lashes out at Katya in her impressive Russian, gargling the words like a native.

I will learn Russian. I will!

Caitlin taps her glass and we are ordered to the tiny drawing-room which opens from the hall. We are just settled in our seats, receiving our coffee from Katya's friend Linia, when the telephone rings.

A slight tension crystallises in the room: despite the advent of *glasnost* the telephone here has so much more significance than at home. There are no telephone directories; there's no way that you know someone's number unless you are given it directly. The telephone is a lifeline, a crucial contact; for these journalists it could throw up a bit of information that might make this week's great story, a satisfying by-lined piece to be splashed across the headlines in a dozen countries.

And here, to add to the *frisson,* we know that the phones in this foreigner's building are still tapped. Caitlin, however, is blasé´ about this. She has a theory that there are so many thousands of calls these days, and the government is in such a bureaucratic mess, that the tapes are not listened to with any consistency.

Caitlin picks up the phone and the room falls into an avaricious silence. My daughter, with her perfect Russian and her wide network of contacts, is often the first to pick up new trembles, new fissures in the fabric of this crumbling society. She is often first with a story. I know this because she has told me that she is famous for it.

She's talking into the phone now, in rapid Russian. There are bright red patches on her flawless cheeks. She raises her eyes angrily to me. 'It's for you, Mother,' she says fiercely, holding up the phone and waiting while I scramble to my feet and make my way across the crowded room.

Volodya's voice booms down the line. 'Olivia? Is that you?'

'Yes,' I mutter hoarsely. 'It is me. What is it?'

'Will you meet me tomorrow?' His voice was urgent. 'Will you be there at the flower stall? You will be there?'

A dozen eyes are watching me. I press the receiver hard to my ear so they can't hear his voice. 'Yes. No. I am not sure.'

'You must come.' His voice is rasping into my ear now. 'I have something important to tell you. An amazing thing. I have just discovered it. A *fa-antastic* thing.'

'How did you know where to ring, Volodya?' I whisper fiercely, turning my back to the company, shutting out their veiled, hungry eyes. 'How did you find me?'

His warm chuckle at the other end of the line

forced a smile to my own lips. 'No problem, dearest Olivia. I just rang your daughter's office and told them I had a hot story for her. So, they gave me her number. *Quick-as-a-flash*, don't you know! You will come?'

'Mother!' Caitlin is breathing down my neck. She is reaching for the phone. I pull away from her.

'I have to go, Volodya!' I say desperately.

'Will you come?' His voice is urgent, insistent.

'Yes! Yes.' I smash the phone back in its cradle before Caitlin can get at it.

The silence in the room is finally broken by Caitlin's slightly nervous laugh. 'Mother, you *do* get in some pickles!' she says. She turns to the company. 'Do you know I had to rescue her once after she had fallen into a canal in Amsterdam, chasing some thief who had snatched her bag?'

'Don't be silly, Caitlin. You came to the hospital and brought some flowers. Hardly *rescuing*.'

'Intrepid!' says Jan the Dutchman. 'You were fortunate not to get your throat cut, Mrs. Ozanne.'

Charles Conrad sits back comfortably in his chair. 'Don't tease Mrs. Ozanne, Janni. In all probability she was gathering copy for her kids' books. *Five Run Riot in Amsterdam* and all that,' he drawled.

There are grins at this. I take a look round at the

keen, young faces before returning to Charles Conrad's bland smile. 'Don't be so bloody *patronizing!*' The words chip their way through my gritted teeth.

Caitlin puts a hand on my arm, 'Mother, I—'

I turn and stump to my bedroom, slamming the door behind me. I stand with my back to it and wait while the talk wells back to its normal social purr. No doubt they're pleased to be rid of me. I relax a little then, stripping to my skin, ripping off the carefully chosen clothes, which I know still make me look too fat. I hesitate a little, but remembering Caitlin's strictures over my nudist tendencies, I pull on my nightie and dressing gown. Then I go to stand at the window and lean my head against the cold pane. Eyes wet with unshed, angry tears I watch the dimly lit trams as they trundle their way round the terminus, and peer at the shadow of the warehouses against the inky green filigree of the garden ring.

Green! There *is* some green, of course. I suppose I was wrong to tease Caitlin about there being no green.'

There is a knock at the door and I keep my back to it as it opens, waiting for the douche of Caitlin's icy contempt.

'Madame?'

It's Katya with a small tray covered with a lacy

cloth, on which steams a cup of frothy hot chocolate. I sit down hard on the narrow bed, scrambling in my pocket for my handkerchief.

Katya places the tray on the bedside table, and then she puts a hand on my arm and glances angrily towards the door. She says something in Russian which I don't understand.

I smile then, and my tears dry back into my sockets. 'You're right, Katya. They're silly people,' I say. 'Bloody silly people.'

She nods and glides quietly out of the room.

I reach out for my chocolate and begin to lick the sweet froth from the top. One thing is sure. Wild horses wouldn't stop me meeting Volodya by the flower stall tomorrow.

Outside in the hallway someone has put on some music, drowning the chatter and spurts of laughter. Miles Davis. Cool. Mellow. I brought the compact disc with me to Russia as a present for Caitlin. It strikes me that, in playing it now she is making one of the complex, inexplicit apologies she always offers when she knows she has gone too far.

Content at last I slide down onto my pillow, wondering what *fa-antastic* thing Volodya was so excited about.

I'm just slipping off to sleep when I remember that tomorrow Caitlin will be on her two-day trip to this city called Perm. That's a blessing. I won't have to worry about her at all for two days. I tuck the thin blanket under my chin. At least the coast will be clear. That is, if I can head off the delightful Piotr, who will no doubt be here at the crack of dawn, to get his bodyguard briefing.

'Now close your eyes.' Volodya's wiry hand grips my elbow as he guides me along.

It's an hour since we met at the flower stall and since then we have been walking the streets. He's showing off the unseen places of his city and I am drinking it in not just with my eyes, but the very pores of my skin.

From time to time I ask him what is this *fantastic* thing, this thing he wants to show me? But he just shakes his head. On one corner we pass a man with the large hat and the insignia of a general carrying a briefcase. It strikes me that I've never seen so many military men with briefcases in any city.

(Last night, tucked up in my narrow bed, with the laughter of the dinner party dying outside, I read a short story by Gogol called *The Nose*, where the administrator calls himself a major. Perhaps soldiers with briefcases are not necessarily a post-revolutionary phenomenon.)

Now Volodya leads me out onto the Boulevard Ring and we sit on a bench watching as an elegant white dog - a stray —stalks an Alsatian on a lead. The owner finally yells at the white dog, and chases after it. It skitters away with ethereal grace through the sparse grass and the withered, bare trees.

As we walk on from there a ribbon of shock flutters through me at the sight of the chiselled features of Lenin: a relief medallion on a wall. It is actually defaced by a vulgar splash of red paint. I'm used to and amused by graffiti at home, seeing it as the scribblings of the dispossessed, who merely enjoy a kind of power to irritate, like starlings in cities.

Only once have I been shocked as much as this: in a derelict chapel in the North where my mother lives. The chapel was littered with paper detritus used condoms and expended aerosols. My flesh crept as I read foot-high letters scrawling out the words *BLODY VIRGIN MARY WAS A HOOER.*

We wend our way through a series of derelict streets. At last Volodya makes me close my eyes. The streets become even narrower; the walls exhale the breath of ten generations. His hand is on my arm, his dry palm over my eyes.

'Now!' he says.

I blink in the light.

We are standing under a wide gateway at the end of an unexceptional alleyway. A tree to my right, half yellow, half green, wilts under the assault of Moscow's 'fast autumn'. On my left is a battered building, painted peeling cream. Squeezed in between the tree and the building stands an exquisite church, its fine new plaster painted in candy pink and pointed in white, with a high tower and a golden dome glittering in the morning sun.

'Volodya!' I am choking. 'It's beautiful. Exquisite.'

'This is the church of the Archangel Gabriel,' he said. 'Myself, I am an atheist. I have always been in favour of the secular state. But there is something fine, very human, in the way the people are now beginning to restore and repaint the churches, repossessing them clearly as their own.' He pulls at my arm now. 'Come,' he said. 'Come inside.'

We enter through a narrow door, past a cluster of elderly women, obviously the keepers, minders of the church. Inside, the church is surprisingly small. Proportionally, the height is the most important feature. I lift my eye to the inside of the cupola to find the face of Christ peering down on me in all my smallness.

'Such places make you wish you believed, in something,' I say softly.

He laughs grimly. 'Such places make me think of the gentleness and sweetness of the people they enfold. Of the strength of the builders. The delicacy of the painters . . . Not of Gods or false prophets.'

One of the old church keepers shuffles forward. She raises her squirrel-bright eyes to me, and I blink my recognition. It is the 'Brown Auntie' from Volodya's flat.

She speaks to Volodya, gesturing towards me.

'She says she will show you their most precious icon,' he murmurs.

We follow her into an even darker interior space. Reverently, from a carved box, she takes out a small icon. The semi- precious jewels and the gold inlay catch a beam of light from the high window. The serene contours of the face of the saint locked into eternal lines showing a passive strength and a jewelled certainty.

I catch my breath and put a hand towards it, whispering 'Utterly beautiful. So still.'

'It was hidden away during the Great Atheism.'

My head jerks towards Volodya's face, which has not moved a muscle. The voice is not his.

The wavery sound goes on. 'We hid the icon in a secret place, in an outside wall.' My hair lifts slightly on my scalp. The voice is rusty with disuse, but it is clearly an English, not a Russian voice. I put a hand on the shoulder of the Brown Auntie, and turn her towards me. Then I watch her face as she speaks again. 'Not just me, hiding things, pet. There were others as well. And other sacred things. But they were stolen by the atheists, boiled down for their gold..'

I can hear a familiar soft fragment of an accent: Durham, Cumbrian perhaps. I grasp the old woman's shoulders more closely. 'But you're English! But you can't be. You're here in Russia. You're Volodya's Brown Auntie . . .'

Volodya is frowning, watching us intently. The old woman pulls down my hand and turns it in hers. 'Don't take on, pet. No need to take on like that.' She is smiling, her scanty teeth turning her grin into a grimace.

'But how . . . when . . .' I am spluttering, excited. My blood is pumping through my veins.

Her hand tightens on mine. 'Wait for me, will you? Go home to the apartment with Volodya. My work here finishes here at three. Mebbe we can talk then.' She turns to Volodya now and pushes my hand into his, talking to him in rapid Russian.

54

He smiles down at me. 'We must do as the Brown Auntie tells us. She will come home at three.'

'Will she tell me, Volodya? Talk to me then?' Suddenly I need to know it all. I have to know all about her. I know I am ridiculously eager: like a child who has to have all the sweets in a packet at once. 'Did you know about her?'

He shrugs. 'I hear her voice in your intonation when you speak. She talked to me this morning, about you, who you were. That you must be fromher place. She heard your voice yesterday . . . there must have been *something*. I knew that she and her sister were different, of course. They speak old-fashioned, superior Russian for a start. And the Brown Auntie sings songs in French to the Grey one. But I have only known them ten years. They gave me a room in their apartment and now I pay their rent. I know little else about them. It's like that in Moscow. You are secret from each other. In some ways it always was.'

I turn back towards the Brown Auntie, but she's already turning away, to talk to more visitors, tucking the precious icon deep into the pocket of her bulky coat.

We walk out of the crepuscular space into the dusty sun-shine. Volodya is grinning broadly. 'That is a fine surprise, is it not? Two surprises. The lovely church and the intriguing Brown Auntie.'

'Did she tell you to take me there?'

He nodded. 'She said she would have a fine surprise for you. I thought it was one of her precious icons.'

'So you were surprised too?'

'I always know she is different. A very gentle soul. And sharp, with those bright eyes. But the aunties have never talked to me about who theyr were, about their past.'

'Well,' I say with more certainty than I feel. 'They will now. We're going to your place and I'm not budging till she tells me who she is and why she's here.'

'They will only tell you if they wish. The Grey Auntie will tell you nothing. She is what you call *gaga*. She must be ninety-five if she's a day. Ten years ago she was not so bad. But the Brown Auntie is younger, she has – how do you say it? – still got all her marbles? Got all her buttons on?'

'But she must intend to tell me about herself. Why else would she choose to speak to me like that?'

'You're so right, Olivia! Who could disagree with you, with that earnest face of yours? Now! Have you got dollars?' he says changing tack.

I frown. 'Yes! Why?'

'*Champienski*! We will celebrate the rebirth of an old Englishwoman, and the bubbles will loosen her tongue.'

'And,' I say firmly, 'you will tell me about yourself. Luckily I have escaped my captors . . .' Caitlin must be ploughing around the permafrost of Perm by now. She assigned Piotr to take me to see Lenin's tomb, but I've given him the slip. '. . . and have been trailing around with a man I don't know from Adam. You could be a mass murderer.'

He flushes, and his arm drops from my elbow. 'You think that I am like that, I—'

'Don't get *huffy*. That's an English joke.' I put my arm through his. 'Now we will get the champagne and go to the apartment.'

We stride along in companionable silence, successfully obtain the champagne from the unlikely Irish supermarket and flag down a car to take us straight back to the apartment. The driver, wearing a worn suite and mild eyes, smiles his appreciation of the dollars.

It's only when he is turning the key in the lock that Volodya speaks to me directly. 'This *huffy*, Olivia. What is that?'

THREE

I have to tell you I was inexperienced when I was married – a rarer thing even then, than I realised at the time. I tended to think everyone 'saved themselves' for the one true man. It turned out of course that I was wrong. They just made the right noises in public and fumbled their way into each other in private. In black alleys and doorways, in cars and under bushes; on staircases inside and out, in some way very uncomfortable places. My mate Janey tells the tale of doing 'it' under a canal bridge with rush hour traffic roaring overhead. 'Very damp and slimy it was, too.'

So what a pity it was that my first introduction to what I subsequently discovered was a delightful activity, was with Kendrick. Even when he was young he was self-obsessed, unimaginative, leather-obsessed and only able to sustain his passion to the point of his own satisfaction.

My first experience of true lovemaking as a delightfully self-indulgent pastime was at a literature conference in Paris. At the time I was a primary school teacher, but had also published my first two children's novels – about, respectively, a child who is battered and a child who runs away from home. In the euphoria of confidence induced by receiving money for something as pleasurable as writing, I booked myself into a conference advertised in Kendrick's Sunday paper.

This was my first blow for freedom. Kendrick laughed with disbelief when I told him. 'On your own? It's stupid. You'll never survive.'

'I'll be fine,' I said airily, not really believing it myself.

'What about Caitlin?'

Caitlin was seven at the time, voluntarily doing too much homework and insisting on weekly piano and clarinet lessons. She was also in a gym club and read *The Times* from cover to cover, every day. She tested me on its contents over tea every night. I never did score very highly. I was becoming redundant; she was already almost entirely independent of me.

'What about Caitlin? Janey will have her. She's running a play scheme at the school. Caitlin can play along.'

'Play along? Play along? You don't think I would let our daughter just play along, do you?'

I came in for my second line of attack. 'So, Kendrick, what are *you* going to do about our daughter, then?'

He stared hard at me, those full eyes gleaming.

Then he shrugged. 'If you insist on this wild-goose chase, Olivia, I'll have to take time off work myself.'

'Good,' I said. 'It's only for five days. You have holiday due, don't you? You'll have a wonderful time, the pair of you. The music lessons and the swimming baths. You could take her to the zoo.'

So I went to Paris. It was the first time I'd been in any city on my own and I loved it. In the mornings and evenings I listened to the lectures and in the afternoons I walked the streets of the city, miraculously invisible and free.

Over dinner at the conference centre people would asked about my writing, and I found myself holding forth quite eloquently on the portrayal of child abuse in fiction. This lead to invitations to speak at other conferences, and this theme was to become the main strand of my doctoral thesis and has been the source of my fortunes ever since.

In recent years though, I've moved away from the bad experiences of childhood into future fantasy. Some people have commented that this is something of an ideological retreat. Of course, one might argue, as I occasionally have, that future fiction is a metaphor for, rather than a flight from, the bad experiences of childhood.

Despite all this I wouldn't identify myself as

clever, not like Caitlin. Rather, my career has fallen steadily in one lucrative, interesting direction, like stacked dominoes, or the playing cards in Alice in Wonderland, The degree of success has been modest but it finally liberated me to kick the protesting Kendrick in the direction of his leather-knickered primary school teacher. And now so long as I write my books and give my lectures, I am a free agent.

One feature of life as a so-called academic or literary expert in the inner life of children is the curious way in which it is viewed on the part of the broad group of what you might call 'clever' people: people like Caitlin. They seem driven to infantilise you. (I have been asked more than once whether, when I grow up, I would be writing 'proper' books.) More frighteningly, I tend to act up to all this, taking up the part of a naughty child with glee, and watching myself do it, as though through an upside-down telescope.

So, it was in Paris that I learned that you could spend a languorous afternoon not-quite-making-love before you actually performed the act. My educator on that occasion was very a clever professor from Beirut called Edi some-thing. That was when Beirut was a beautiful city with wide boulevards, before it was shot to pieces in the Middle Eastern turmoil. I see the city is undergoing a rather glam renaissance these days.

I was not 'in love' with Edi, did not even love him in any accommodating, temporary fashion for the duration of the conference. But oh, I *liked* him, with his charming, lisping French and his gleaming, honey-coloured back, and the delicious sensual fun he could evoke from the basically comic act of making love.

After that experience, when I came home I found it better to sleep alone than to make do with Kendrick's rough and very ready search for his own satisfaction. First I slept in a separate bed. Next, inevitably, living in a separate house.

Not that I am forced to be alone. There is always Lee Compton, my good friend and occasional lover. And there have been other occasional encounters.

So I wouldn't like you to think that I end up lolling on the floor or on a heaped-up sofa in every foreign city I visit. However, here I am in Moscow now, on the Azeri rug on Volodya's floor, half naked, propping my head up on one elbow so I can make out the marble length of his body, which measures the length of the cramped space between his table and his bed.

Apart from a rough gathering of skin around the collarbones and the eyes, I am looking at the body of a much younger man. He is lying back now, in slack, trusting pose, after a forceful explosion of passion which made up in power what it lacked in control.

Volodya opens one eye and says dryly, 'I am too quick for you. There is still a feast in your eyes,' he sighs. 'It is a long time . . .'

I hesitate. 'How long ago . . . who . . . ?' The words drop from my mouth softly, like petals from a blossoming tree.

He sits up and lifts some hair from my cheek and cups my face in his hands. 'How long? A long time. Five years and three months. Who? A French woman. Visiting lecturer in epidemiology. I was her interpreter and translated her papers for her. Before the Frenchwoman, three years. That was a German woman. Before that, one year. An Australian woman.'

I pull my face away from his hands. 'They - the government - let you do that? Get close to these women?'

He shrugged. 'Well, I had to write private reports for the bureaucrats. But these were innocent professional women, no threat to the state. The reports were drenched in innocence. But they had to be watched.'

'So, you only make love to foreign woman?'

He shook his head. 'My first wife, she was a woman from Peter.'

'*Peter?*'

'St Petersburg, which has just now retrieves its old name. She left me for a Hungarian army captain here with a delegation. Since then, no Russian women for me.'

'So why did you decide that?'

'I didn't. He did.' He takes his limp penis in his hand rather tenderly. 'He will only work with foreigners,' he says sadly.

Then I start to laugh, so much that I have to hold onto my ribs, my breasts bouncing slightly on my forearms. After a second he starts to laugh too, and soon we are clutching each other, roaring with laughter. We are roaring so loud that we do not hear the door open quietly, and only through our tears do we see the Brown Auntie standing there waiting patiently for us to stop, with the Grey Auntie like an insubstantial shadow behind her.

Volodya laughs and says something to them, and they withdraw. 'We make ourselves respectable and they come back,' he says. 'In five minutes.'

The two ancient ladies do return in five minutes. The Brown Auntie carries a tray covered with a lace cloth, on which stand four exquisite wine glasses. Volodya takes the tray and makes them sit, side-by-side on the torn brocade sofa. He places me on the single hard chair and, having poured the champagne and placed the glasses in our hands, he perches up on the table. He raises his glass and says, '*Bottoms up!*'

They smile and nod and drink heartily, the Grey Auntie swigging all the glass at once and gargling it down her throat. My eyes are on the Brown Auntie. She is wearing the same shapeless brown jumper and skirt, the same clumsy felt shoes. But a pretty lace collar is peeping out above the jumper and she is wearing a gold locket which twinkles in the dingy light of the flat.

'You are English,' I say.

She nods.

'The Grey Auntie too?'

She shakes her head. 'We are sisters, but not of the blood. She is a Muscovite, born and bred.'

Volodya fills her glass, but ignores the Grey Auntie's waving hand.

'What is your name?' I say.

The Brown Auntie frowns. 'Ah've been Marie Samsonova for sixty years, and me sister here is Nina Samsonova.' She speaks with a curling Russian accent and her voice is a wispy thread in the air. She sips her glass thoughtfully. 'Well, that really *is* her name of course. But it's not mine. She is not my blood sister.'

'So what is your name, then?'

'Me name is Mary Martha Johnson.'

At the sound of her name the Grey Auntie leaps towards her and clamps a claw-like hand over her mouth, gabbling away.

Volodya pulls her off and holds onto her shoulders, talking to her in a soft soothing voice. He looks over her head at me. 'I will take Grey Auntie for a little walk on the corridor,' he says. 'Perhaps you could pour Miss Mary Martha Johnson another glass of *champienski*, Olivia?'

I take the bottle across to the sofa and sit beside her. 'Hello, Mary Martha Johnson,' I say it softly, wonderingly, knowing I am in the presence of some kind of miracle.

A first smile glimmers in her eyes. 'Hello, Olivia Ozanne,' she says.
'And how do you come to be here, Mary Martha,' I say, 'disguised as a *babushka*?'

Then her words come out in a torrent, tumbling over each other. Sometimes she says the Russian word then substitutes it for a vaguely similar English word. Sometimes she leaves in a Russian word as though it is English and expects me naturally to understand it.

I learn that Mary Martha Johnson has been here in Russia since she was fourteen. She and a cousin were once servants in the London house of Oskar Samsonov, an anti-Czarist Russian lawyer in London. When the Revolution broke out, bringing with it the promise of overdue, much-needed change, he hurried back to Moscow with his wife and his daughter Nina so he could be part of it.

His daughter Nina had taken a fancy to the little English maid and begged her to return with them, offering her a great gold watch inscribed for her mother. 'It was a bribe, like.' Mary Martha laughed. 'It was as big as a turnip. He knew how much I loved my mother. I couldn't resist it. I couldn't resist her neither. My Lady Nina! She was that beautiful, so full of life. I loved her from the minute I first saw her.'

I glance at the door through which the babbling Nina had been dragged by Volodya.

Mary Martha shakes her head. 'That thing there's not my Nina. That thing there is a shell: a house where my Nina lived up to ten years ago. Then the Nina I know died inside there. Inside that shell of flesh and bone.

That was just before the man Volodya came to live here at the apartment. We needed his rent. He had to come because I couldn't work no more, as I had to take care of the shell of Nina. And the church. Even in the Great Atheism. When the church was a warehouse for carpets I always have to take care of the church. The priests who were the foremen of the warehouse gave us a bit of money for cleaning it. That was before things changed and they took out the carpets. A new priest came and started to do it up, like.'

'So you came to Russia with Nina and her father? In 1917?' I venture, trying to send her back into the deep past.

She ignores me. 'So anyway, at the beginning I had the watch engraved and sent it to me Mam. I sent it home for her and set off for Russia with them, the Samsonov's. With my lady Nina.' She puts the back of her veined hand to her forehead. 'Mind you, that was surely the wrong time for them to come home.'

In the silence that follows the click of Volodya's clock sounds blunt, muffled by the dust settled in the room.

'And what happened then, Mary Martha? What happened when you got back here? The Revolution would be in full cry then, surely . . .'

Now the old woman seems to wake from her trance and turns to me and Russian words tumble from her mouth in a meaningless torrent.

My head spins. 'In English Mary Martha! In English! I can't understand you.'

Still she gabbles on, her hands gesturing

helplessly and her head shaking from side to side.

I go to the door and shout for Volodya.

He rushes in. 'What is it? What is it?'

He kneels beside the old woman and listens, then looks up at me. 'Her English is gone. She says she can find no more English words. She says her head is tired.' He hauls her to her feet, and puts an arm round her. 'Come, Auntie. You're tired. I will make you some tea.'

I stand looking at the panel of the door as it closes behind them. Now I am buzzing, buzzing with what I have heard. Now I'm overwhelmed with panic.

What am I doing here? Is this a trap? Does Volodya set it for all his female conquests, lulling them into a sense of security with the babblings of a mad old Englishwoman? *Befriending*. Wasn't that the way they trapped diplomats and turned them into spies? I scrabble for my coat and make for the door, race along the corridor and down the stairs. I am on the bottom level when I hear him calling from the top.

'Olivia! Olivia!' His voice bounces off the peeling walls, pings along the ornate iron banister. 'Come back. Oh come back! You . . . woman!'

The front door clashes behind me. I take a breath before I look around and decide which way to go. I go in the opposite direction to that which we took the other day and start to run.

Having turned round three corners I slow down. I'm drawing too much attention to myself, racing so quickly. No one moves this quickly here. Anything beyond a steady tramp, a square placing of one heavy foot before the other will betray itself as alien.

I find myself in a narrow street with shop windows containing very little: some of them are boarded up, some gaping open and empty. A long-haired young man is staggering towards me, his head wagging from side to side. He stops in my path, his mouth slack, his eyes rolling.

I move to one side, and he blocks me. I move to the other and he blocks me in that direction too, talking away, shouting at me. He cups his hand and thrusts it in my face, a very importunate begging bowl. I pull back. He touches my shoulder bag and cups his hand again. I feint to one side then dodge in the opposite direction and run for my life.

I don't stop running until I come out into one of the wider boulevards. I stand out in the road and put my hand up in the same way as Volodya did. In just one minute a small car stops and the driver leans his head through the window.

I falter when I see his military uniform with so much braid her could only be a major. Or a general.

'Can you take me to Oktoberskaya Ploschad?' I venture, hoping desperately that English will do.

He opens the door. 'No prob*lem*.' The voice is heavy, guttural, but the words are English. 'Three dollars, hard currency?'

'Yes. Yes.' As I scramble into the back seat I know this is a mistake. It must be a mistake.

He puts the car into gear and we set off smoothly. He glances at me through the mirror. He has very heavy brows which almost meet in the middle. 'You are holiday in Moscow?'

The car smells of some kind of floor polish. I button up my coat. Pat my hair. I might as well be tidy for the Lubianka. 'Yes.'

'You enjoy?'

I take a breath, 'I enjoy it very much. A beautiful city.'

He nods and his brakes squeal as he turns a corner. Then he turns on his stereo and I am treated to a four-speaker performance of the Beatles singing *She loves you, yeah, yeah, yeah*.

Yeah! I sit back against the plastic car seat and surrender to my fate. Caitlin will certainly have to do a rescue job on me this time. That should please her. More ammunition in this lifelong battle we call a relationship.

'Madam?' The car has stopped. Before us is an as yet unblemished statue of Lenin (his finger pointing ever onwards for the workers), which graces the centre of Oktoberskaya Ploschad.

The general has brought me home.

I scramble out of the car. 'Thank you. Thank you!' I babble, thrusting three dollars into his willing hand.

'No problem.' The deep voice echoes like a clanging bell. 'Enjoy your stay, madame.'

Katya, thank God, is still at the flat. She's wearing her coat and fake-fur hat and that grim look my mother used to have when I first started staying out after seven o'clock. Katya's tone is scolding, but I'm so relieved to see her that I hug her and start to cry. She frowns and then she takes off my coat as though I'm a five-year-old and pushes me into a chair in the little hallway. She tells me in gestures to stay there and vanishes into the kitchen. When she returns with a steaming cup of hot chocolate I have blown my nose and dried my eyes and am sitting up straight like a good girl.

'Thank you, Katya, thank you.' I nod wildly to show her what I mean.

She thrusts a note in my hand. It is typed from Caitlin, obviously left before she went.

Dear Mother, just to remind you, I will be away overnight and when you get back from the museum you should stay put . . .

Museum? Little does she know.

. . . and tomorrow Piotr will come and take you to Lenin's tomb. I should be back some time in the evening but I don't know when. C

I nod up into Katya's concerned face. 'I am all right now, Katya. You must go home.' I gesture towards the door.

She takes my hand then and leads me to the kitchen and shows me the meal she's left for me. Then she nods again and takes up her bag. She makes gestures telling me to lock the door behind her and quietly leaves.

I realise I'm ravenous and sit down and do more than justice to her cold meat and potatoes and the bottle of French wine so thoughtfully opened in time to breathe. When I'm finished I take my wine through to the sitting room and put on a video of *Yes, Minister* that I brought from home for Caitlin. I let the arcane decadence of English politics flow over me and soothe away the last dregs of my panic.

My mind begins to focus on one of the women who is meandering across the screen, the light rhythms of her North Yorkshire accent penetrating my brain.

And I hear again the reedy voice of the Brown Auntie, Mary Martha Johnson, who must come from somewhere near this fictional place. I drift off to sleep wondering what really did happen to Mary Martha in the Revolution.

It's eleven o'clock when I wake up to the rasping ring of the old-fashioned telephone. I feel certain it will be Volodya but I make no move to answer it. Not tonight.

FOUR

I wake up with a headache to the smell of coffee, the murmur of voices and the clash of dishes pricking at me through the thin wall which divides my bedroom from the kitchen. I can hear Katya's placid, musical tones. The other voice is too deep for Caitlin. It couldn't be her, anyway. She's probably strapped into her seat on some string-and-chewing-gum aeroplane, travelling back to Moscow.

Piotr. It must be Piotr. Oh, the deception of that curly soldier-with-a-sense-of-humour tone. I know this man if mean and watchful, regretting the day that Caitlin put him in charge of me. I drag up my hair and push it through an elastic band. Then I pull on a thick jumper and heavy shoes, under the delusion that the sheer weight of these items will provide some kind of armour against what I know must be the driver's disapproval.

Their heads, close together over the tiny kitchen table, whip round at my approach and they both stand up. Katya raises her brows, her expression not unsympathetic. Piotr starts to grunt and rattle away at me. I feel as though he's about to explode and radiate some deadly black substance into the tiny room. I imagine it spilling over me and down the wall in a

75

black tide. I pity now any poor soul who came across Piotr in the old days, when he had some degree of real power.

I wait until he has finished and shrug, turning my hands out. 'I can't understand a word you say, Piotr.'

He starts again, and Katya puts a hand on his arm. She turns to me. 'Piotr says you put his job in danger by going away like that, madam. Miss Ozanne will blame him. She will report him to the agency.' A shock runs through me. Katya's English though heavily accented is perfect.

I feel betrayed, deceived. 'You speak English?'

She looks uneasily at Piotr. 'Yes, madam. But we are not supposed to say . . . The agency . . .'

Piotr starts again, the grunting stream of his words projected towards me like a sour douche.

'Piotr says you must go to see Lenin's tomb today as planned on Miss Ozanne's list. And also you must give him the name and the address of your of the man you visited yesterday. He says Miss Ozanne will want it checked.'

I relax, lean against the wall and fold my arms. 'Tell him I do not choose to go to see Lenin's tomb, Katya. I can imagine Lenin's tomb. That's what I do for a living. Imagine things. And most definitely I will

76

not tell him where . . . who my . . . friend . . . is nor where he lives.'

Piotr flaps the typed sheet of paper under my nose.

I stare him in the eye. 'I don't care if Miss Ozanne has given you a thousand orders, Piotr. I don't care if the agency says you must only obey her orders and report back to them. I will do what I want. I am *not* a child.'

Katya translates and Piotr goes even redder. He tears up the piece of paper up and grinds it under his heel in a melodramatic gesture. This achieved, he stands there looking lost, his hands hanging loosely before him.

Katya puts her hand on my arm. 'Piotr is worried about his job, madam. Miss Ozanne, if she report him to the Agency they get rid of him. She has great power.'

I doubt this. The boot is very probably on the other foot. The agency is still a powerful tentacle of the bureaucracy that acts to observe and even to control the actions of foreigners. But I play along with them. 'Well, why not pretend that yesterday we followed her orders and today we followed her orders? Why does my daughter need to have chapter and verse on all I do every day? This doesn't happen at home.'

Katya frowns. 'Chapter and verse?' she says.

'To know *everything*. Absolutely everything.'

She translates, listens to Piotr and turns to me. 'He says that would be improper. His duty is to Miss Ozanne.'

I shrug. 'Well in that case he can blame me. I ran away after all. He can tell her I am a really *bad* woman. My daughter knows this. She will not blame him.' He nods belligerently at this. 'And you can tell him that today I will go out on my own again.'

Now the words rattle from him like machine-gun bullets. There is saliva at the corner of his mouth.

Katya regards me apologetically. 'He says in that case he will have to restrain you. You are not allowed.'

'Restrain me?' I draw myself to my full height. 'So how will he prevent me? Handcuffs?'

'He will bar your way.'

He folds his muscular arms and scowls at me. An image of me exchanging fisticuffs with this bear of a man comes before my eyes. Once, Kendrick shook me till my eyes rattled in my head. That was a terrifying experience, not alleviated by his abject apologies and the offer of a day in Paris as compensation.

'He means it, madam,' says Katya quietly, with conviction.

'Well, you may tell him I have no intentions of going to see the petrified Lenin. I will stay here and do some work. And if he wants to hang around, he's not to stay here in this matchbox. He can hang around outside, with the militiaman in his box.' The militiaman, in his small hut among the puddles, packing cases and rubbish of the inner square, was another piece of detritus from the cold war culture of surveillance.

Katya frowns. 'Hang?'

'Stay near. He can't say here at the apartment. He takes up too much space.'

She translates this and Piotr picks up his cap and stumps out of the apartment, clashing the heavy door behind him.

I collapse into a chair. 'Well, that's a relief. Now, Katya, this speaking English, is it a secret?'

She glances round the tiny kitchen. 'Not any more a secret. We are told to listen, not to talk. It is an old rule.'

'You make a report?'

She nods. 'It is an old rule. I am not sure who reads them any more, but still we must write them.'

'And they still eavesdrop?'

She nods. 'There is a room in the basement. There is equipment and tapes. Hundreds of tapes. But perhaps now there is no one to listen.'

I unlock my hair from its restraining elastic band and shake it down. 'Well, I'm just going to have a quick bath, Katya. And wash my hair. Then we'll have breakfast together and discuss just how I'm going to get round that big klutz down there.'

She raises her finely arched brows. 'Big Klutz?' She reaches into the fridge and pulls out bacon and eggs. 'English breakfast?' she says.

'You have the bacon and eggs,' I say. 'I'll have bread and coffee. I love your bread.'

I've acquired a taste for the huge workmanlike loaves of fresh bread that are in the shops here now even when there is nothing else. This bread costs the same now as it did in 1952. Don't they say that bread is at the root of all revolutions? If that's so, cheap bread in Russia has probably delayed the present revolution by thirty years.

'I eat your egg and bacon?' says Katya. She never touches any part of Caitlin's provisions. Caitlin is as tight with them as any nineteenth-century bourgeois housewife. She is not alone here. The problem of pilfering servants is an issue alive and well in twentieth-century Moscow. They talk about nothing else at diplomatic and journalistic *soirées*. Caitlin has told me this, scorning those women, yet she is guilty of it herself.

'You have the egg and bacon, Katya. I'll have the bread. And we'll decide what we'll say to Caitlin. It's time for a bit of good old-fashioned mendacity here.'

She raises her brows. 'Mendacity?'

'Lying, Deception.'

Half an hour later my hair is washed and back up into its elastic band, the curls drying to a frizz round my face. In the kitchen Katya is tucking into a pile of scrambled eggs pitted with shards of bacon, sprinkled liberally with black pepper. I can smell dill. 'Hardly the 'English Breakfast', Katya. Much nicer. You must be much too sensible.'

She points with her fork at the plate of ready carved bread on my plate flanked by Irish butter and strawberry jam with a Harrods label. We eat in companionable silence for a while. Katya puts her knife and fork neatly side by side on her plate. 'About the lying, madam,' she says. 'The mendacity.'

'Yes?'

'You must not tell Miss Ozanne that I talk with you.'

I spit on my finger and trace a cross on my left breast. 'Cross my heart and hope to die.'

She frowns.

'Don't worry Katya. It's just a thing that children say in the playground at school.'

She begins to gather up the dishes. 'Is Miss Ozanne your only child, Madam?'

'No. There's Joseph. He's younger than Caitlin. Much more of a scatterbrain than his sister.'

Kendrick blames me for that, of course. 'The boy is a journalist also?'

I splutter with laughter at this. 'Too wild for that. A bit of a painter, bit of a poet, a lot of a drop-out.'

'*Drop-out?*'

'He lived on the streets at one time. In squats – that's flats . . . apartments . . . that's where he and his friends lived. Without paying rents. Without permission. Then they would be thrown out. So he would find another squat.'

'We have such in Moscow now. Even outside, under bridges. It is a bad thing.'

'Bad? Perhaps not always.'

You might say Joseph has always been my ewe lamb. Even as a child he was easier to be around than Caitlin. Easier to love. True, that episode with drugs finished his college career at Hull. But being sent down didn't stop him painting and for the last two or

82

three years those meticulous paintings of his, of stringy nudes lying around among strange animalistic flowers, have begun to sell. Some of them have been used for record sleeves and they are becoming quite collectible.

Caitlin, of course, is rather embarrassed by them and says loudly in company that, really, they're not her taste. She is rather keen on the later Russian realists, and typically has become something of an expert in them.

'Joseph is an artist, now,' I say to Katya. 'His paintings are becoming very popular. But sometimes he goes for months without painting even one.'

She puts down her dishcloth and claps her hands. 'You must be pleased with your son.'

'Do you have children?' I say.

She has been waiting for the question. She nods. 'I have Ulli, who is nine and Viktoria who is fifteen. They stay with their grandmother in the week. Ulli is a great scientist. He speaks English better than me. And Japanese. All his teachers praise him.'

'And Viktoria?'

She shrugs. 'She is fine, but I think now she is like a bird who wants to fly. My mother and I have great trouble to keep her shackled. She neglects her studies, and all she only dreams of is jeans and those decadent American singers. We have many arguments.

83

I tell her I would much rather be teaching little children but when I cook and scrub and clean for dollars it is not to buy her jeans, but to save for a better future for us all.'

I laugh. 'Bravo!' I stand up. 'Now, Katya. I need to see someone. My friend, the one I was with yesterday. How can I do this? With Piotr out there protecting me from the world?'

She frowns. 'Is it mendacious? Can we lie about it?'

'Of course we can.'

She clicks shut the dishwasher. 'Well then, if you can't go out there, why can't your friend come here?'

'But Piotr has seen him. He will recognise him. And the militiaman. They will stop him.'

'You must meet him, by the Metro perhaps, and bring him into the block. Walk with confidence.' She is reaching for the phone. 'You have a telephone number for him?'

I hand her the scrap of paper that Volodya tucked in my pocket. She dials the number, then hands me the phone. 'Tell him.' Her lids droop over her eyes. 'I have big shopping to do this afternoon, two markets, before Miss Ozanne returning from her long journey. She left strict instructions.' As she left the kitchen, a German glass-cleaning spray in hand, her smile was conspiratorial, ironic. 'I clean the balcony windows first. It is very quiet, very safe on the balcony.'

My heart jolts on hearing Valodya's voice again. It's as familiar to me now as Kendrick's, but infinitely more precious. He doesn't mention my running away. He listens attentively to my request for him to bring Mary Martha Johnson across to Caitlin's flat. He mentions the story of Rapunzel in the tower, suggesting I should let down my hair, so he could climb up. My whole body flushes with the ridiculous romance of this.

He goes on more soberly. 'Seriously, Olivia, your guard will not let us through your door.'

'I will meet you outside Oktoberskaya Metro and bring you in. The militiaman cannot stop you then.'

'Right! We will come in . . . how do you say it? Our Sunday best! This is is all very cloak and dagger, is it not?'

As I return the phone to its hook I reflect that it must be twenty years since I have heard that phrase. *Cloak-and- dagger.* What fun.

Half an hour later, Volodya, Mary Martha and I are making our way into the interior quadrangle of the blocks of flats. Volodya is smartly dressed in a heavy coat and a well-brushed hat. Mary Martha has her old brown coat on, but is wearing rather a smart hat with a feather in it.

The militiaman strolls over and blocks our way. He ignores me and starts asking questions of Volodya in rapid Russian. Now he's shouting and pushing at Volodya, who cringes back, then thrusts some papers under his nose. The steam seems to leak out of the militiaman who shrugs his shoulders and returns to his hut, passing Piotr who is leaning on the Volvo, smoking a cheroot, watching the scene with taciturn interest. Game over.

The two of them bring in a smell into the immaculately aerosol'd flat - of dust and old clothes, of wine and cabbage-y spices. In the face of this, I feel shy and clumsy, over-clean and effete. My recent flirtation with this man seems now to be the action of a deranged woman. My cheeks are red at the thought of it.

'Won't you sit down?' I say, hearing the echoes of those women on Palatine Close. Mary Martha looks around in wonder and perches on the edge of Caitlin's pink linen sofa. Volodya lowers himself into a carved chair that Caitlin has had made, very cheap, here in

Moscow. It has a tiny carved hedgehog hidden under the seat. Caitlin has told me that it will be a collector's piece in ten years.

Volodya has brushed his hair back in an untidy mass, and looks absurdly young in his workman's denim. Katya comes in with a tray laden with a steaming coffee pot and silver dish full of Kit-Kat biscuits with Dutch writing on the labels. She says something to Volodya, and he replies, smiling broadly. Then she says something else and he laughs out loud.

I remember now, how good it was, making love with him. 'In English!' I say. 'You must say it in English.' I sound like a spoiled child.

'She asks if I am KGB and I say no, not in a thousand years. Then she says you are quite a character. Not like an English woman. I do not tell her that the Brown Auntie here is English. It would not do for her to know.'

I laugh out loud at this. 'She does know now! You speak English, don't you Katya?'

Katya is staring at Mary Martha with interest. 'Yes. So I do,' she said.

'Can you keep a secret? Will you write it in your report?' I say, my voice hardening a little.

She nets the room in her familiar glance. 'I can keep secret, but what about the tapes in the basement?'

I laugh. 'You said yourself. They are unmanned now. No one to hear them.'

'Still they record . . .' she was suddenly uncertain. 'If I do not report it to the agency, and they cross-check it with the tapes . . .'

I go over and hug her. Her body is hard and unyielding under my touch. 'That won't happen, Katya. I promise you. Now put on your hat and go to the market. You know nothing about this anyway. If you want to put in a line about me having visitors in your report do that. But look at her.' We all look at Mary Martha. 'She could only be Russian.'

Mary Martha says something to Katya and all three of them laugh. 'What did she say?' I demand.

Volodya wiped his eyes. 'She says that I am insane, a madman, and I do not know my neck from my toe. So Katya must take no note of what I say.'

Katya nods, and the door clicks behind her and we sit in silence until the outer door slams.

'And where is the Grey Auntie today?' I ask.

Volodya glances at Mary Martha. She moves her bright eyes from the steaming coffee in my hand, upwards to my face. 'I took her to the church. Left her with the old women there. They have tied her in a chair. She will be safe.' Once again her English sounds rusty with lack of use.

Volodya drinks deeply of his coffee, slurping slightly. 'So, Olivia, what are we to do, up here in Rapunzel's eyrie?'

I give him my best, schoolmistress look. 'You are to sit quietly. You may drink coffee and eat Caitlin's biscuits. You may make us fresh coffee and hunt more biscuits. But what we will mostly do is listen to the Brown Auntie. To Mary Martha Johnson.' I place a tape in one of Caitlin's little voice-activated recorders and push it onto the glass-topped table. She frowns at it. 'No! No!' A lifetime of fear inundates her anguished voice.

I look around and then remember Katya's comment about the balcony. 'Look, why don't we put our coats back on and sit on the balcony? Then no one will overhear. Then you won't have to worry, Mary Martha. This is just to make sure I miss nothing. Honestly. Trust me.'

In a flurry of activity we put on our coats, pick up rugs off the beds and decamp to the narrow uncomfortable chairs on the balcony. I wrap a rug round Mary Martha's knees, and set the recorder on it. 'Now Mary Martha, right from the beginning, when you first came here? Before that, even.'

FIVE

Volodya is leaning forward: a shadow against the light. 'The tape-recorder? Why do you need the tape-recorder. Olivia?' For the first time in our short acquaintance there's a hard note in his voice, a dry questioning of who I am and what I'm about.

'Mary Martha's story is history, Volodya. Archive. English history as much as Russian. Her voice itself is history, not just a few notes that I might scribble.'

Mary Martha holds up her hand and rattles off something to him.

'What did she say?' I ask sharply.

'The Brown Auntie is no fool. She says she has no children so perhaps *this* can be her child. Her own voice on a recorder. A reel of tape.' He laughs and sits back on the fragile verandah chair. By turning his head very slightly he can keep his eye on the militiaman down below. 'And she says you are to take it to her family in England and present the reel of tape to them. She also told me to mind my own bloody business.'

Mary Martha is sitting there in the chair, a heavy wave of sleek grey hair escaping from her feathered hat on her head, Her eyes are sparkling above her sunken cheeks. 'From the beginning, Olivia Ozanne?' she says. 'You will forgive. The language is hard. I am translating from my head.' She smooths the cloth of her dress on her knee. 'Well, there is not much to tell, about the beginning, Olivia. I grew up with my mam, and my little sister Ellen Alice.'

The story proceeds. It was the Great War. Mary Martha's father was dead, killed in an accident when he was beating for a landlord's shoot. Her brothers had volunteered and were off fighting the Kaiser with all the other lads.

The words begin to flow faster now, as though an engine has been saturated with oil and the pistons are thrusting and humming, singing their song.

'I've dreamt that dream many times through the years, Olivia – the glitter on their cap badges as those lads marched away. For a second I forgot the cracks and clouts they'd given me, and was very proud of my brothers. That glitter o the badges is maybe the only thing that stays. I remember the glitter, all right. For years after I used to dream of it. The glitter of the badges stayed with me longer than the faces. Those faces took just a few years to fade. Just a few years and they were gone from my head. Those lads. Entirely dead. All that was left was dreaming the glitter of cap badges.'

Both of Mary Martha's brothers survived that war. But she never did get to see them again. By the time the war ended she was here in Moscow. 'They could be alive now. And Ellen Alice my sister.' Her voice fades a little. 'Her too.'

I ask now if she'd like to see them. Does she care about her brothers, now?

'Care? I don't *care*, Olivia. I didn't like them then, big brutes that kicked you soon as look at you. Should I like them now? I don't think so.'

I ask how, then, had she ended up still here in Moscow, seventy- odd years later. She laughs a deep cackle, a rusty sound full of humour and salty secret knowledge.

'Here? All this? Well, to be true, me own mother was like them lads, hard. Hard as any man. And she and me were often up against each other, though she used her tongue rather than her feet. Well, one day we had a barny.' She glances at Volodya. 'That's a fight, Volya. A big quarrel. So I picked up a knife, a knife we used for gutting fowl, and went for her. Give myself a fright, I can tell you. I ended up with me hiding in the privy and her threatening me with the constable.'

The next day Mary Martha went off to Darlington, to a Lady Gomersall, - who did this kind of thing - to get fixed up with a 'place' to work, as far away as possible.

I have to smile. 'So you have a temper, Mary Martha?'

She sat back in her chair. 'Oh yes, I have a temper. And my temper's stood me in good stead, through the years.'

I lean forward, reducing even more the distance between us, feeling the thread linking my time to hers, the past to the present. 'You came to Moscow then, Mary Martha?'

She laughs that rusty laugh again. Volodya glances down at the militiaman and lights a cigarette, watching me and the old woman with veiled eyes.

'Not to Moscow right then, Olivia. But Moscow was pulling me, sure enough. It was pulling at me, cunning as me Da when he was setting his snares for those hares of his. Do you know, Olivia, once, he lay me alongside a dead hare and measured me against it? Same length top to toe. That was before he died himself, caught in someone else's snare.'

So Mary Martha got this 'place' in London, working in a house in Bryanston Square. And one morning she found herself standing on the edge of this crowd of servants there, waiting for an important visitor to the house. 'Russian, they said. Fluttering like a covey of grouse they was. Me own mouth was dry

93

and I didn't know what I was expecting. I had to lick me lips.' Mary Martha licks her thin lips now, in almost lascivious remembrance.

'A right vision she was, her ladyship's guest. She was all got up in velvet, frogged lace, this big veiled hat, fur muff standing out fine as cobwebs in the cold air. She smelled foreign if you know what I mean.'

So, this was the Russian Nina stepping down from the carriage on her tiny feet, distaining the hand of the footman, even though he wore white gloves. The servants fell back as she swept up the steps into the wide hall, followed by the footman carrying a vanity case and a hat box. Mary Martha had peered into the dark carriage which was piled with trunks and boxes, 'Black as licorice, it was, Olivia, the clasps and keyholes shining brighter than cap-badges.'

Now here on this bleak Moscow balcony I feel as if I am peering too, right back into a well of time, into an age which was out of date even then and doomed not to outlast the Great War that was rumbling away in France.

Mary Martha goes on with her story. Mrs. Beswick, the housekeeper, who ruled the roost in that all-female household, strode forward to the guest like a great farmer, planting her feet flat in her powerful way. She bowed before this fluttering, scented vision. 'Miss

Samsonova? Lady Geary expects you.'

Mrs. Beswick turned and led the way towards the shallow steps of the staircase. Like all the others, Mary Martha bobbed a curtsy as the Russian lady swept past.

'Her smell, deep flowery scent, like old roses drenched in pepper, looped towards me like a noose. My head was giddy with that scent, and I shivered as she threw her fur over her shoulder and it prickled across my face. Then, finally I dared to glance upwards and see that face more closely. That white face, fine boned as any kitten. Those sooty black brows. Do you know, Olivia, in that minute my very hair stood on end? And I could feel sweat trickling down my back?'

Mary Martha's hands grip the arms of her chair. We can hear the Moscow trams grinding as they turned round at the terminus outside.

Volodya uncoils himself from his plastic chair, glancing casually yet again down at the militiaman, who is deep in conversation with Piotr. 'Shall I make tea?' he says. 'You must not tire yourself, Auntie.' He addresses her in English. Their relationship is clearly different now. No longer is she an eponymous Grey Auntie, only slightly less irritating than the Grey Auntie, who is clearly gaga.

Mary Martha stirs 'Tea? Yes I'll have more tea,

Volodya. Is there sugar? I would have sugar. My head's dizzy, drunk with all these things running through it. And talking English is that hard you know. Only now have I stopped translating in my head.'

She closes her eyes for a moment then snaps them open. 'D'you know my Mam used to say if you thought too much your brain would burst. She was safe enough, like/ She never thought a thing beyond plucking the birds and stoking the fire. She sent me letters, you know, asking for a bit of my wages. I was pleased enough to send her money.'

She says she thinks that the money made up for having a go at her mother with the filleting knife.

'Everyone did that, you know. Sending money home. Think of all of those bits of London money shooting all over Britain.' She cackles again and shakes her head. Fronds of hair escape her hat, trembling in the air like dandelion seeds. 'There was Irish maids there too, in that house in Bryanston Square. Nice girls, singers all. I liked them. But I can't bring a face or a name to mind now.'

She drops her lids and the orbs of her eye roll and move under their skein of flesh, as though she is watching a scene. I lean over and put my hand on hers, which feels dry and papery. 'Are you too tired for this, Mary Martha?'

Her eyes snap open and blaze forth so brightly that I leap back in shock. Then she takes the thick Swedish mug from Volodya who moves to the rail to take up his watchful position.

'So one day I was sent for next day by the old woman, Lady Geary.'

Lady Geary asked her if she would like to see the Queen. 'Would you like to go to see the Queen, Mary?' she says. The echoes of that ancient patrician twang, held in Mary Martha's voice like flies in aspic, reverberate through the room, pinging off the walls of this cramped foreigner's flat in the middle of Moscow. The echo very precisely down seventy years that separate then and now. I shiver as though a ghost has touched my neck with a cold finger.

'Well, Madame Olivia, there I was, standing there, hiding my hands behind my back, my nails digging right in my palms. 'The Queen, ma'am?' I says. My voice croaks.'

Then Mary Martha tells me how Lady Geary was very close to Her Majesty, because her son, Sir Matthew, was some kind of secretary to the Queen. As well as that, her grandson, now off fighting the Kaiser in France, had also played some small part in the Royal Household.

'The cook had actually called it the Royle *Arse-*

hold!' Mary Martha cackles again. 'I wrote all about that on one of these cards I sent to my mother. I bought these ten picture postcards with pictures of the Tower of London on the back. I sent all ten. Then afterwards, nothing. Once I got here there seemed nothing to that they would understand.'

She holds up her cup for more tea and, obediently, Volodya fills it to the brim. He glances down at the square before he returns the teapot to the little table.

Up till then Lady Geary it seemed that had never spoken directly to Mary Martha, except to comment to Mrs. Beswick on the strength of her legs, as though she were a prize horse, or one of her pug dogs.

'She actually mentioned 'good northern stock'.' Mary Martha's tone is contemptuous. I decide that Mary Martha must have been very much at home in the Revolution.

'Anyway, that time I was up this ladder, mad as a trumped up cockerel. I could have killed them then, talking about me like I were a prize heifer. And deaf. But I just spat on my brush, hooked another cobweb and said nothing.' Her voice fades.

'To see the Queen, Mary Martha?' I prompt her now, to bring her back to the thrust of her story.

It seemed the Queen was to be at an antique

shop in Marylebone at ten-thirty that morning. And her Ladyship thought Mary Martha might like to see her.

' "Well, child?" she says to me. " Would you like to see the queen? "Yes, ma'am. Yes indeed," I says, but try not to sound too enthusiastic."

Mary Martha turns to me. 'Have you seen this new Queen, Olivia? This Queen? Elizabeth the Second?'

I nod. 'She's very small,' I say. 'Kind of demure.'

Mary Martha stares at me for a second, then nods. 'It's all gone, that grandeur,' she says. 'No bad thing.')

She plunges back into the story. 'Anyways I was to accompany Miss Samsonova, the Russian lady to Marylebone. Seems she was to be her ladyship's guest while her father is in Paris. Now she wanted to see the Queen. And I was to accompany this Miss Samsonova so we could both peer at the old dear. Queen Mary, that was. Well, Lady Geary waved her hand then and Mrs. Beswick dug me hard in the back. So I bob this curtsy and backs out of the sitting-room.'

With the door safely shut, Mary Martha looked up at the housekeeper. 'Marylebone? Where's that?' she said. In her six weeks in London she'd never been across the Geary threshold. The city to her was a noisy landscape of buildings and the green square seen through the window.

So it was that young Mary Martha and the Russian lady were driven to the appropriate place. Mary Martha had to rehears her full instructions to mrs Beswick, The driver was to drop them at a special corner and he would wait and drive them back.

The Russian lady ignored Mary Martha's presence, even when they were dropped off. They placed themselves in a doorway a discreet distance from the shop.

'It seems like, that the Queen and them did go shopping in them days. Of course they went with maids and flunkeys and that. Anyway, this shop was called *Arlington and Buckley's*. It had one of those bright polished curving glass fronts. Right in the middle of the window was a pair of silver wine flasks standing on a velvet podium. I remember them now: glittering, like, in the low morning sun.'

Mary Martha, standing slightly behind Miss Samsonova, had to move a bit to get a clear view of the gleaming motor car as it chuffed and sputtered to a halt.

'They made such a noise, those cars, but they were a great miracle and you didn't worry about the noise. The driver, all in royal livery, jumped out to hold the door open. Then a middle-aged lady in a fur stole climbed out.'

Mary Martha smiles now, her eyes blank, looking inward, focusing now the scenes from the past which are unfolding before her. 'So this woman, like, she stood there to straighten her hat, case it had tipped a bit when she got out of the car. This was when my Russian lady clapped her hands. 'Bravo! Bravo! *Vive la reine!*" Her voice was fluting, like a bird. I loved her voice'

The French intonation on Mary Martha's voice is perfect.

'But I get hold of her arm and shake my head at her "No, no, Miss! That's not the Queen," I say. I point at this older lady getting out of the motor car:- an erect figure in greys and floating blues, furs up to her neck and the generously cut, old-fashioned toque hat on her head.

"That's the Queen," I say to my Russian lady. "That's our Queen Mary."

So now the Russian lady clutches me hand and says the words again like she was in church. "*Vive la reine.*"

And me, I got carried away meself, shouting "Bravo! God save Your Majesty!" at the top of me voice.'

Mary Martha pauses. 'Though, to be honest, Olivia, I cared nothing for her, for anyone of that class. Anyway, the old lady in the grey hat shoots us this chilly regal glance and sets her eyes right ahead.'

In seconds the royal party had entered the shop, ushered in by an oily fellow in a black suit. The shop door shut behind them and the chauffeur, a strong, muscular feller relaxed, lit a small black cigar and stood at ease beside the door of his car. Mary Martha imagined he must have got exemption from the Army, being the Queen's driver.

'Miss Samsonova was still clutching my hand. Now she starts to chatter away in that strange language which is now my own. Her pale face is alight with excitement, her black eyes sparkling. I take this big breath. I had never, ever, seen anyone so beautiful as her, Olivia. Never before, never since.'

My own eyes are pricking to tears at this sincere confession of falling in love. There are tears now in Mary Martha's eyes as she looks at me. 'Do you see, Olivia, before that I'd never been touched by any other person except in anger?' No one. And there I was standing holding hands with a stranger in a

London street. Now here is a peculiar thing. That feeling. I let my hand lie in her soft palm for a while. Then I pulled away, shaking her head, saying she couldn't understand the Russian words.'

'Then she seems to see me for the first time. She says something and touches my cheek and her touch singes me like a searing iron. I draw back, just like I'd been burnt. 'We must get back, Miss," I say. "Her ladyship'll be waiting."

So Mary Martha turned and started to march back to the corner, leading the way. The Russian girl followed her, fine leather boots tapping. Lady Geary's car followed them and the chauffeur shouted that they must get in, get in! Back at the house Mary Martha bolted out of the car and across the hall, leaving the visitor with Mrs. Beswick. She fled down the steps to the kitchen where the cook plied her with questions about Queen Mary – what did she look like? What did she wear?.

Mary Martha smiled. 'She was a funny'n that old cook. Hard. But that day she went all soft. "I seen the queen meself one day you know, with the King," she says. 'But it was a cold black day, driving rain and fog. An' they were in a closed carriage. So it might have been the Queen o' Sheba, for all I'd a' known." '

Again Mary Martha renders an exact voice; this

time, a very different, rolling cockney voice comes winging to me down the years. Mary Martha is an amazing mimic.

'The cook was holding a pie plate up before her eyes like a chalice, and started to cut off the extra pastry with a knife, so that it shimmered down onto the table surface like potato peelings. "An' the young Russian *lidy*." she says. "D'she like seein' our Queen Mary?"c'

The young Mary Martha was in a tumult. She did not want to talk about the Russian lady. She tried to divert the cook into another favourite topic.

"That steak and kidney pie, Mrs. Beaver?" I says. "I always like your steak and kidney pie. I told me Mam about it when I wrote to her. She made steak and kidney pie for the lads on a Wednesday at home. Before they joined the Army, like." Me mouth watered at the thought of the pie. The food that Mrs. Beaver made for the servants' table in that house seemed like royal food to me. I described it in detail in the postcards I sent home to my mother.'

It seemed that night, after servants' supper and just before the household dinner, Mrs. Beswick came and told young Mary Martha to tidy herself, as her ladyship wished to speak to her. She leapt up, tidied her hair, straightened her cap and scurried off after the striding figure of Mrs. Beswick.

'It passed through me mind that the housekeeper would make a fine figure in a butler's long black coat and big black boots. I wondered if it had ever occurred to her to cut her hair and dress the man and really *be* a butler. There was a butcher back home, a woman, who did that. Every inch a man, she was, with a booming voice and these great hammy forearms. Everyone knew she was a woman, like, but they didn't take much bother over it.'

'Her Ladyship was in her usual chair in the drawing-room. Standing by the fireplace was a tall man with great side whiskers and a body like a big barrel. Miss Samsonova, the Russian lady, was sitting on the chaise, her emerald dinner gown setting off those white shoulders of hers and showed off this lovely collaret of pearls and emeralds.

The door clicked behind Mary Martha. Mrs. Beswick had left the room. Lady Geary waved a fragile hand. '"Come here, child, come here," she said to me.

'Her voice was kind of powdery, no single line of sound. I thought she must be cross at something I'd done.'

Mary Martha walked over and bobbed this uncertain curtsy. 'Ma'am,' she whispered.

Stiffly, the old lady turned her head towards the man. 'There you are, Count.'

'Here, girl!' he said commandingly, waving a cigar. She walked over to him and stood still.

'The smoke from his cigar wreathed round me, making me want to choke. His great heavy hand came towards me and landed on my shoulder. I could smell his sweat. I looked ahead but through the corner of my eye I could see his thick ringed, fingers. I comforted myself with the thought of the lady butcher back at home.'

The Count said something to Lady Geary in French, and nodded towards his daughter, who was sitting on the couch, watching Mary Martha with her snapping black eyes.

Her Ladyship sighed and nodded. 'Come here, child,' she said in that powdery voice.

Mary Martha looked her hard in the eyes.

'It seems Miss Samsonova has taken a great fancy to you, child,' the old woman said.

Now here on the balcony Mary Martha stirs in her seat. She's leaning eagerly towards me. Down the funnel of these seventy-odd years, I can hear, now, that powdery, patrician English voice ventriloquised through the lips of this old woman who - it seems -

might not be Russian..

'Her ladyship says, "It seems Miss Samsonova here wishes to take you from me, so that you can be her maid. She is somewhat bereft here without her maid who, unfortunately . . . er . . . succumbed to an attack of seasickness on the boat on the way from France. Mrs. Beswick tells me you have been adapting here very well, my dear. So you will be missed in this household. Perhaps I could send up to Lady Gomersall for one of your sisters?"

I didn't bother to protest that my own sister Ellen Alice was too young. A child still. "To be her maid, ma'am?" I says, all innocent, "But I can't understand a blamed thing she says."

Lady Geary spoke then to Miss Samsonova in French. The Russian girl laughed and responded with a torrent of words. Lady Geary smiles at us, and then says, "Miss Samsonova tells me that she will have you taught. She will teach you herself. Russian. French.'

I protested hard at this, saying that I was unschooled and that I left school at nine years old to help me mother in the house. Me mother had to take washing, see, when Dad was killed. "They say I am quick. I can read and write, your ladyship. But I've no education." '

"Then it is time to start that education." Lady

Geary nods to the Count. "It is done. You may have her."

It was like I was a bolt of cloth, displayed, bought and sold. From her perch on the couch Miss Samsonova claps her hands.

Mary Martha's cheeks burned. 'You can't do it just like that, ma'am,' she protested. 'I'm not a packet of bacon nor a trussed chicken.'

The Count spoke rapidly.

Lady Geary turned to Mary Martha. 'The Count very generously says he will give you ten guineas and a gold watch right away, to send to your mother. And will pay you each week two shillings more than Mrs. Beswick pays you. Most generous.'

Mary Martha looked from one of them to the other, her flesh creeping at the hungry look in all their eyes.

"'Right, ma'am," I says. "Me mother could do with that money.' I stop talking and make them wait a while. "So when will the lady want me to start?" I says.'

Miss Samsonova stood up then and spoke rapidly in French. It seemed Mary Martha was needed at that very moment. Miss Samsonova was eager for her to start right away.

" 'I'm sure Mrs. Beswick can spare you.' Her

ladyship waved her hand and sat back in her chair, seemingly exhausted.

That wasn't untrue. Mary Martha *could* be spared. She had thought from the very first that there were more hands than jobs in this house. Except for this present Russian guest, there was only this old lady to care for.

Mrs. Beswick, when she heard the news, was put out. A decision made without her 'say so'! But she merely told Mary Martha she'd better mind her *p's* and *q's*. The Russian count was a friend of Sir Matthew and was up among the bigwigs in the Russian Royal Family. She would find herself in Russia as soon as blinking.

'So I said, I didn't think so. Nobody was getting me out of England. It was bad enough all those lads going off to France,' Mary Martha cackles. 'Do you believe I said that, Olivia? There I was, bought and sold like a trussed chicken.'

Mary Martha asked Mrs. Beswick what she would have to do for the young Russian lady. Mrs. Beswick stroked her whiskery chin.

'"That'll be getting Miss Samsonova undressed and into bed,' she says. 'Just go up there after they've had their dinner and wait. There's no linen to see to, as that goes out by box every day to Harrods and comes back laundered the next day. Just wait there in the bedroom and she'll tell you what she wants."

Mary Martha complained that she couldn't understand a word the Russian girl said so how could she tell her what to do?

"'She'll show you. An idiot could understand. Probably hair, dressing-table. Check the kettle on the fire and the water in the bowl on the washstand. She'll show you.'

But I was scared. "She can't." I starts to wail then. 'I can't understand a bleeding thing she says.' I say it again. Then my jaw explodes as it comes into contact with Mrs. Beswick's heavy mit. That stops me bawling as I was too busy rubbing my sore jaw, tears still in my eyes. Mrs. Beswick wipes her hand down her black dress. "No language like that in this house, Missy.' she says. "I won't have that. Now get upstairs."

Once upstairs Mary Martha wriggled her aching jaw and started to poke around in Miss Samsonova's bedroom. She went into the little dressing-room and peered into the wardrobes, finding just how she hung her dresses and furs, how she lined up her shoes and little boots.

Back in the bedroom, she lifted the perfumes and potions on the dressing-table and ran one of the silver-backed brushes through her own hair. The steam was rising from the little copper kettle on the dainty fire hob.

The bed had already been turned back by Clara the housemaid, and across a stool lay an elaborately ruffled and starched nightdress.

'Fresh in from Harrods laundry service, no doubt,' says Mary Martha now.

The little French clock on the mantelshelf was ticking on to ten o'clock when she heard light steps on the corridor and watched the door handle turn. Miss Samsonova came in and sat down on the boudoir chair without looking at her. She stretched out her feet in front of her, and then finally looked up at Mary Martha, speaking sharply.

'So I kneels beside her and undo the little pearl buttons that fastened her kid shoes. I cup her heel in my hand, slip the shoes off and place them side by side.'

What followed was a lesson for Mary Martha in how to do everything for another human being, bar go to the lavatory. She removed Miss Samson ova's necklace and tiara and unpinned her black hair; and brushed it. She unhooked Miss Samsonova's dress and lifted it over her head; she unlaced her corset and rolled it, still warm, in her hand. She poured water from the kettle into the flowery bowl, and stood with the towel while the lady splashed water on her face and took a flannel and washed her arms and her throat before she held out her arms to be dried as though she were a small child.

'I was really jumpy as I dabbed at her arms and shoulders, frightened of doing the wrong thing. Suddenly she was smiling, laughing out loud, and I jumped as she took the towel from me and scrubbed her own face with great vigour.'

The young Mary Martha breathed out then, relaxed, and started to gather all the dropped clothes in her arms, planning to sort them out later in the dressing-room.

' "Maree Mart'a!" Her voice was low and throaty. I turned round to see her slipping her shift from her shoulders and stepping out of it, naked as a new bairn. She threw the shift at me so that it landed on the pile in me arms.'

Young Mary Martha muttered 'Thank you, miss,' and fled to the dressing-room, only to be called back by that low throaty voice. "Maree Marta!

'So I dumped the linen on the floor and when I returned to the bedroom she was still in the same place, in the same state. Looking her directly in the face, avoiding the sight of that white body and its shady places, I say, "Yes, miss?"

Miss Samsonova said something and gestured towards the stool by the bed. Mary Martha ran to pick up the ruffled night dress and hand it to her. Miss Samsonova pulled it over her head and fastened the ribbons at her waist.

'I almost blink, looking at her, I can tell you. Just a dark-haired child. Innocent. Not muc older than me.'

The Russian girl sat at the dressing-table and gestured towards her with the silver-backed brush. Obediently Mary Martha took the brush and started to brush the hair, taking out the tangles at the ends first, as her mother had taught her.

'In five minutes it's smooth as silk. In the mirror the Russian girl mimes a plaiting movement and I plait the hair loosely, tying it with a white ribbon.'

The girl nodded and beamed her approval, then said something, climbed into bed and sat still smiling slightly, while Mary Martha smoothed the covers.

'Then I went back into the dressing-room and sorted out the clothes as far as I could, the soiled clothes into little string-tied muslin bags and then into the Harrods box. I turned down the dressing-room lamp as I came out, and shut the door behind me.

Then I turned down all the lamps in the bedroom. All except the little bedside lamp.

She stood by the bed. "Well, I'll say good night, miss.' I says. And, glad to be off, I make my way towards the door.'

"No!" The voice was sharp behind her. Mary Martha watched Miss Samsonova mime her instruction to stay here, and sleep on the floor beside her bed.

' "That's it!" I shake my head like a donkey. "No, no miss," I say. "I'm not doing that, not sleeping on the floor like no dog. I'll sleep in my bed like any good Christian."

With Miss Samsonova wailing and shouting behind but Mary Martha walked steadily downstairs and along the corridor towards the kitchen. There was a little room behind it that contained her own little truckle bed. As she made her way along the dimly lit passages Mary Martha smiled a little to herself. 'I had to admit that, well; this certainly beat cleaning doorknobs for a living. I hadn't enjoyed myself so much in a long while, I can tell you.'

And now here on Caitlin's balcony I lean across and turn off the tape-recorder with a click. Mary Martha drops back on the sofa, eyes closed. I glance

114

across at Volodya.

'Enough?' I say.

He nods, hauling himself to his feet. 'Enough,' he says, glancing down yet again to the militiaman. Mary Martha opens her eyes. 'There is so much more, but—'

'Another day, auntie,' says Volodya. He pulls her to her feet and guides her back into the sitting-room.

I nod. 'Another day. Then you can tell me all about the Grey Auntie.'

Seated on Caitlin's sofa she blinks at me with those tortoise eyes. 'But I have told you about her, Olivia. Miss Samsonova. Her name is Marie Louise Lydia Samsonova. She was always called Nina. And we changed my name to Samsonova in 1921. I became Nina Samsonova. It was wise to make that change.. For safety.'

This makes sense now, But it is hard to grasp, that the Grey Auntie, that shuffling, sniffling madwoman is the beautiful Nina Samsonova. But she is now a shell, as Mary Martha has said.

Mary Martha relaxes again and I gather the cups and take them to the kitchen, Volodya close behind me. He takes the dishes from me and pulls me to him. I can feel his lean length and the urgency of his flesh. He is whispering in my ear. 'Is that not a great love story, Olivia? Such passion?'

I return his kiss, glad of some way to express the heat of my own delight, my own amazement at all this stuff that has come tumbling from the lips of that very old woman. His hands fumble to the buttons on my dress and he brushes aside my protests about Mary Martha. 'She is old. Telling the truth is very tiring. She will sleep a good time now.'

My hands move to his shoulders, to the inside of his collar. His hands move round and slip onto my bare back under my sweater as he presses me to him. So we make love there and then, standing up: a rough and ready experience which has its own attractions. Somewhere in the back of my mind is the slightest tingle of concern, like a whisper in the wind, as I wonder just when Caitlin will come back from the frozen wastes of Perm.

SIX

Caitlin Ozanne's rather challenging day had started with a heart-stopping flight back from Perm, clinging onto her seat in the string-and-chewing-gum aeroplane. She had grabbed some sleep the night before on a bench in the dusty, freezing airport, deserted apart from a regular patrol of moon-faced, uniformed adolescents who had Kalashnikov sub-machine guns drooping over their arms like steel chrysanthemums.

That morning she'd had to kick-start her photographer to get him into the taxi, dismayed to find that he had made too free with her bribe-vodka. 'To keep out the chill, Miss Ozanne. I promise you. Only to keep out the chill.'

Caitlin had some worries about the quality of the photo-graphs. She was never happy about using Russian photographers after a bad experience with one who forgot to put a film in his camera and had tried to fake pictures in the old Soviet style and nearly got her the sack.

Even while she was interviewing these last three prisoners (whose personal histories were the now-familiar litany of accident and ill luck, malevolent persecution and bureaucratised malignancy), she experienced a sinking feeling.

Here was no drama, no platinum hook. It was true that the mere existence of these men had poignancy and human interest. But the men themselves lacked charisma, they were draine of drama. They were mere hollow husks, not starving, not even (in these enlightened times) visibly abused. And despite their satisfyingly dramatic shaved heads, and their tragic personal histories, for Olivia they committed the unforgivable sin of being ordinary, even boring souls.

She had to admit that this story was not going to set any world on fire or win her any prizes. So it would be a chore, not a buzz, to write the piece and send it down the line. She was not even a hundred per cent sure that her paper would print it. The London desk had been enthusiastic about the idea at first but had in recent days become markedly less enthusiastic. Her relationship with the foreign desk editor, Malcolm Self, had never been brilliant, but was deteriorating by the day.

Malcolm had fancied Caitlin once, even made a play for her, despite the encumbrance of a beautiful wife who went round in a trance induced by the rapid production of four children.

For a while Caitlin had succumbed to the tiniest of flings with him, just as a bit of insurance for her, regarding the prominence of her copy. As an independent woman she would have denied this. But she had a pragmatic streak which judged such actions as distasteful but inevitably useful.

While she was in Moscow she and Malcolm had indulged in some rather elegant coded faxes which obliquely referred to their special relationship. But recently, her physical absence was definitely making his heart grow cynical.

Now, despite the fact that all she wanted was a hot, soaking bath to heat her blood back from lizard to human, she told Piotr to take her straight to the office rather than back to the apartment. The cold, soiled feeling she was enduring might just add the right tone to the piece. Perhaps for once she should make it more personal. A colour piece, perhaps, capitalising on her own feelings about the drab wilderness out there. No. They wouldn't like that. *Hard* they wanted and *hard* was what they would get.

Absently she looked at the way Piotr's hair curled down over his collar. The driver had been rather grimly silent at the airport.

'So, how are things, Piotr?' she asked, not really wanting to know.

His eyes snapped at her through the mirror, pleased that at last she had taken notice of his glowering looks. 'It has been difficult, Miss Ozanne.'

She sighed, her eyes wandering to the car window, picking up a long queue of people outside a china shop that was selling garish gilded china from packing cases: part of a flood of useless goods that would be sucked up into cluttered sitting-rooms in crowded apartments, or sold at a big profit to souvenir-starved Westerners. She dragged her glance back to Piotr. 'My mother?' she said wearily.

'Mrs. Ozanne was missing again.'

'But Piotr, I told you to keep close, not to let her—'

'It was not possible. Your mother is not logical.'

Caitlin stifled a smile. It must be a hard for Piotr. Keeping tabs on Westerners was so much easier in the old days. But she herself had never managed to keep tabs on her mother so why should Piotr, whose dealings so far had been with the more *logical* flotsam and jetsam of the international scene?

'She returned to the apartment?'

'I believe so. But . . .' This through clenched teeth, 'I believe Katya conspires with her. There are people who . . .' He left that in the air. He never spoke directly of the agency, part domestic, part surveillance, which supplied the staff for foreign residents. But its residual power was sometimes invoked.

Caitlin yawned. 'There is no need to tell anyone, Piotr. I am sure Katya has not been conspiring.'

'Well,' said Piotr swinging off Kallinin Prospekt into the yard behind the office. 'This behaviour makes our life very difficult. You know this, Miss Ozanne.'

She jumped out of the car, and waited while he wound down the window. 'These are different times, Piotr.'

He smiled grimly at her. 'Is that so, Miss Ozanne?'

She stood very still for a moment and then said in a flinty voice, 'You can wait in the office, Piotr. I'll be through there in an hour and will need to go to the apartment then.'

She knew he would be pleased to stay in the office. He liked nothing better than lounging on the low Sixties' couch, flirting with Elizabeth and showing off to young Roger Flett-Smith who, Caitlin was sure, was secretly writing a spy novel based on Piotr's distinctly fictional exploits.

But there was something about Piotr. Something which was both sly and mean. When she was tired, this quality put her more on edge than she liked to admit. But she needed Piotr, as she needed Elizabeth, to fix things, to smooth some of the ragged edges of this very difficult life.

As she climbed the stone steps to the office she had an exaggerated awareness of his presence behind her: she knew his heavy eyes would be lingering on her back and her bottom. And she was furious at herself for letting him prickle her into annoyance.

In the event she stayed much longer than an hour in the office, her mind tangled up with oblique assertions of the new Russia, the queue for gilded china, and the redeployment of KGB operatives. She had to rescue herself by scrapping her first draft altogether and writing an informed, straight – and she had to admit it – faintly boring piece about the last political prisoners at Perm.

A whisper faint as silk crossed her mind that writing fiction, compared with this, must be easy. Even fiction about children who suffered the cruel vagaries of adult attention. And there was more than one way to consider that as well. Cruelty. Mistreatment. She tried for a second to think of a time when her mother had been less than a pain in the neck.

At the apartment she refused Piotr's offer to help carry her overnight bag and her bulky computer, leaving him to chat with his friend the militiaman who spent his time in the little sentry box in the inner square. As she went up in the lift a short piece was forming in her mind about the changing role of the militiaman.

The militiaman was undergoing subtle changes in his official surveillance function since the August coup. Bullying resident Russians who visited the building remained a favourite sport, but no one was interested in his reports, any more than they were regularly listening to the tapes in the basement.

The militiaman knew that soon his official pay would dry up and he'd have to look elsewhere for income. Perhaps soon the residents would pay him themselves to guard their property in the proper traditions of capitalism, against the burgeoning mafia gangs who were extending their attention now to the occasional unfortunate Westerner. Yes. An armed paid concierge in uniform - that's what he would be then.

Up till then the Russians operatives who drove cars for the Westerners in the block would gossip with him about their employers and share the small thimbles of vodka that kept him warm through the day and into the night.

Caitlin let herself into the apartment, dumped her over- night bag in the hall and went through to her sitting-room. She blinked hard at the old woman, dressed in the layered clothes of extreme old age, snoring on her sofa.

'What the ...?' Caitlin glanced round, then leaned down and shook the woman's shoulder hard. She withdrew her hands very quickly from the fragile bones, wrinkling her nose at the smell of dust, soap and old person's sweat.

The old woman didn't stir.

Caitlin heard movement, muffled laughter from her own bedroom. She flung the door wide open to see her mother up on one elbow, naked under the Egyptian cotton sheet, talking to a man whose long silver hair spread across the pillow.

'Mother!'

'Caitlin!'

Knowing my poor daughter's tendency towards embarrassment, I pull up the sheet to cover myself properly. The standing-up sex was so funny, so nice, and Mary Martha was so fast asleep that we had been tempted to further, more leisurely, intimacies.

'Caitlin I . . . This is Volodya,' I say.

Volodya rolls over and pulls on his jeans which are in a crumpled heap by the side of the bed. He hops around, finally managing to zip them up. 'Miss

124

Ozanne! I am a great admirer . . .'

Caitlin doesn't take his proffered hand. She glares at me, looking curiously young: a picture of rage, frustration and sheer temper. Muffled up in a military-style grey silk parka, her perfect face is small and grey with tiredness. And at this moment I must say I love her like crazy. I am grateful for the feeling. It is so new.

'Have you a minute, Mother?' She says grimly, and marches off towards my bedroom. I pick up her dressing gown and scurry after her.

\she turns towards me. 'What on earth's happening here? Where's Katya?' she explodes.

'I won't tell you anything till you make a promise.' I clutch her dressing gown around me.

'A promise? Don't be ridiculous.'

I sit down on the dressing stool. 'I won't tell you then.'

She takes off her parka, folds it carefully and lays it on the bed. 'Right then. You have your promise.'

'Promise you'll do nothing to Katya over this? No shouts, no words, no sack? Promise.'

She laughs bitterly. 'I wouldn't do that anyway, but she might get the sack whatever we say. Piotr's bent on reporting her to the agency, though he wouldn't say so in so many words. But I'm not the one to report her. How could you think I would do that? I know you're a law unto yourself so why should I blame her? So on my own behalf that's an easy promise. Now tell me about it. Who's that creature in my bedroom and who is the old woman snoring in my chair?'

'His name is Volodya. And he is a man, not a creature, sweetheart. He translates for a joint venture publishing company. As far as I know. He was down in Kiev doing some teaching for a long while, before that he did some interpreting for government agencies. Came back to Moscow ten years ago and has lived with the two aunties ever since.'

I realise that that, literally, is all I know. I'm not quite sure if Volodya married someone else, after the wife who ran off after the Hungarian, if he has any children . . .

'The old woman is his aunt?'

I shake my head slowly, uncertain of the wisdom of the next revelation. 'No. She is not. And now it seems she's actually English, though he didn't quite realise that—'

'What?' Caitlin's face becomes keen, loses its tiredness.

I go on, 'Her name is Mary Martha Johnson. She came over . . . well I don't know the whole story. She's

126

only started to tell me. She was employed by a Russian family in England during the First World War. Somehow she must have stayed here, become a Russian. Her English was very rusty at first, but when she got started she managed quite well. Old-fashioned English, northern accent. It was like sitting with your ear to a time machine. She got very tired though. So we had to let her sleep.'

'Talk?' Caitlin's whole demeanour has changed. Her aggression has leaked away from her, like water into sand. Her face is now bright and sharp. Once, I saw a police dog being given the clothes of a missing child and starting to strain at the leash. The dog had just such a look. 'Good heavens, Mother! What a story!' She is already at the door.

I grasp her arm. 'Be careful, Caitlin. She's an old woman.'

She shakes off my arm and bestows me a look of withering patronage and contempt. 'Mother! Really.'

In the sitting room Volodya already has a yawning Mary Martha up on her feet, her scarf tied round her neck. His own coat is on, his scarf is already tied round his neck. He bows to Caitlin and smiles at me. 'We must really be going. The Brown Auntie is very tired.'

'There is no need to hurry,' says Caitlin heartily.

She turns her keen eye on Mary Martha. 'My mother tells me you're English . . . Mary Martha, is it? English! How amazing.'

Mary Martha looks blankly at her and mutters in rapid Russian to Volodya. Caitlin proceeds to talk to her in Russian but still Mary Martha stubbornly shakes her head. Then she speaks very sharply to Volodya.

Very deliberately he turns away from Caitlin and towards me. 'We must go, Olivia.' He frowns. 'The old one is worried about the Grey Auntie, tied to her chair in the church all this time.' He half turns towards Caitlin. 'And she is nervous at the hard questioning. She says she has had enough of that in her life.'

Caitlin stands, impotent, as they ignore her and start to make their way towards the door. I put a hand on Volodya's sleeve. 'I'll come to see you tomorrow,' I say.

Keeping one arm around Mary Martha's shoulder, he pulls a battered card from his inside pocket. 'Come to the right place, Olivia,' he says. 'Moscow is still not a good place to become lost.'

Caitlin bangs the door behind them and turns towards me. 'Well!' she says. Her eye drops to the tape machine, its tell-tale light still glittering like a red eye. 'You taped it! You've got her on tape! Mother, you are a wonder.'

I watch her warily, not very sure how to handle this. Caitlin is alarmingly excited. The Brown Auntie's story to me is a wonderful historic story for the archive. To Caitlin this stuff is pure 'scoop' for her journalist's brain - tomorrow's fish and chip wrappers to be sure, but for one day, gold leaf. Front page stuff.

What have I done?

Caitlin sees me watching her. Her face is smooth. 'Now then, Ma. Why don't you pour us both a glass of wine, and I will have a very, very quick shower and then we can listen to the tape together. And you can tell me all you know about that strange pair,; she says very sweetly, dangerous honey in her voice.

I pour the wine but I'm in a tumble of revolt. So I lean over, take out the tape and go into the bedroom to change into proper clothes. I slip the tape into an envelope and put it in the back of my writing case with all the other envelopes. Then I go back and sit down quietly, glass in hand.

Caitlin returns, her head in a towel turban, her face glossy and shining. 'Now!' she says.

I should face it out, admit what I've done. But to tell you the truth I've often found that lies – or implicit lies – save a lot of hassle. That was so with

Kendrick. It is so with Caitlin. When faced with an implacable force it's much easier to slither round it, than to batter one's soft snaky head in its way.

She leans over to turn on the machine. The clicks and whirrs told their own tale. 'There's no tape inside!' she says accusingly.

'No tape?' I say innocently. 'Oh dear!'

'Did you know there was no tape?'

'I thought you always left a tape in. You were using it before you went away.'

'I took the tapes with me to work on. You saw me.'

I take a sip of my wine. 'I didn't realise.'

She flops back in her chair, wine in hand. 'I never know when to believe you, Ma. Never have. I once heard Dad say that you made things up as you went along. I thought it cruel at the time, but now I'm beginning to see some reason in what he says.'

That was the funny thing about Caitlin. She's so like her father yet right throughout her childhood she would defend me against him. He would be reduced to some white-gilled rage at my alleged infringement of his right to have a quiet orderly life and she would shout about him being rigid and deterministic, manipulative and obsessed with control. In this way she ensured that his cold anger would turn on her. So

130

then I would became an onlooker, as they locked intellectual horns in an icy battle for supremacy.

'Mary Martha is not just *a story*, Caitlin,' I venture now. 'It might be very dangerous to turn her into *a story* at this juncture. It could kill her.'

Caitlin throws up her hands. 'I know that, Ma. No incident is *just* a story. But people need to know about these things. They have a right.'

'Not if Mary Martha doesn't want to tell her story, they don't.'

'It would be a wonderful story, Ma. Life enhancing! Surviving seventy years as Lenin rose and then died. As Trotsky won the civil war. As Stalin . . . The Terror . . . The Cold War . . . Glasnost . . . what happened to her through all that? The mirror of history in one life.' Her voice is almost dreamy. She is already writing the piece.

I pour myself some more wine. '*She*'s not history, Caitlin. She's living, breathing, now. Just a very old woman near the end of her days. Leave her in peace.'

Caitlin lifts her towel turban and starts to rub her hair dry. 'Don't you think you're being very patronizing, Ma?' She says this very quietly and I sense battle lines being drawn, on quite a different front.

I'm offended. 'Me, patronising?'

'You are deciding all this for her. Whether she will or won't talk to me. Whether she would or would not like to tell me her story.' She took up a brush and started to trawl it through her thick hair. 'Wouldn't she like to go back to England? Out of all this? It must be hell to be old in the middle of all this business. You've seen the queues. Food is short—'

'Stop! You're not making a broadcast now.'

'Be sensible, Ma. You have the tape haven't you?'

I shake my head. 'You can't hear her or see her unless she wants it. And as for her going back to England, she must be well into her late eighties and she's been here more than seventy years. What would there be there for her now? And what about the Grey Auntie?'

'The other one? Is she English too?'

I shake my head and lie. A Russian high *bourgeoise*! Flavour of the month now. Poor old Nina. 'I don't know,' I say. ' You'd get nothing out of her anyway. She's gaga. Off her trolley.'

Caitlin stands up and stares at me for a minute, a look of blank frustration in her eyes. 'Will you at least take me with you when you go tomorrow? Just let me talk to her?'

I shake my head. 'No.'

'I can find out where they are. That's not difficult any more in Moscow.'

'How would you find out?'

'You say he translates. There are not that many Joint Venture publishers around yet. It won't be too difficult. Of course it might make it a bit difficult for *him*, with his company. They're easily spooked, these new companies . . .'

I put down my glass. 'I'm surprised at you Caitlin. Reduced to blackmail.' I pause, and then sigh. 'All right. All right. But you must talk in English, not Russian, so I know what's going on. And you must do exactly what she wants.'

She leans down and kisses me, laying her soft lips on my cheek, where just an hour ago Volodya had run his finger and rehearsed for me my unique and extraordinary sensual characteristics.

An hour later I am sitting leafing through old copies of *Paris Match*, listening to Caitlin talking on the phone in the bedroom. She's talking to her editor, who appears to have appreciated the piece on Perm. Now I listen to her talk of next week's piece. Apparently she has a lead on a terrific human interest story. This woman, believed to be English, who has survived here since the Revolution. A meeting is being set us as they speak, apparently.

133

I let the betrayal sweep through me, but I take note.

The second after she puts down the phone there is another call. She puts her head round the door. 'It's your erstwhile hippy son, Ma. Seems a bit put out by something.'

Joseph? That brings a smile to my face. Joseph might be unreliable, prone to seeking support from noxious substances, and too frequently broke, but he doesn't use people and he has a sense of the ridiculous which is like a tonic amid the pompous, over self-important people with whom Caitlin surrounds herself.

Like Caitlin her brother Joseph calls himself Ozanne, not Kerslake. 'Nothing against Dad, ma,' he told me once. 'But like Caitlin I think it's much cooler than Kerslake. Got a zed in it, hasn't it? Cool.'

Caitlin has never bothered to explain to me why *she* has always written under Ozanne. My own mother, when she was still compos mentis, used to be pleased about that.

I pick up the phone. I can talk to Joseph. Always could. 'Joseph? Darling, I have such a tale to tell you!

SEVEN

Joseph Ozanne turned off the engine, rocked the bike back onto its stand, planted his heavy boots on the ground and surveyed the house. The paint on its doors gleamed like fresh red cabbage. A single tree, a shrimpy, fragile thing, stood beside the drive on the trim lawn. Its branches were bare now but in the spring its blossom must match the red doors.

He pulled off his helmet, shook his hair free, and marched down the drive. The bell pealed through the house, ringing on in his head like the bell that called them in from playtime in his first school. *School bell peals on and on through my head, through the years.* He would use that. Then terror. He could use that. Into it. He could draw fear on the air. A bell being rung held by a hand with hair sprouting on its back.

No one came. He rang the bell again and watched the shiver of the frilly nets hanging at the door that would herald Naomi's approach. There was no shiver of net.

He put his mouth to the letter-box. 'Naomi, I know you're in there. Open the door. I'm a good boy now, clean as a whistle.' That wasn't technically true, if you counted drink as opposed to other stuff.

'Stepmother, stepmother!' he shouted, using his fairy-tale voice. 'Do let me in.'

Still no response. He returned to the bike, unlocked the security box, took out the chainsaw and carefully assembled it. Yellow enamel glowed and gleaming steel teeth shone back at him in the autumn sunshine: a tribute to the oiling and tender-handling that were among his favourite pastimes. He positioned himself by the puny stalk of the single tree, braced his knees and set the saw away, treating himself to a few feinting waves before positioning himself for a cut.

'Joseph!'

He turned off his saw; the puttering, dying engine echoed around the close like the last ticks of a winding down clock. Two women wheeling pushchairs stopped and eyed him closely.

He waved his chainsaw. 'Hi!' he said. Then he turned to Naomi, who was standing in the doorway; her legs, rather plump of ankle and clad in pink leggings, were like sticks of seaside rock; her fluffy sweater above them a cloud of cerise candy floss. Her hair, done up in a topknot, sported wisps which floated gently down around her slightly heavy jaw.

'What the hell do you think you're doing?' Her voice was high pitched, still laced with the embedded panic of extreme youth sustained too long.

He grinned. 'Just trying to get your attention, miss.' He touched his ragged forelock with his forefinger. 'Cut down your tree, miss? Very competitive rates!'

She glanced round the *cul-de-sac*. One or two of her neighbours were peering openly out of their bay windows. The two women with pushchairs and child cargoes continued to watch with keen interest.

'You'd better come in.' Naomi opened the door and the warm smell of baking wafted over him, bringing with it a memory of one Saturday morning. He and Caitlin are making scones with Olivia. Then his heart is sinking with disappointment when the scones come out of the oven burnt on the bottom and dry as cardboard. And he is angry at his mother for laughing at the catastrophe.

His mother never could bring off anything in the house. It was clean and bare and his mother, unlike other mothers, did very little *to* or *in* it. Years later, when it dawned on him that his mother did this deliberately, to distance herself from the domestic realm, he suffered a belated bout of paralysing anger against her. This gave him yet another excuse to get stoned and forget the obligations of the day.

That was what his counsellors had always said anyway.

137

When he told his mother he was seeing a counsellor (a condition of probation for that incident at the local off-licence), she had clapped her plump hand on her forehead and said dramatically, 'It will all be my fault, Joseph. It is always the mother's fault!' Then she had put her hand on his, smiling apologetically. 'For which I am truly sorry, love. We can regret the past but we can't remake it.'

But for him her tone was too knowing, almost smug.

Now he looked down at Naomi's three delicately poised fingers trying to push the chainsaw to one side. 'And you're not bringing that thing into my house!' she bleated.

He clutched the saw to his bosom. 'This? My baby? She won't do any harm to you or anyone else. You've been watching too many late night films with my father, honey. An' if you think I'm leaving this beauty outside for those grinkles to nick, you're up a tree.'

'Grinkles?'

'Can't you see them? Peering through their windows. Aliens have planted them here in this close, with their pushchairs and their sets of *Le Creuset* in Mediterranean blue. Always beware of blue *Le Creuset*, Naomi. Satellite signalling devices from outer space, don't you know?'

She looked at her stepson for a moment. Joseph was not at all like his father. It was Caitlin who had inherited her father's fine, almost delicate good looks. But Joseph was infinitely more attractive than either of them. He shouldn't really be attractive with his lanky body, his long tangle of hair and his face criss-crossed with scars from unresolved teenage acne. But these blights were more than redeemed by large bright eyes and an anxious darting presence which breathed excitement and danger. She wondered in passing if this sense of excitement, this attraction, came from his mother, Olivia whom she'd never met but who looked distinctly plump and plain on her photos.

When Naomi spoke her tone was reluctantly affectionate. 'You do talk some rubbish Joseph.'

She led him into the through lounge.

He bounced on the black leather couch. 'Still got the old boy's couch? I'd have thought this was a bit . . . well *naff* for people of . . . well, *our* generation.' Naomie was only five years older than he was.

Scenes rolled before him of the first time he met his stepmother. Naomi is standing there in a full-length cream wool coat. She is twenty-three but looks fifteen. His father, elegant in a handmade lounge suit, has put on a tasteful hotel luncheon to celebrate his marriage to Naomi Madon.

Blissful on skag, Joseph hugs his new stepmother's unyielding body, chuckling away, mumbling, 'Another little sister, and a little child-wife. If I didn't know you better, pater, I'd suspect you of breaking the law here.' Joseph kneels at Naomi's feet and puts his cheek to Naomi's stomach. 'Can I hear it? Can I hear that little heart beating? A new life, a little brother.' He starts to chuckle. 'A new wife . . . a new life.'

His father hauls his son to his feet and plants him firmly in a chair, telling him in his hard blank fashion that he must either sit down and behave himself, or leave. But Joseph is relishing the deliciously unusual uncertainty in his father's voice.

In this situation, entering into this shotgun wedding, his father has forfeited his accustomed moral high ground and he knows it. In fact he is glad to have Joseph there at all. Caitlin has sent her regrets. Something about a United Nations meeting in Vienna which she just has to attend, though she would have been charmed, charmed, to meet her father's new wife.

Now here in his father's house Naomi was standing, in front of her Mastergas nearly-real fire, her arms folded her eyes wary.

Joseph glanced round. 'So, where're my little half- brothers?'

'They're at the nursery. I've to collect them soon. What is it you want, Joseph?'

'Well, first, a bed, please. I've nowhere to lay my weary head. Police raided the squat.' In fact a girl who'd cadged gear from him had dropped dead on the dance floor and the police were claiming Joseph had supplied her, for money.

'Kendrick said you were working,' said Naomi. 'Some poetry things or something. Pictures for record albums. And chopping trees or something.' She tucked a curl behind her ear. 'He can exaggerate, your father.'

'Well the poetry gigs don't pay much more than a pint for a set. And I only do the paintings now and then. And the have-chopper-will-travel gigs rather depend on the state of the hangover. A shaking hand is no good for the bush.' He waited in vain for a smile for his witty transposition of the proverb. But none was forthcoming. Naomi was terminally literal in all her dealings in the world. She must be bloody good in bed, he thought.

He went on, 'On the plus side I've two tickles for covers from a record company. But I need to have a shower and go and talk to them.'

Scenes roll out for him now from his Art School

141

days. He's in the office of his tutor, Archie Lawrence, whose red shirt and riotous beard are the only visible relics of a youth spent experimenting with allegedly free sex and the mind-expanding capacities of certain substances. In his lectures he throws in references to The Stones and calls things *cool*, oblivious to the cynicism of his students who find him uncool in the extreme, and despise him for the fact that he stoops to speak a language he doesn't own.

In fact Archie Lawrence's allegedly *free* sex has cost him a lifetime shackled to a female Napoleon who has created an elaborate behavioural code, based on politically correct Sixties ethics: a code that he continually strains to transgress as with middle age he has been transformed into his own father, who was a fussy trade union official who liked his tea on time.

Joseph's own easy entry to the Art School had been a certainty, with his facility for drawing and his raging imagination that fed on and spewed out surreal images by the hundred.

'You have talent and you should nurture it,' Archie is looking at his manicured fingernails, unsullied now by anything as creative as paint. 'Yet you've not been in the studio for a fortnight, Joey. I know it's a turn-off, perpetually being expected to produce something. I've been there, buddy. And I know the old rock-and roll-is a seductive siren; you should have been there when it all started . . .'

Joseph blinks. 'Crap artist,' he mutters.

Archie's head comes up. 'What was that?'

'I've got this cold, Archie. Clearing my throat.'

'Don't think I don't know a hangover when I see one. Like I say, buddy, I've been there. Anyway. ..' The tutor's voice is icy now. His eyes return to his fingernails. 'Anyway. This is a warning that you must produce something or—'

'I'm leaving,' Joseph's voice rushes over that of his tutor.

'Why?'

Now he has Archie's full attention.

'I'm so bored, Archie. Going to the lav is a highlight of my day.'

'You will be bored, buddy, if you're doing the stuff every three hours. And it shows. When you do manage tp get back in the studio you're blanked out.' He pauses 'Anyway, you leave and what do you propose to do?'

Joseph notes that Archie has no intention of fighting to keep him. He makes something up. 'The thing is that this agent's got a whole line of gigs fixed up for me. My poems and Jim Rank's guitar.'

Archie frowned. 'Is this real, Joey?'

'Well, they have done a couple of pubs and the students union.' Joseph embroiders the lie. 'And this guy has someone interested in putting the poems together into a book, with some of my drawings.'

That night, by the time he is snorting his last line, in his cupboard of a room, Joseph believes it all himself. He can see himself making the victory salute as hoards of screaming boys and girls bay for more. Now he's being interviewed on television about his cross-disciplinary creativity and how he's taking the meaning of performance forward. He's running down Oxford Street, ticker-tape sticking to his hair, his shoulders. Or is that Fifth Avenue?

After his interview with his tutor Joseph dropped out completely, happy to rescue himself from Archie and his like. For a time he was indeed seduced by the music scene where his poetry, as surreal as his pictures, is in demand as lyrics from the musicians around him. Then that world moves on from him and he conceives an idea about chopping down trees. He gets his father to cough up for the chainsaw and the bike which was to be his professional transport. Kendrick even wangles him a year's enterprise allowance. But that doesn't even keep him in Charlie and the enterprise fades as fast as it started. But he still has the bike and he still cuts down trees for people, when asked. And when his hand is steady enough.

Naomi reached out and shook his arm. 'Joseph! Come back, come back! Where the hell are you? Are you on this planet at all?' Her voice was cross, even higher pitched than usual.

He stood up and came just too close to her. 'Do you know you have one brown eye and one green one?'

Naomi ducked away from him and put a chair between them. 'Don't try that again, Joseph.'

She had quite enjoyed it last time, giggling as they ended up wrestling rather amicably on the floor in the dining- room. On that day he, the worse for drink, had proved unequal to the occasion, and she, - offended and relieved at the same time - began to redefine the experience as Joseph taking liberties.

Secretly she admitted that it had been a laugh. Kendrick was so limited in his lovemaking: it was all over so quickly, despite being so seriously embarked upon, with all that dressing up. Just for a moment she'd wanted to try it again with a younger man, not worrying too much for a moment that the younger man happened to be Kendrick's son.

But all that was not on Joseph's mind today. He collapsed backward onto the couch. 'Don't worry, Naomi dear. You're safe from . . .' His glance strayed behind her and he frowned. She whipped her head round to look behind her but all there was blank white wall.

'What is it?' she said urgently. 'What is it, Joseph?'

He closed his eyes tight, and then opened them. He smiled. 'It's all right now. It's gone.' Then he smiled his enchanting smile, which had always been so effective with boys and girls, men and women. 'To be honest, Naomi, it was a kind of bird. Its beak is edged with diamonds and it has bright teeth in white gold. There are steel hooks at the end of its feathers and its eyes burn furnace bright with fire. In its talons is a small baby, blood dripping from—'

She struck the back of the seat with her hand. 'That's not funny, Joseph.'

He shook his head, bewildered. 'No it isn't. It's terrifying.'

She put her hands over her little pink ears. 'Stop it, stop it, you idiot. Tell me what you want and get out of this place or I'll pick up that phone and get your father here.'

146

'And what'll he do? Wave a computer report at me?' he sneered. Then he relented. 'Look Naomi. I'm not here to torment you. Honestly.'

'You can't stay. You want money,' she said flatly. 'I know it.'

'Look, Naomi. I've not been so well. There was this thing happened with the police. At the squat. I want to go to my mother's. Stay there a while. I've no money for petrol. Well. The fact is I've no money at all.'

Naomi pursed her lips. 'Your mother's not at home. She's in Moscow with Caitlin.'

Kendrick had exploded over the cost of the trip, saying it was his money Olivia was going with. Gallivanting about! She didn't change, Olivia. Naomi had listened patiently to all this but knew perfectly well it couldn't be Kendrick's money Olivia was using. Hadn't she typed the divorce agreement herself, gloating over the tight conditions? Apparently Olivia had said she'd be all right as long as she had a roof over her head. And Kendrick had made sure that that was what she got – a smaller and infinitely more modest roof than the one she and Kendrick had originally shared with Caitlin and Joseph; a roof with a very modest house underneath it, on that nasty little estate on the edge of the town.

Well, as Kendrick said, she was never there, was she? Olivis never was interested in the house, was she? That was part of the problem. So what did location matter?

But Kendrick had never paid Olivia any money, Naomi was sure of that.

'Russia?' said Joseph thoughtfully. 'That figures. Poor Caitlin. She'll be on hot coals, Ma being there. . I'd have thought she'd rather have had the Gorgon staying with her.'

'Your mother went a week ago.' In her honest moments Naomi resented the way that Kendrick still kept tabs on Olivia. The purpose of this peculiar activity seemed to be the search for extra opportunities to be disgusted with his ex-wife, to sneer at her conduct.

Once Naomi had summoned the courage to tell him he was obsessed with Olivia. 'Obsessed? Nonsense! I loathe the woman.'

Joseph was standing before the mirror, stretching his cheeks this way and that, looking for signs of embryonic spots. 'In that case I can stay at her house without bothering her, can't I?'

'So, you're going to break in?

'She'll have left a key with Janey. And Janey is putty in my hands.'

'Aren't we all?' Naomi sighed and made her way through to the neat little computer corner Kendrick had set up in the dining-room. She reached inside an envelope which had *MILK* neatly printed in one corner and extracted a ten-pound note, two pound coins and a five-pence piece. She thrust it towards him. 'There. That's all there is in the house. You can't stay here. You can buy petrol to get you to Olivia's.'

Kendrick, in his own perverse way, might quite like to see his son. But she couldn't face her husband's moaning all night long about his disappointment in his son and the exact ways in which Joseph resembled his mother.

Joseph grabbed the money and tucked it into his black leather pocket. 'All you've got? Keep you barefoot in the kitchen does he?' He grabbed her and kissed her on the nose. 'Well, everyone to their inclination, stepmother. Everyone to their fancy.' He paused. 'Why d'you *marry him*, Naomi?'

She blushed. 'I fell for him, hook, line and sinker. The works.'

'And now?'

'Now I am married to him and have his two sons.'

He followed her into the hall. She reached across to the hall stand and pulled down a pink striped parka with a fluffy hood. 'I have to get Leo and Gareth. I'm late for the nursery,' she said.

'I'll give you a lift,' he said, expecting her to turn him down.

'OK,' she said. 'Do you have a spare helmet?'

Later, as he roared with unnecessary speed through the quiet suburban streets, with Naomi clinging to his back, his long hair flapping into her face, he reflected that though it was so easy to despise Naomi, he felt sorry for her, stuck with the old man for life. Fancy opting *into* that life sentence.

As for his mother, being pushed out of the nest by Kendrick's urgent need for younger flesh had been the best thing that had ever happened to her. By far the best.

He waited at the nursery to have a laugh and a joke with his little stepbrothers and to give them a pretend ride on the bike. Then he was off. As he stood at the petrol pump waiting for his tank to fill he speculated on the possibility of finding money left lying round his mother's place. She was a bit careless about money. There might be a bit of booze, although she did hammer that a bit herself. Anyway he could have a couple of night's good kip and steady himself for a tree job he was booked for in Hereford. And he'd keep out of the way of the police, of course.

Things would calm down; he was sure of it.

Later that night, having consumed the last half of a very dusty bottle of Dubonnet and three miniatures of some very obscure Spanish liqueur from his mother's shelves, he was visited by a powerful desire to talk to her. He made a mess, turning out papers from Olivia's bureau, trying to find Caitlin's number. He couldn't find it. In the end he telephoned Caitlin's paper. After a big tussle with man on the desk he finally got Caitlin's number.

Olivia was delighted to talk to him. He let her words wash over him. How amazing Moscow was, and how, unlike ordinary tourists, she'd met people who actually lived there. Something about this old woman who was actually English . . .

'I was thinking about that time you, me and Caitlin made those scones, Ma. They tasted like cardboard and were burned on the bottom.' He giggled.

'Joseph? Are you drunk? Where are you?'

He giggled again. 'I'm in your house and I am a very clever boy, getting drunk where there's bugger-all to get drunk on.'

'Joseph? Are you all right?'

He put down the phone and closed his eyes.

'Joseph?' Olivia looked at the dead phone and shook it, as though she could shake - *squeeze* - Joseph himself out of the old- fashioned plastic ear piece. 'Caitlin!' she called. 'Caitlin? How do I ring Janey?'

Caitlin came into the sitting-room, pulling a comb through her beautiful hair. 'Why? Why don't you ring Joseph back? You must have lost the line.'

'No. I couldn't get any sense out of him. I want to ring Janey and get her to go round to my house. He sounds as though he could explode any minute. He's babbling.' Olivia put her hand to her head. 'Don't let it be drugs again. Please don't let it be the drugs.'

Caitlin frowned at the rare look of uncertainty on her mother's face. 'That boy is so stupid, so irrational, I . . .'

Olivia relaxed a little then, and put a hand on her daughter's arm. 'We all know that you are the only rational person in this family, dear. You have to forgive us lesser people for being so fallible.'

Caitlin snatched her arm away. 'Don't be so bloody patronizing! Ma. Anyway. What are you doing tomorrow?

'Well dear, I thought I might go to Red Square with Volodya. We can take Mary Martha. I was wondering ... for lunch. That would be a real treat for them, and—'

'Perhaps I should come. We could take them to TrenMos. It's the place...'

'No Caitlin. Volodya and Mary Martha are my friends.   You *cannot* have them.'

For a moment it looked as though Caitlin would stamp her foot. Then she shrugged. 'Suit yourself. But I'm warning you, Ma, I'll get my story. You watch me. And I'll find outyou're your creepy Russian really is. I promise you.' She picked up the phone. 'I'll get Janey for you. What's her number, again?'

EIGHT

'Is everything in this city designed to make you feel small?'

Volodya stands still while I put on my glasses to get a better perspective on this vast space. Red Square is at once more vast but, with the high walls and red-brick towers, warmer and more human than I'd expected. My own expectation is based on the May Day processions I've seen on television - never-ending cavalcades of tanks and nuclear warheads, trucks and immaculately turned-out soldiers performing their high-kicking march.

I remember once sitting on a sofa with Caitlin (trying without much success to get her to breast-feed) feeling so much despair as I watched miles of bristling hardware on the screen, roaring past three politicians - more Toby Jug than human - who were taking the salute from a balcony. At that point Caitlin bit my tender nipple with her hard gums, I shot a foot into the air and she started to wail her *I-am-offended-wail*.

'That's it! That's it!' I roared, forgetting the procession, tears of pain and frustration in my eyes.

'It's a bottle for you, lady, no matter what those frigid, do-gooding midwives say.

A lousy mother. I'll settle for that, I thought.'

I can see the Toby Jug balcony right beside me, now: a harmless enough lump of marble. Red Square looks reassuringly tame now, with its gaggles of tourists hopping about the great space like misplaced sparrows, and its collection of red-brick, turreted buildings like the abandoned set of some Nineteen-Thirty movie.

I touch Volodya's arm. 'Did you ever take part in one of the May Day processions?'

He nods. 'Yes. I was a very young officer. 1959.'

I have to smile. 'I was watching that year. Caitlin was a baby. She bit me.' I pause, thinking of a question that I might ask. 'What did you feel like, Volodya, marching along there, after all that weaponry?'

'One part of me felt very bad. You say the word *ropey*? It is a good word for that feeling. Too much vodka the night before.'

'The other part of you?'

'Pride. We had in our brigade men who had defeated Hitler. And we knew we were part of the Soviet Union, the most exciting country on earth.'

I stir at this. 'And did you believe all that guff?'

'Did you believe your own propaganda? That Britain ruled the waves? That Britons never, never, never would be slaves?'

'We might not rule the waves any more. But we never have and never will be slaves.' I was surprised at the patriotic heat this raised in me.

'Not slaves to America? To the almighty dollar? To hedonism, to the soft luxuries bought on the backs of the poor and oppressed? That's what we were taught about slavery in the decadent West.'

'But that's all lies. You know that. Just as I know we don't rule the waves. But where was the truth in all that? Where is the truth?'

He puts a hand on my arm. 'The only truth we know, or may know, is what we see or hear, touch or smell.' He moves closer and his lips are on my ear. 'That is why playing with children and making love are the only truths worth talking about.'

He is wrong about the lovemaking. How many times, in the early years of marriage, did I fake enjoyment when I made love to Kendrick? There was no truth in that either. Funnily enough when I stopped faking it Kendrick hardly seemed to notice it, so busy was he demanding the tiny excesses which led to his climax.

'Did . . . do you have children, Volodya?'

'Yes.' he said. Then he took my arm. 'Now do you want to see Lenin or not? Will you participate in this continued orgy of necrophilia?'

'Certainly. I will. Caitlin'd not forgive me if I didn't. Especially as they'll be dismantling the old boy soon.'

At least this would be something to talk about over dinner tonight. I firmly turned down her offer to ride shotgun with me on this visit to Lenin's tomb, so Caitlin has dragooned me into going to dinner with Charles Conrad and her. And I am invited to take Volodya. Obviously this is all part of her scheme to get her hands on Mary Martha, no doubt. I feel that Volodya should go, if only to prove that he wasn't some snaky ex-KGB colonel.

He still hasn't said whether he will come.

Mary Martha was quite keen to come to Red Square. She is here with us, the Grey Auntie in tow. Volodya said she had not visited the tomb mausoleum before. 'I very much doubt whether it will last many more months. They should bury him. It is an obscenity. He did not wish it himself.'

'Have you ever seen inside?'

'Many years ago. I was in a group of young soldiers. And we saw Mr. Stalin, who used to lie beside him.'

'What did you think then, when you saw him . . . them?'

'Like the parade, it was an honour. I wept. They were gods, these men, in my childhood. Listen, for her newspaper in these days your daughter talks to many people who will swear that they never believed in all that, how they were forced to play what you call 'lip service'. I tell you that is not the case. These great men, bad or good, were the fulcrum of our society. Like the spider they spin the whole web of this society through their own stomach. They *are* it and *it* is they. We, the people, are the filaments of the web. They hold the centre. When you take them away the centre will not hold. As you know, it is not holding now.'

'But you were not the filaments, Volodya. You were the flies caught on the web. There to be devoured. Millions were devoured.'

He shrugs.

I make up my mind at this moment that, once we are on our own I will get out of him, once and for all, who he is and how he came to be here in this place at this time. There is a good deal I need still to know about this man. I feel that I know every nook and cranny of his body, but as for his mind, that is strange country indeed to me.

But then, I am such an unreconstructed woman

158

aren't I? Why can't I be more like a man, and enjoy this encounter on its very pleasant sexual level and leave it like that? Own the body without preoccupying myself with the soul? Women are so predatory, when you think of it.

'Will you come inside with me, Mary Martha?' I look into the brown eyes.

'Yes, I would like to see him. Mr Lenin.' The soft voice of Mary Martha whispers in my ear. She is standing quietly beside us, her arm tightly through that of the Grey Auntie. 'He was a very big man in the beginning was Mr. Lenin. A great man.

I glance at Volodya. 'Will you come?'

He shakes his head. 'No. I will wait by the corner. It is only a small queue. You go. Take the Aunties.'

'Small? There must be fifty people in it.'

'Sometimes the queue used to go right around the square. A thousand people would be nothing.' His hand goes to his pocket and he pulls out a battered paperback. 'I stay here on the corner. I will read Mr. H.G. Wells. *The War of the Worlds.*'

I take my place in the queue with the two old ladies. 'Did you ever see Mr. Lenin?' I ask Mary Martha.

She shakes her head. Her sleek hair framed by

the little woollen hat she wears instead of the usual head scarf. She has dressed for the occasion. She is wearing black suede gloves which have little mends all over. And silver earrings with crystal drops.

'What lovely earrings!' I say.

She puts a hand up to her ears. 'They were a present from Nina on the tenth anniversary of the day we met.' As she turned in the light the earrings glittered with white fire. Perhaps they weren't crystal. Brilliants perhaps. They might even be diamonds. 'They are the last precious thing. All the rest is gone, bit by bit.'

I remember seeing her sell the fine dress with bugle beads. I glance around wondering if she is safe. 'They're diamonds Mary Martha, aren't they? Are you sure it is quite wise? They could be snatched from you.'

She shrugs. 'They were a special present,' she says. 'I could not let them go.'

'You loved Nina, didn't you Mary Martha?'

'So I did. And she loved me. Every day of our lives. We shared a bed and a life. The good and the bad.'

Now I'm not very up on all this stuff between women. I've seen some very respectable devoted relationships in my time. A pair of women teachers

160

living a delicate and specifically ordered life with their cats; one or two loving friendships at college which, I only realised afterwards, must have had sexual as well as affectionate content. Joseph has brought gay friends home from time to time; they were remarkable only in a combination of sparky gentleness and jollity which made them good companions over a late-night drink. I'm not a hundred per cent sure that Joseph himself is not what Janey sometimes calls one of 'our feathered friends'. But then he has brought girls home as well: girls who were obviously besotted. Perhaps he likes his bread buttered on both sides. Perhaps he just wants to be everybody's sweetheart.

Then again perhaps he is ahead of his time. Perhaps the next surge in civilisation will be when the human race acknowledges that there is no great division between the sexes, other than by our own manufacturing.

In any case, is it different between women than it is between men? Women have the custom of intimacy on their side. They can have affectionate and sub-erotic relationships with each other under the umbrella of what is called ordinary society. Even that is just one element in a whole spectrum of friendship with men and women, which women, with any luck, enjoy.

For men I imagine it's different. Just a sniff of the over- affectionate or the sub-erotic between men and they are wondering whether they should upscuttle their life, with its wife and their two-point-four children, and come out as gay. This is such rigid thinking.

One time I tried to talk this out with Caitlin and she accused me of being a fellow-travelling, politically incorrect, out-of-date pragmatist. Funny, then, that she hasn't spotted that thing between her beloved Charles and the lanky Dutchman.

A wall of heat meets us at the entrance to the building. I take off my coat and drape my cardigan round my shoulders. As we get nearer to the entrance of the mausoleum a quasi- religious silence descends on the queue and we squirm a little as the beautifully accoutred soldiers focus their attention on us. These boys have full round faces, shining and polished and the hair beneath their caps is closely barbered. (These are soldiers in a different league to the youthful army conscripts in dusty fatigues, country boys from the Southern Republics, who I have seen digging up roads and building walls, in an ineffectual, desultory fashion, all over the capital.)

I jump as one of these glorious military beings steps forwards and stops me, a hand on my shoulder.

He says something. I understand the tone but not the words.

Mary Martha, her eyes lowed, murmurs. 'He says you must remove your jumper, Olivia.'

My cardigan is draped quite neatly around my shoulders. 'Why?' I say, clutching it with my Westerner's lack of deference.

'Because it is disrespectful. Do it, Olivia.' There is the iron thread of authority in the soft northern voice.

I obey, slipping the cardigan off and folding it carefully, respectfully, over my arm. We step inside and are funnelled further and further down along a railed-off carpet into an eerie, domed space at the centre of which, half propped up, is the figure of the man who, almost accidentally, succeeded in imposing his brutally surreal design for living on a nation, an empire. The bier is somehow designed so the face appears to radiate a white light from within. It is such a familiar face, etched on a thousand statues; an emblem illuminating a thousand documents. Amazingly, his hair is red; I have a sense of how young this man was when, no longer the spider, he was caught in stillness like this, like another fly on the web.

Tears of rage and pity prick at my eyes: rage at the man and the callous system which he set in process, and pity at the fact that his chemicallised, distilled remains have not been put to rest. The Soviets certainly got their mileage out of the last poor rags of this being who was merely human, after all.

Behind me a muffled sob broke the silence and I could feel rather than see Mary Martha put her arms round the shaking shoulders of the Grey Auntie. Under the eagle eye of the nearest soldier we shuffle on and on and on until we are at last into the daylight. The grey September light seems like a brilliant dawn and the fresh air is sweet and wholesome in my mouth.

Across the square Volodya pushes his book back into his pocket and strides towards us. Mary Martha, clutching the wailing Grey Auntie, scuttles on ahead of me and passes Volodya at speed. He raises his eyebrows and, taking my arm, we chase behind them. We catch up with them right at the other side of the square.

I put a hand on Mary Martha's shoulder and she slows down. 'What is it Mary Martha? I know it was awful in there, but . . .'

She looks anxiously behind me, but when she sees we aren't being followed she stops, pulling the Grey Auntie to a halt, murmuring, stroking her friend's face and muttering to her until the wailing stops.

'What is it?' I repeat.

Mary Martha lets out a long, relieved sigh. Then a small smile breaks across her face. 'Do you know what she did? In there, in that sinful atheist's church?'

I shake my head.

'She wet herself. Right there on the carpet near the old feller's head.' She laughs out loud. The Grey Auntie starts muttering. 'Showed him what we think of him, didn't she?'

I laugh with her now, looking into her face, leaning on her shoulders and our laughter slides into excess because of the contrast between the ghastly museum of the past and the dead and the wide open freedom of the square.

Even Volodya is smiling. 'She might have been arrested,' he said. 'Even in these days.'

'No wonder they were running away,' I say, putting my arm through Mary Martha's. Volodya links his arm through mine and the four of us walk on, linked like the best of comrades. So many comrades in this square. So many years.

I look down at Mary Martha. 'We must get the Auntie home now, so that she can . . . well . . . sort herself out. So she won't be . . . uncomfortable.'

Just outside the wrecked elegance of the great

GUM store I step out in the road and hail a car. I am getting used to some small feeling of power in this city. With friends like these and fifty dollars hard currency in my pocket I can be queen of this city: buy anything, go anywhere! I have access to its past. I am enjoying its present. And as for the future, I have a certainty that my three companions are bound up with that.

Back at the apartment the Aunties vanish into their rooms and Volodya makes coffee for me on his small stove. I sit up on the bed, my back to the wall, my feet straight in front of me.

He brings the steaming cups across and smiles down at me. 'Ah, the lady rests,' he says.

'There are such long distances to walk in this city. My feet are killing me. Those cobbles on Red Square might just have been daggers.'

He puts down the cups, sits beside me, slips off my shoes and takes my feet in his hands. For a second I wish my feet and legs would have the smooth, unused beauty of those limbs on the Polly Peck advertisements. But I close my eyes and forget all that as he massages first one foot and then the other with his hard, firm touch.

I drop off to sleep for what must be just a few seconds and Joseph is there in a dream. He has brought me the small branch of an oak tree, in full leaf. Winding round it is mistletoe, its fruit hanging in waxy clusters.

My eyes snap open. Volodya has stopped rubbing my feet and is staring at me.

'Do you have a son, Volodya?'

His pale skin reddens. 'I had one. He was killed in Afghanistan.'

'A daughter?'

'She lives in America. I do not hear from her in many years.'

'A wife? After the one who ran away with the Hungarian?' The pause is too long. 'Yes. No. She killed herself with vodka after our son was killed. I was in Kiev at the time. I could not help her.'

My life has been so trivial compared with this. I take his hand in both of mine. 'I'm so sorry, Volodya.'

'It is past,' he said briefly, slipping my shoes back onto my feet. He hands me my cup. 'Here, drink the coffee. And we can get the Brown Auntie to tell more of her story for your tape. And then we will go with your daughter to dinner.'

Very clearly put in my place, I swing my feet to the ground. Better off sticking to the sex. This personal stuff drives you apart. Gets you nowhere.

'I told your mother she shouldn't go. It's on the television, the trouble out there. Queuing for food. No electricity.' Janey sat in the peacock chair watching Joseph fiddle with bits of wood and glue on the low coffee table. 'Er, just what was it you were doing there, Joseph?'

'I'm building an aeroplane. I was scrounging about in the loft and I found this kit in a box. It was addressed to me.' He threw across some torn packaging which had To Joseph. Happy Christmas 1975 scrawled across Santa and his sleigh. 'It was unopened. I never received it.'

'Olivia's always losing track of things,' said Janey, watching him carefully.

'Tell me about it' he murmured, squeezing a line of glue onto the fragile edge of a wing.

'That's not just an excuse to play about with glue,' said Janey suddenly. 'Is it?'

He hooted with laughter at this. 'Must have been at school when I did that stuff. Didn't like it even then.'

'What about the other stuff?' said Janey cautiously? 'Olivia said—'

'I'm off it. Months now. Went through a programme, counselling and everything. Off it all. Apart from grass, which doesn't count? Clean as a

168

whistle—'

'So why are you here? Lurking around in your mother's place?'

He frowned at her, and then shrugged. 'I was at this party and this bloke asked me to pass this tablet to his girlfriend. Anyway the girl freaked out, had some kind of seizure, the boyfriend's vanished and the police are looking for me.'

Janey offered him a cigarette and took one herself. She lit hers, drew on it very deeply, and then allowed a fine billow of smoke to drift from her mouth. She screwed up her eyes and looked at him. 'You should go to the police and tell them.'

'To be honest, I can't be bothered to argue the point with those bozos. They won't believe me.'

'They'll catch up with you.'

He shrugged. 'Another day.'

'Olivia rang to ask me to check that you were all right. She said you were stoned when you rang her. Are you all right?'

'Well, you can tell her I am. It was just booze. I had emptied all her bottles.'

'You ring her. You tell her.'

He pressed the second wing in place and held the fragile aeroplane up against the light. 'OK Janey. I'll do that if you go out and get something to drink and some crisps. Then when you come back we can get drunk and have a game of draughts.' He pushed a battered box towards her. 'I found this game of draughts in another box in her loft. We used to play that for hours on end when we were waiting for Olivia to come home from some late session at school. The only thing I ever beat Caitlin at. She cheated like mad at Monopoly.'

Janey gathered up her bag. 'And I have to pay for this booze?'

'I would pay if I could, Janey. But I can't.'

He waited till the door crashed behind her and picked up the phone. It took some time to get a line and when he did, there was only Caitlin telling him what a twerp he was.

He broke into her barrage of talk. 'Just tell Ma I'm all right. Not a thing the matter with me and that Janey and I are just about to embark on a game of draughts.'

'She'll be here any second. She's supposed to be back for us to go out to dinner.'

He picked up her annoyance. 'Being a bad girl, is she? Never could stand anyone disobeying orders, could you, Caitlin?'

'Don't talk such rubbish, Joseph.' The phone clicked with crisp finality at the other end of the line.

Joseph looked at the receiver for a second then placed it carefully in its cradle. Then he cleared the aeroplane debris to one side of the table and laid out the counters for the draughts. This bit of fun with Janey would calm his nerves. Stop him picking up the phone to talk to Mick or Garthie to ask what was happening down there. He wondered how the girl was, if she was out of hospital. No point in letting anyone know where he was. There was time enough for all that.

He found himself staring at the white wall above the table which was starting to move, stretching this way and that like a great lump of chewing gum, as though something or someone was battling to break right out and leap into the room.

He clenched his hands and the sweat poured down his face. He could feel it, hear it, like a great ocean swishing around in the hollow of his throat below his Adam's apple. Now he could see a great jewelled wing break through the chewing-gum wall. Then he screamed a high-pitched child's scream and Janey, coming through the door, dropped her clinking plastic carrier, walked towards him and took him into her arms. 'What is it, babe, what is it?'

He was gulping now. 'It's nothing, Janey. Nothing. But it keeps coming back.'

'I thought you said you were clean? Off all that?'

'I am! I am!' he wailed. 'I haven't done any stuff for months. But still I see this thing. It keeps coming back. Time and again it comes back. And I don't know what to do about it.'

NINE

The wrinkles on Mary Martha's face concentrate themselves into a frown. Then she began.

'We travelled to Russia from a port in the North of England. Hull – do you know of it? I was that excited at first. We were in the North. Perhaps not so far from where I grew up. But they told me it was far too far to call into Darlington, or even to get my Mam to come, to wave us off from the quay. I cried about that and Nina put her arm about me. Strange even then, Nina doing that. Ladies didn't do that, you know. Touch you.' She paused. Volodya's French clock whirred and clicked and started to strike the hour. 'When I think now, of those times, me, a little bairn going into that cauldron of trouble. I can weep for that little bairn that was me.'

Volodya glances at me, a faint smile of sympathy on his face. But what I am feeling is my own shame. I am shamed now, thinking of myself at that age, at just the age when Mary Martha was embarking for Russia: my own self-pitying melancholy. At fourteen years I was playing truant from my grammar school; writing false notes to teachers; lying on a hard couch listening to a record of Elvis Presley singing *Heartbreak Hotel*.

I try to tell Volodya about this. How it is our privilege at this end of the century, in the West, no longer to suffer tragedies of any significant scale. So what do we do? We create epiphanies of inner destruction, such as anorexia; sicknesses of self-abuse through drugs; involuntary hatred of our children. Even worse, we submit ourselves to vicarious substitutes for real experience, mediated by screens of one size or another: baffled by the scale of two world wars and a hundred minor wars, by being the helpless witnesses of genocide and famine as wide as continents, we have invented minor hells in our selfish universe to convince ourselves of our sentient, suffering existence.

Mary Martha puts her hand on mine, stopping my rush of words.

'Let the Brown Auntie tell her story, Olivia,' says Volodya, and I wince at the note of reproof in his voice. I turn my hand so I am holding that of Mary Martha, crisp as paper and fragile as a bundle of twigs.

On the long journey to Moscow Nina and Mary Martha became friends, never out of each other's sight for more than a few moments; fascinated by each other's strangeness; drawn together by the unmistakable magnet of attraction. They went by train to the North of England to board ship to Finland, then on long train journeys first to Petrograd, then on to Moscow.

From the moment they first got on the train together Nina insisted on beginning Mary Martha's French lessons. She drew pictures, she pointed at objects and people, named them, and made Mary Martha repeat and repeat and repeat. She sang French nursery songs to her, and folk songs about unrequited love, acting out the passion in comical excess.

After days of feeling utterly in a fog, it started to dawn on Mary Martha that she could use bits of this new code and when she did the language worked: if she concentrated she would crack it. From that point she made great progress, a progress endorsed by many kisses and hugs from a delighted Nina. The lessons continued on the boat across to Helsingfors, even though Mary Martha was seasick and cried for her mother. Nina calmed her down by promising they would return the next year and they would all visit her family at Darlington.

Now Mary Martha laughs. 'Not much hope of getting home, though I didn't know then. Fancy them at home seeing me in my fine duds and Nina with her hats. They wouldn't know us!'

It seems to me that with every gale of words Mary Martha is getting younger and younger. She stumbles very little with the English now and the more she speaks the more she remembers.

It was hard at first to understand why Nina should be so kind. It wasn't common. That class of person. But Russians are different. I didn't know that then, but I have learned it since. I suppose you might say she treated me like a doll. Something to play with in those long days.

In the Count's house in Petrograd her bedroom had twenty-seven dolls in it from all over the world. Perhaps for a time, I was to be just another doll. I thought she would get sick of me, of course. Much later on she told me she always loved me, from the moment when we watched the English Queen together. And I believed it in the end. But in the beginning I wasn't to know that, was I?'

The Count's party paused briefly at his mansion in Petro- grad; in those days Kerensky's Provisional Government was holding temporary sway. The chilly streets, scoured by the wind from the Gulf of Finland, and carpeted with dirty slush, were pulsing with people – workers, peasants and soldiers moving in to attend a great meeting which would seal the fate of Russia.

But even then at the height of the Revolution,

176

anything was available for money and the Count had
no difficulty renting a modest carriage to take them
from the great Railway Station to Moscow, to the
Samsonov house by the canal.

Mary Martha shudders now as she talks of those
crowds and the grey cold of the day, the slushy
uncleaned pavements. But people let them by. Only
one group, a gaggle of lads in muddy conscript tunics
challenged them, pulling the horse to a stop.

Mary Martha's voice fades and I think of the
soldier labour battalions I have seen in Moscow just
this week: swarms of young lads in muddy conscript
uniforms performing the most menial communal
labour in this great city. Even now.

I wait a moment, and then push her on a little.
'So what did they do, those lads?'

Mary Martha shrugs. 'We had to get out of the
carriage. They pushed us around a bit, and took Nina's
case. But the Count talked to them and showed them
some papers, which they held upside down, the wrong
way up. They couldn't read them, you see? He showed
them money. Then another fellow came up, just a year
or two older than them, who could read. He took the
money to let us through and he made them give Nina
her case back.'

The Count hurried them into the house and bolted the door behind them. The staff had fled, all except a squat, low-browed young man . . .

'. . . built like a frog, he was . . .' says Mary Martha. 'Alexei. He was the Count's second cousin or something, wrong side of the blanket, of course. But really acted like a secretary.' She glances round Volodya's room. 'Alexei it was who lived here in this room before you, Volodya.'

'The old man? The old man was Alexei?'

Mary Martha nodded. 'That old man.'

'So you came to Moscow?' I push her on again.

'We came straight on to Moscow. In Petrograd Nina had rooted out some plain clothes for herself from the servants' chests. Really drab they were. And we had spent a whole day sewing her jewellery into our petticoats. Then the next night the Count rode with us and Alexei to the station and we caught the overnight train to Moscow.'

'The Count too?'

She shakes her head. 'The Count had great hopes of that first government. Like plenty of them he thought he had something to offer for Russia. Change. Modernisation. He said he would send for us when things quietened down again. But they didn't

178

quieten down, did they? The Bolsheviks got the upper hand, and then there was the civil war. They killed the Royal Family didn't they? Beat the Whites and that was that. The new age.'

She sighed. 'The Count and his Countess just vanished. They said he had been thrown into the Neva with stones tied to his feet, but we could never find out. It was dangerous even to try.'

'So you were in Moscow with Alexei?'

'We came here,' she looked round the room, frowning, trying to think back.

'This house?'

'This was the Count's house. It stretched the whole block then. But when we arrived it was already pillaged. That was lucky really. They never came back. There was nothing to get.'

'So you set up home here?'

'Where could we go? The streets were running with people who didn't know what they were supposed to do. There were boys – children – with guns. Blood-lust. There were posters telling them to kill the likes of Nina, even the likes of foreigners like me. Landowners and shopkeepers were clubbed to death. But somehow not us.'

She and Nina unpicked their jewels from their petticoats and went out with Alexei at night and hid them in the ground at various points on the outside of their building. Alexei started to teach Mary Martha, and Nina, the kitchen Russian of his grandmother who had been a slave, in the service of Nina's grandfather in more ways than one.

Mary Martha smiles slightly. 'Such spoken Russian was a better credential than a gun, in the new way of things. And Alexei got us papers to show that we were his sisters, and we shared his credential of a grandmother who was a slave.'

And then?' I say, clutching Mary Martha's hand even more tightly.

'And then? Nothing. Keep going. Survive. Live. The house was split up in the democratic fashion and we were allowed the top rooms. We always claimed that we had been servants here; that Nina was my sister.' She sighed. 'And such we came to be. Sisters. All in all. Everything to each other.'

'And Stalin? The Terror?'

She shrugged. 'Mr Stalin? We were little mice up here. We made no display of wealth. Alexei found some work as a cook in various communal kitchens and later in a state restaurant. We had papers. There was nothing to blame us for. We were true comrades. Sometimes we went to the new theatre and the new ballet. Very cheap for comrades, but Nina said it was not like before.

Nina and I sewed things for people in the house and we got bread and potatoes. We queued. We still queue. Alexei brought us things from the kitchens, although he could not manage without his vodka, so there was little money.'

Then one day Nina fainted in the street and was brought home by a thickset man in black clothes.

Mary Martha smiled her wide gap-toothed smile as she told us of the man in the black clothes. 'He was a priest. Not openly of course, but he was a priest. He came to us and he made us see outside our little lives; we began to see the eternal pattern of it all. We told him our true story and he took us into the bosom of his church. We let him see our icon. We put it into his safekeeping. The one I showed you.' She cocks her head at me. 'It was the little church where you and I first talked, Olivia. So all these years Nina and I had a purpose. We cleaned the church and polished the holy icons. We kept watch on our own icon. So lives which had no worth were given worth. Beauty where there was none. Colour in the dark world. Even when no services were allowed, even when it was used to store carpets, the building had to be kept up. History of the people, see?'

She frowns, trying to bring something to the front of her mind, some memory gnawing at the fabric of her recall. 'The priest brought there an Englishman, a great big man with a blood-mark here.' She touched her cheek. 'Just before the Great Patriotic War. That Englishman said he could get me home, back to England, if I wanted. I said yes, and I would take Nina. But that was not allowed. Nina could not go. So I stayed here, with Nina and Alexei.' She lies back against the cushions, her eyes closed.

Volodya's clock ticks away.

'What about Nina's jewels, Mary Martha?' I say. 'Surely they would be some use?'

She shakes her head. 'Not a bit of use to us. We had some fights but I would not let her touch them.' The shadow of a smile of satisfaction crosses her face. 'We had many a fight. But they would have betrayed us, those things, wouldn't they? The slightest sign of wealth and someone would inform. We thought of giving them to the church, but even there, there are informers.'

'A pity,' I say. 'You could have had a better life, more. Comforts. A more comfortable life.'

She shakes her head. 'We sold a few bits of clothes. But the jewellery? We'd have vanished in the night, like thousands of others. You get in the habit of

182

secrecy. All the time. You have to live for yourselves.'

Volodya stirs in his chair. 'The jewellery is still there?' he said, frowning.

'Under concrete now, Volodya. Under the pavements. Not even you could know, Volodya. It had to be secret. What was the point of you knowing? That's what we did, Nina and me. And Alexei. Kept the secret. Alexei was a worry now and then, with his drinking, and the funny women he brought here to 'play house'. Wives he called them. He was a fool in drink.'

.'But he died?'

'He died. Ten or eleven years ago.'

'Was he sick?'

She shakes her head. 'Too drunk to come home one winter's night and died of cold. We found him the next day in a back alley. Stiff as a board.' She shakes her head, and then nods across at Volodya. 'Anyway, we had to let the room and that's how *he* comes to be here. We said he was our nephew.'

'And Nina?'

The animation fades a little from her face. 'I told you once. My Nina has gone, the lovely beautiful lass I knew. She left her little body behind and I tend the body to honour my Nina's memory. But I am alone now.' She heaves a great big sigh and I think of the

Grey Auntie sleeping her vacant dreamless sleep in the room along the corridor. 'I saw you that day here with Volodya and felt I had to tell him to bring you to see the icon. The beautiful icon. That is why I spoke, and now the secret is broken. I recognised you, like my Nina recognised me in London all those years ago.'

I put my arms around her and we rock together on Volodya's daybed. Her body is as fragile as a sparrow's beneath my hand and I can smell on her the old aroma of dust and incense which is the essence of the little pink church with the golden dome. In this moment I love her more than I loved my own mother, more than I love son, daughter, husband or lover. In this moment she is part of me and I am part of her for all time.

Caitlin is trying her best to be really nice to Volodya as the car bumps along the road. Piotr is taking his bad temper out on the car, screeching to a stop on corners and muttering at pedestrians who jump out of his way.

The dark night streets are only spasmodically lit. Piotr encounters a dead end, and has to reverse. Caitlin glances at the map on her knee and speaks to him sharply. He settles for a more sedate speed and she shouts instructions to him at every corner.

We finally screech to a stop in a rare surviving

street of old houses set beside the rearing wall of a high residential block. A shaft of light emerging like a silver sword through an open door spotlights a dinner-suited doorman talking to Charles Conrad, bulky in a heavy coat and scarf.

Charles beckons us.

'There is never a table,' said Caitlin, 'without a little lubrication.'

Coming into the restaurant from the cold, ill-lit road it seems that we have moved on fifty years in time and across a continent in territory. This could be any middle-range city restaurant in London or Vienna: he familiar smells dominated by pepper and garlic, the tinkling of jazz piano, the clatter of cutlery and the bustle of men in long white aprons.

The foreign customers, the majority, stand out, the men in lounge suits, the women in sub-designer clothes with subtly cut hair. Two tables are occupied by Russians: the women are very young and stunningly beautiful, their make-up too highly coloured for Western taste, their hair over-lacquered, the men in Armani suits and gold wrist-watched.

I am learning. Tonight I didn't need Caitlin to whisper 'Mafia' in my ear.

And the steaming trays emerging from the kitchens give the lie to the contemporary legends of

185

food shortage in Moscow. In my mind's eye I can see Mary Martha patiently queuing yet again outside bread- and food-shops with crowds of other equally patient souls.

I think of her saying how, during Red October, at the height of the Revolution, 'anything could still be had for money'.

We settle ourselves round the table. Volodya looks handsome, if not quite up to Mafioso standard, in his very decent suit with its unfashionable 1970s cut. Caitlin introduces the men and they shake hands and nod. I'm not sure whether the slight guardedness is because they instantly dislike each other, or whether it is Charles being reserved, the reserve I have noted here with all Westerners when they are around Russians.

They start to speak in rapid Russian but I tap the table. 'In English if you please. I'm here as a participator, not an onlooker.'

Caitlin and Charles exchange looks. Volodya grins at me. 'Charles is, as they say, attempting to get my level. Isn't that what the English always do? Especially English journalists. Find out if a person is worth talking to and if he is worth talking to, then what the subject matter may be, so he may have a product from the conversation.'

Charles laughs heartily. 'A lot of leeches, that's all we are, dear boy.' He turns to me. 'Your daughter told me that Volodya had to go away from Moscow once. I was curious as to why.'

'I told my daughter, it was about papers he had written.' My uncertainty shows in my voice. I still do not really know what he does now or did before.

Volodya flicks a glance at all of us. 'The paper was my notes from a trial in camera, where I was translating. An American businessman who was in the wrong place at the wrong time. They got him to admit much. In fact what he admitted was true. Anyway the paper got into the wrong hands by accident. So they hassled me a bit about it, and then offered me a job which I couldn't refuse down in Kiev.'

'Do you have that paper now?' said Caitlin eagerly. 'And were there other times? Did you—'

He shrugs. 'History overtakes it, Miss Ozanne. Yesterday's news is very old news, is it not? The archives are being opened. With *glasnost* what was hidden becomes open and we see it as the boring stuff it is. . It fills us with *ennui*. What would have earned me many dollars in the old days is now common knowledge. So much paper. No story.'

'But . . .' Caitlin is positively sparkling across at Charles. 'My dear mother, with her aptitude and

187

intuition for fiction, has uncovered something much more fascinating at the human level.'

I am surprised at my disappointment as I witness her in this seductive mode. I'm used to her being strong and self-assertive. It's odd seeing her laid low by Cupid. That's for us lesser mortals.

She turns to me. 'Why don't you tell Charles about your old lady, Ma?'

I exchange glances with Volodya, uncomfortable at being asked to perform in this fashion, to offer Mary Martha as some kind of votive offering on the altar of Caitlin's desire to seduce Charles.

I have to say something. 'I've met this old lady who's English. In her eighties. She's been here since 1917.'

Charles whistles.. The burly Russian at the next table twists round, then turns back to get on with his conversation. 'Well, darling,' says Charles, looking across me to Caitlin, 'no doubt you've got her tied up, signed up and all that?'

'Nobody's got anybody tied up.' My annoyance is making my voice too loud. 'Or signed up. She's just an old lady who's decided she can stop being a secret after seventy years.'

'She will not wish the spotlight,' said Volodya. He pushed his foot against mine under the table. 'She is a very old lady.'

Charles laughs heartily. 'They all like the spotlight,' he bellows. 'Every last one of them.'

Even Caitlin raises her brows.

'*Them*? *Us*? Do *we*? I think not,' growls Volodya.

'How very rude!' I glare at Charles.

Volodya and I speak together.

Charles's pale, handsome cheeks redden at this and it is as though he is seeing me for the first time. 'Sorry, sorry, no offence meant.' he mumbles. He picks up a piece of tough black bread and chews it before speaking again. 'So, Mrs.Ozanne, will you just keep this lady to yourself? Do you intend to write a book about her?'

I smile my best lets-all-be-friends smile. 'I intend to do nothing. All I'm doing, Charles, is listening to her. It is a lovely story but it belongs to her. I'm not going to borrow it or steal it.'

We have finished the first course, a rather fine pate´ and the waiters are clearing our places with a flourish and relaying cutlery for the fish course.

When the flurry has settled down, Charles looks across at me. 'It's rather odd that you've bumped into that old woman, Mrs.Ozanne, because tomorrow I'm to visit an old fellow called MacIntyre, who is in a not dissimilar situation. An Englishman staying on here.'

Caitlin perks up. 'Herbert MacIntyre?'

Charles eyes are still on me. 'He's been here since the Thirties.'

'His existence is no secret.' says Caitlin. 'But I thought he was a recluse. Never gave interviews.'

Charles winks at her. 'Well, normally he doesn't.' He turns to me. 'Have you been out to a *dacha* yet, Mrs.Ozanne?'

I shake my head.

'Would you like to join me? Would you like to meet old Herbert?'

I am wary but interested. Volodya's foot is pressing very hard on mine. 'No strings?' I say.

He shrugs. 'No strings. Perhaps we could exchange notes on the way back.'

'But I'm interviewing Lebed tomorrow!' wails Caitlin.

That charlatan!' mutters Volodya.

'It's taken me weeks to set it up.' This is not the daughter I know, bleating like a lovelorn kid-goat.

'The old hypocrite?' Charles laughs. 'I wish you luck. But never fear, Caitlin. Your mother and I will manage very well on our own. She will tell you all about it when she returns.'

Our fish course is arriving. Peering over the snowily clad arm of the waiter I say, 'Well, thank you,

190

Charles. I'll be delighted to come with you.' I smile a kind smile. That smile which reassured children in my classes when they were eager to make amends.

The fish course is carp in a tomato sauce. We all tuck in, giving the food the concentration it deserves. By the time we plough through the next course of veal and then tackle the ice-cream we have, between the four of us, eaten more protein than the average non-mafiosi Russian family gets in a week.

During the meal, Volodya - shoes off - is making a very seductive play with my ankles and feet. His face is bland as he listens very attentively as Caitlin and Charles show off to each other about their respective foreign assignments.

Me? I'm just about fainting with sensual excess, eating all this delicious food and enjoying a very specific foot massage at the same time.

It turns out that Caitlin and Charles are to go on afterwards to a private party at the American Embassy. They will drop me off at the apartment. Caitlin smiles sweetly at Volodya. 'Perhaps we could drop you on our way Mr... Volodya?' Volodya glances at me. She thinks we're stupid. What a chance to locate Mary Martha. And anyway I'm not having my feet tickled for an hour and a half and leaving it at that. It's like mixing a cake and not putting it into the oven.

191

I smile sweetly from Charles to Caitlin. 'No, no. You young things go and enjoy yourselves. We'll have a little nightcap at the apartment. Just to round off a perfect evening.'

Charles opens his mouth to say something and closes it again, before calling up the bill in a very lordly fashion.

In the car, Caitlin, looking very pretty in her silver- grey trench-coat, snuggles beside Charles, while I squash into the corner with Volodya, who, greatly daring, takes my hand.

Volodya says nothing until we are alone inside the flat. 'Mr.Conrad wished to warn you against me,' he says softly, pulling me towards him, taking off my coat and hat with deft precision.

I lean back against his arm, looking up into his eyes. 'And should I be warned? Are you dangerous? Is there a mystery around you?'

He roared with laughter. 'Dangerous? Here is the truth about me, Olivia Ozanne. I am an ex-Pioneer who did well at school and was permitted to learn languages because I was such a good boy, such a clever boy. An ex-soldier who never fought. An ex-civil servant who mistook the temper of the times and ended up just a little out of favour. You people from the West always want a great conspiracy; you always ascribe great mystery to the simplest things. You read too many spy books!'

I breathe out. This is surely the truth. 'So you do not threaten me?'

'Of course I do. I want you for mine.' He kisses me! 'I want to make love to you now, on this floor which Katya shines so clean.' He kisses me again. 'Then in that kitchen pressed hard against that cabinet.' He starts to unbutton my Marks & Spencer's satin-look blouse. 'Then three times in your little orphan's bed.'

I pull back to smile at him. 'Confidence! Isn't that what the new Russia needs to surge forward? Confidence!'

It is three o'clock in the morning when Caitlin returns. I know because I check the luminous dial of my little travel clock, my hand dropping to Volodya (who has finally rolled onto the floor) to stop the slight whistling breath which is his version of a snore. I hold my breath as Caitlin pauses outside my door. 'Mother?' she whispers.

'Asleep, darling.' I slur my speech for effect and turn over, satisfied, when I hear her door click.

I have only been lying there for a minute when Volodya climbs back into bed, jamming me rather effectively against the wall. His lips are on my ear as he breathes the words 'Do you think she make love with Mr.Conrad tonight?'

I struggle to get my lips against his ear. 'I hope so, for her sake. She needs taking out of herself.'

'What?'

'Nothing. An English expression.'

'You must teach it to me.'

'Too complicated,' I whisper. 'Tomorrow.'

I nod my head against his shoulder. He groans slightly and his hand starts to move from my armpit, along my body and down the length of my thigh to the hollow behind my knee.

At some level of abstraction I wonder just how we are going to manage all this without being heard. I can only hope that Caitlin had a great deal to drink at her Embassy party.

Then the thinking stops.

TEN

Since I was a child I have been able to induce dreams: I would lie down, think myself into a reverie and then move on to a full-blown dream. The dream itself then detonates of its own accord and I end up with impressions and experiences which I did not know were mine. I've long said (in my lectures) that a story is a dream trimmed somewhat, tidied up, and written down. I have been subject to rather bossy assertions by regression theorists, that, when I write my stories, I hypnotise myself and regress myself into someone else's experience. I do hate the limitations of that explanation, which clings neurotically to linear time as the way to understand all things. Why can't the dreams be other lives not lived within this consciousness? Why can't they be metaphors which allow us complex access to the billion interior possibilities of a single personality?

'Do you think my mother is mad?'

Janey woke with a start as Joseph's voice pierced the predawn gloom. 'What?' She shot up in bed, reached over to pick up her sweater and pulled it hurriedly over her head. Then, keeping the sheet over her embarrassingly flabby nether regions, she hopped around the room looking for her knickers and tights.

Joseph sat up and watched her, leaning over to pull a packet of cigarettes from the pocket of his jeans. 'My mother. Olivia. Do you think my mother is mad?'

Fully clothed now, Janey sat at Olivia's dressing-table and peered at her face in Olivia's mirror. 'Mad? Have you looked at yourself? Have you looked at me? Here? After last night?'

'I think she *is* mad actually. Not quite properly connected to things. At heart she's a bad girl. That's why my father left her for the Naomi popsy and Caitlin, finding madness so untidy, can't stand her, though she plays the loving daughter, and might even love Olivia in her own way.'

'You are very wise, for such a baby.' Janey dropped her head into her hand and groaned. 'What have I done? The wine, it was the wine.'

Joseph drew on his cigarette. 'Now what's the matter?' 'What's the matter? What's the matter? I've just about committed incest with my best friend's son and you ask what is the matter?'

'Don't come that 'old enough to be your mother' shit. There are only twelve years between you and me. And there are twelve years between you and

Olivia. I worked that out long ago. Fancied you since I was thirteen, matter of fact.'

Janey picked up a towel from the back of the chair and threw it over her head, moaning.

'Take that thing off your head, stop moaning and come here,' said Joseph, grinding his cigarette in an empty wine-glass. 'We're not finished yet. I want to thank you for stopping the nightmare. I'm bloody sick of that bird.'

In my dream I am standing in what I know is Volodya's room but his shelves and papers are not there. In the centre of the room is a table with chairs; a dying fire moves and shifts in the hearth. Under the shallow window is a rocking horse which is moving gently to and fro, being ridden by a beautiful girl in a blue silk dress: she is dark haired, the Rose Red of the fairy-tale. She turns towards me, her eyes wide with tears and full of fear.

And I am saying, 'don't worry Ninochka, I will . . .' I hear a banging on a far door and the thunder of footsteps on wood. I reach towards the girl, thrusting dark and dingy clothes in her hands, shouting 'Put them on, darling! Put them on!' Through the window I can see young men, boys in shabby army fatigues pouring into the house. The knocking gets louder.

'Mother! Mother! Can I come in?'

I sit bolt upright in bed, blinking down at Volodya who is curled in a foetal position on the floor. 'No, Caitlin. No. Wait.'

I grab my wrap, squeeze through the door and shut it behind me. Caitlin is standing there, polished and elegant in a green trouser suit and well-polished, sturdy boots.

'You look elegant, darling.' Fending off words.

'Is he in there?' She says fiercely. 'The Russian?'

I push my hair out of my eyes. 'I'm afraid so. It was a bit late for him to get across Moscow when we—'

'I don't want to know.' She pulls me into the hall and faces me, holding both my arms, hard, above the elbow. 'Now, Mother, just two things. Charles will call for you here at ten. Why he wants to take you careering across the countryside I don't know. But you've caught his fancy. Or your story about the old woman has. But I want you to promise me something.'

'Yes, dear?' I am trying to struggle out of her grip.

'You do not let Charles Conrad have the old woman, do you hear me? If she's anyone's she's mine.'

I pull away from her. 'Mary Martha. Her name is

198

Mary Martha Johnson. You can't *have* her. And she's not mine to give to anyone, you silly girl. I certainly wouldn't 'give' her to Charles Conrad. But I won't give her to you either.'

'Oooh.' It comes out as a yelp over ground teeth. Then she pulls on a very fetching felt hat and thick coat and makes for the door.

'Caitlin?' I say.

'What?' she snarls.

'Charles Conrad is very attractive, but I wouldn't trust him an inch if I were you.'

'You? You? What would you know about anything you . . . madwoman!' The door clashes behind her.

'She is very beautiful, your daughter, Olivia.' Volodya is leaning on the frame of the bedroom door, fully dressed.

'She is very like her father,' I say sulkily. 'Her father was very beautiful.'

'Then why did you leave him?'

'There is an English saying about beauty being only skin deep. It was like that with him. His skin was very thin. You could see right through him.'

He is frowning at me. 'Sometimes it is hard to know whether you joke or not, Olivia.'

'Sometimes I don't know myself.' I step towards

the kitchen and he follows me, watching me as I move about fixing some coffee and toast. I hand him a steaming cup. 'When you've had this you must go, Volodya. You must be gone when Katya comes. We don't want to give her another moral dilemma about reporting any of this to the agency or not. She has enough on her plate and she needs this job.'

A companionable silence blossoms in the small space while we munch our toast. I am more at home with this man than with anyone I have ever met. 'I am worried about Mary Martha,' I say. 'Those two, Caitlin and Charles, I think they're about to operate a pincer movement on her. Is there a place where you can get her away? Can you get the Aunties out of the flat?'

'There is a little place—' he says thoughtfully.

'Can we take her there? First thing tomorrow?'

'Will you come?'

'Yes. Mary Martha and I aren't finished yet. Not by a long chalk.'

'Not by a long chalk. Another English saying? You will explain that to me please.'

I like to think I am not a judgmental person, but on the way to visit the old English bloke, I find myself looking at Charles Conrad as he pores over his sheaf of faxes and the heap of last week's English and

200

American newspapers.

Charles is very personable, really. With his dark wings of grey hair he is a familiar face on the English television screen, giving measured, informed judgment of these crucial events in the East. Actually he's not that much younger than me. Twelve, thirteen years perhaps: Janey's age. And Janey's my close friend. Odd that. I wonder who his best friend is. The Dutchman? Caitlin? No. He seems so much the man who walks by himself.

Perhaps I was wrong about that young Dutchman. Perhaps Charles is charming, almost seductive with everyone, but is intimate with no one. The *confirmed bachelor*. I've met some of those in my time. The academic world has a fair sprinkling of them. Nice men. Single by choice. Not impotent, but somehow born aloof from human desires. If that's the case Caitlin is definitely barking up the wrong tree. For a very intelligent girl she can sometimes be quite blind.

The car, driven smoothly along the road by Anatoly, Charles's driver, who is a much more affable presence than Piotr. I find myself dropping off to sleep as we wend our way through ugly, dusty suburbs pock-marked with high blocks of flats rising out of the great sea of grey concrete.

Volodya's busy attentions, pleasurable as they

were, have robbed me of half of last night's sleep and I need my seven hours to keep me going these days.

*

I wake with a jolt to find a face crowned with a military cap staring at me through the side window of the car. Charles has the window down on his side, and he is talking to another militiaman, showing him papers. In the driving seat Anatoly is balancing a bottle of vodka and a carton of red Marlborough on the flat dashboard.

The militiaman folds the papers very precisely and hands them back to Charles. His colleague reaches in the front and takes the vodka and cigarettes, exchanging a chuckling, dismissive comment with Anatoly.

We're soon on our way again, going off the road onto a bumpy rutted road that makes the Volvo lurch from side to side. The landscape is opening out now. I can see scrubby fields and lines of birch trees dripping with rain.

Charles tucks his papers away and peers out. 'Not long now.' He says something to Anatoly, who throws a comment over his shoulder.

'Anatoly says ten minutes.'

'Tell me about this man,' I'm pleased at last to get his attention. 'Herbert MacIntyre they call him?'

'He's just someone who has . . . well he's been forever. I met him in Moscow once. He has this little house in Moscow. You would like it. It has a perfect English cottage garden.'

'Why would I like that?' I say crossly.

He ignores me. 'I have been after an interview for a while. He has finally invited me to come out to his dacha. Bit of a dark horse, to be honest.' His smooth voice tells me he's being anything but honest. I am on the receiving end of an edited version of some kind of truth.

'Tell me more about him,' I instruct.

'Well he's an ancient, is old Herbert. Been here since the year dot. Has been an occasional stringer for the heavies for, well, it must be generations. Reported on the Revolution. Knew the Americans. Knew John Reed. You know they made a film of his involvement? Your genuine Red on top of the bed, that one.'

'I even read the book,' I say dryly. 'Ten Days That Changed The World.'

'What? Yes. Sorry. So used to talking to people who never read a book. They either read the reviews and bluff, or go on endlessly about *film noir* and the European tradition.'

For a second I warm to him.

'Anyway, Reed was mostly in Petrograd, where

the whole thing broke, of course. Herbert was back here in Moscow.'

'But he didn't write a book?'

'There's a legend that he did. His story did not end with the Revolution, of course. But nothing has turned up. Not that anyone knows of.'

'What kind of a man is he?'

He shrugged. 'Queer old stick. Anyway, here we are! You can make up your own mind.'

The car bumps along, following a long wall one and a half times the height of a man. Along the top of the wall shards of glass are set in smeared concrete. You used to see that at home a lot, when I was little. I think it's illegal now.

We stop before an archway that contains a tall wooden gate strengthened by iron banding. Charles gets out and opens it and as Anatoly drives slowly through a buzzer sounds, not stopping until Charles closes the gates again. A man raking the neat gravel drive puts down his rake and looks across at us.

My hands are suddenly very icy.

I peer out at the house, which is modest enough, wood-walled and verandah'd in the Hansel and Gretel style. Up on the roof, straddling the apex, there is a man dressed in dusty farm worker's clothes a hammer in his hand, knocking in pegs of some kind.

204

He stands up and shouts at us, waving his arms. We must go on. We must not stop there.

'Blimey!' The ejaculation is drawn like a tooth from the urbane Charles, as Anatoly drives on past the cottage.

We peer out of the back window of the car and realise that the 'cottage' is no cottage. It has enormous doors on this side which are pulled back, allowing us a glimpse of three gleaming cars. These must be thirty or forty years old but even in this dark winter light their gleam advertises mint condition: a Rolls Royce, a Bentley and a Jaguar.

We purr around another corner and come onto the house proper. It is a long, immaculately kept building in pale green stucco. I whistle. 'A *dacha*?'

'You're right, Olivia,' says Richard. 'Not quite a country cottage. A very special kind of dacha. In Russia only politicians and diplomats have this much space to themselves.'

'What about *mafiosi*?' I am learning.

'Not even them. Not yet. But just give them a year or two.'

As we approach it the door is opened by a small woman, bundled rather than dressed in black, her head bound in a dust black scarf. As we step over the threshold we could be stepping into one of Chekhov's plays or Tolstoy's short stories.

The hall is high, encircled by a beautifully carved wooden gallery and warmed by a great stove covered in deep red tiles. Padded chairs with elaborate carved backs and velvet-covered tables are scattered almost at random across the shiny wooden floors. The air is suffused rather than scented with cedar overlaid by the smell of oranges and cloves.

'Madame?' a croaking voice squeezes its way through the old woman's lips. Humbly she holds out her arms. 'Madame's coat?' she says. The voice and the attitude is calling down the years from the time when a soul could be owned by another human being, when servants and soldiers, artists and actors, could be bought and sold like so many sheaves of corn.

I twist a little to get out of my coat. 'Oh, My God!' To my left, towering over me, standing on its back legs, is a great black bear. In its outstretched paw is a silver tray containing a couple of calling cards.

Charles coughs. 'It's stuffed, Olivia.' But there is the faintest thread of uneasiness in his voice.

'Ah, Conrad! Safe journey, eh?' Bearing down on us from the dark nether regions is a great lumbering man who rivals the rearing bear for height. He has little hair but his scalp is wrinkled, as though his skull has shrunk and there is too much skin left over. He

206

wears a three-piece suit of immaculate, if dated, cut and an Old Etonian tie.

Charles, who, I notice now, is wearing the same tie, shakes his hand heartily. 'A fine journey, sir, no problems. Although the last road was a bit of a nightmare.'

'I keep it like that. Keeps the marauders out, what?' The man chortles in that immoderate way confined to old people who have no one to listen to their jokes any more. He turns to me. 'And who have we here, Conrad?'

'This is Mrs.Ozanne, Mr. MacIntyre. I believe I told you on the telephone. She is a very famous writer of literature for children, now visiting er daughter in Moscow . . .'

I put out my hand and it is crunched in the paw as big and dry as the bear's. 'Mr.Conrad exaggerates, Mr. MacIntyre, I—'

'Nonsense, Mrs.Ozanne. I know the name. I have read reviews—'

'Mr. MacIntyre reads all the Western papers, Olivia. Every single one,' cuts in Charles.

'You sometimes write those queer pieces about the collective unconscious and fairy-tales . . '

I put my other hand on his. So strange to have to come out here to this Addams family house in the wilderness to find anyone who doesn't think my only claim to fame is giving birth to the amazing Caitlin Ozanne.

A lump of birch wood in the great hearth cracks and falls and then flares up to illuminate Herbert MacIntyre's cheek and throw into sharp relief the port wine stain which mars his left cheek from eyebrow to jaw line.

'I have some books which you will like to see, Mrs.Ozanne,' he says. Then he lifts his head and bellows, 'Margaret! Margaret!'

A tiny wizened figure glides down the stairs, dressed in a twin-set and pearls and sensible handmade shoes. Her beady eyes are sunk deep in her head and she wears a wig too full of hair and skewed slightly to the left.

'Mrs.Ozanne, this is my wife Margaret. Margaret, this is Mrs. Olivia Ozanne. We have read her articles have we not? You will give her some tea in the studio and show her the collection. Conrad and I will be in the study, political matters to discuss. Luncheon will be at one.'

Shaking the tiny be-ringed hand I note that Herbert MacIntyre instructs, he does not request. As I follow the old lady down the dark corridor, passing other serf-like beings, dusting, polishing and sweeping,

I decide old Herbert is a nasty piece of goods, even if his presence here in this house, in this country, does present a fascinating conundrum. And there is something, something nagging away at me about him, something I should attend to, but can't quite reach.

'You will want to see the kitchen first, I think.' It has great carved cupboards and china racks laden with fine china. In here are two old women putting the finishing touches to some great dish. Passing over the pristine Moffat electric cooker without comment Margaret MacIntire shows me the two wood-burning iron stoves and the traditional bread oven. Spread across the top of one of the stoves, shrivelling very slowly in the heat, are rows and rows of orange peel.

'The orange peel?' I say.

'For the tea.' she murmurs. 'Always for the tea.'

She goes across to the main table, pokes at the dish, and mutters something to one of the old women and makes for the door again. 'They will bring tea,' she says. 'Now, Mrs Ozanne, the collection!'

She leads the way up to a half-landing and opens double doors into a room, one end of which is illuminated by a skylight with a table beneath it. The rest of the room is furnished with sloping shelves which display books with their covers facing out.

This is a treasure house of first editions in

English, of books by Lewis Carroll, Beatrix Potter, and Arthur Ransome; there are books of fairy-tales illustrated by Arthur Rackham, and Walter Crane. And more. Cruikshank, Greenaway, Caldecott . . . One wall is confined to Russian editions of the artist Viktor Vasnetsov, a famous illustrator of Russian folk tales. I have read about him. Vasnetsov was safe in the times of the terror because fairy-tales belonged to the people, not the *bourgeoisie*, and were models of Soviet political correctness.

Under the wide skylight I take tea, pungent with orange peel, with Mrs. MacIntyre. I wonder what kept this strange English couple safe during the surreal years of proscription and pogrom. Mary Martha and her Nina achieved this by going to earth, by pretending to become, then becoming, the commonest of common people: Russian women at the bottom of the heap.

It has been the opposite with this couple. With their unextinguished English identity, their obvious wealth, there would never be any mistaking who they were.

My eye catches a small, exquisitely executed portrait of Herbert at a much younger age. The face with its heavy prominent bones is unmistakable, but he has a great springing mass of hair and the pulsing glamour of a powerful man in the flame of his young maturity.

'That is a fine portrait,' I say. 'Surely this is not done by this artist, by Vasnetsov? It's in a very different style.'

Mrs. MacIntyre shakes her head. The delicate skin which is pulled across the bones of her eye sockets is white in the strong overhead light. 'No Mrs.Ozanne. That is my work. Many years ago now. Of course I myself was a painter in those days.' She has the stagey, fine fluting voice of those actresses in black and white films of the 1940s.

I stand up and peer closer at the painting The port wine stain is lightly sketched in. Now I remember what has been niggling at me. Mary Martha! She mentioned an Englishman who offered her escape. That man had a stain on his face. 'Mrs. MacIntyre,' I say now. 'In Moscow I've just been talking to an Englishwoman, a woan called Mary Martha Johnson. I discovered that she's actually been here since 1917. I wondered whether you or Mr MacIntire had ever met her?'

The ancient face moves into a tight frown of concentration. 'That can't be so, Mrs. Ozanne. One would have known. No. I have never met such a person.'

I am just about to rush in with the Samsonov a name, when I bite my tongue. That wouldn't be safe even now. These MacIntyres must be, must have been more than mere outsiders to have survived in this style all these years. Clearly, with this house, with this wealth, they were 'inside the loop'; approved by the highest in the land. Whoever that was.I shiver.

A great gong sounds through the house and we both jump. Mrs. MacIntyre stands up, fingering her pearls. 'Luncheon,' she says. 'We must hurry. Herbert abhors lateness. Abhors it!'

ELEVEN

There is no talk of politics at the luncheon table. The issues of Gorbachev's fate and Yeltsin's future and whether Margaret Thatcher would be sorely missed as a 'statesman' must have been safely settled behind Herbert MacIntyre's study door.

That's a relief. These days the masturbatory intensity of what passes for political discussion seems to me to be self-indulgent and lacking in illumination. There are only two or three things to be said on any issue but these armchair experts, 'talking heads' – wonderful term - will insist on saying it again and again. And again.

When Caitlin first started writing her articles – attempting and failing yet again to be the good mother – I read the newspapers comprehensively to get a proper perspective on her writing. After a year I abandoned the practice, merely skimming through the papers to pick up stories about individuals, people caught in the middle of the international political web, but human beings nevertheless.

Like those last political prisoners at Perm, I suppose – that was a eventually a good piece even in the opinion of Caitlin's trying desk editor.

When I tried to explain my preference for this kind of story to Caitlin she gave me one of her kind smiles and told me that such colour pieces were second-level stuff, really. Not hard news. She said she supposed they would suit me, really, given my preference for fiction.

Now in Herbert MacIntire's dacha shadowy women wrapped in black are flitting round the cedar-panelled dining-room serving food, piling plates; one of them is cutting Mrs. MacIntyre's lamb into small bite-sized pieces.

'So what do you think of my book collection, Mrs.Ozanne?' Herbert MacIntyre flicks a glance at the shadowy woman behind me and she refills my crystal glass with the very excellent Georgian claret. I am drinking very fast, as I always do when I am nervous.

I smile too widely at my host, trying to raise a flicker behind that lizard stare. 'It seems to be definitive, Mr. MacIntyre. Mint condition too. I did not realise that such books were available in the East.' It is a question, not a statement.

'I have people who send them to me, Mrs Ozanne. For a price, of course. They burrow away into catalogues and collections and find them for me. I take nothing save perfect copies.' Then he smiles: a cold composition of cheek and chin and gleaming,

214

beautifully made false teeth; a smile which does not reach the eyes. 'Perhaps you will send me a copy of your last book? A story of a child who is hidden away by other children, if I'm not mistaken? A fairy-tale of the future; isn't that how it is described? Such good reviews.'

I blush. 'Just opinions, of course. I am interested that you manage to know of it.'

'I can obtain all the papers and periodicals here – a few days late, but that's of little consequence. I am an old man and it's my favourite sport, reading the papers. *Child of Cyrmra.* Is that not the title? The reviews said it would stand the test of time. Am I right? They got quite excited about it.

I am even redder now. 'They got carried away. Nothing of mine could stand there beside classics such as those you have on your shelves, those …'

He nods. 'Such becoming modesty, my dear. And yet it would be an honour to receive such a work from the hand of the author.'

I note that he does not insist that I am the new Lewis Carroll. I watch his gleaming teeth descend on the succulent lamb, giving us all tacit permission to eat and for a few minutes, to my relief, there is no talk. Mrs. MacIntyre has her head down over her plate and is chewing steadily.

But I am not to escape.

'And what do you think of the Vasnetsov editions in the collection, Mrs.Ozanne?' the old man asks.

In fact those works are not to my taste. In his search for political neutrality Vasnetsov painted pictures lacking that radical anarchic energy which informs the best fairy-tales and is the mark of a good modern illustrator. 'Well, to my shame I cannot read the language, but the illustrations are very . . . fine.'

He grunts, nodding with agreement. 'So how would you see their being translated into English, Mrs.Ozanne? Would they not make very fine books in English?'

'Well,' I am cautious, 'the English market is very fickle, not comfortable with what it would see as . . . images from another age. My own stories reflect the present and a projected future age, of course—'

He interrupts me, flicking a contemptuous finger. 'The English, always so insular!' he growls. 'No, Mrs.Ozanne. I am talking about a very fine limited edition, a volume for which collectors would give their eye teeth.'

'Now that is a good idea, Olivia,' says Charles heartily. 'I am sure it would be immensely popular.'

I throw Charles a glance that asks him what the

hell he knows about it, and say, 'Those limited edition books do seem popular – one might say they are viewed as an accumulating asset.'

Herbert McacIntire barks a laugh at this. 'A very proper capitalistic notion, what? Highly appropriate for these *perestroika* days, don't you think?'

The shadowy ones bring bowls of peaches and plums: round, ripe and wholesome, there is a world of difference between these and the sturdy misshapen fruit I bought for Caitlin at the market.

More wine. White now, if one could call such exquisite golden honey 'white'. I swallow a mouthful of this and ask the question that I have been waiting to ask all through lunch. 'I was wondering, Mr. MacIntyre, whether you were in Moscow in 1938 or thereabouts?'

Charles spluttered over his wine. 'Olivia, I don't think...'

The old man puts out a hand, his dry lids dropping over his eyes. 'Yes indeed, Mrs. Ozanne. I have been here, effectively since 1930. Before that, spasmodically. So yes, I was here at that time.'

I start to peel an apple, concentrating very hard to keep the peel in a single coiling piece. I think of the cook in Lady Geary's household slicing the pastry edge of a plate pie. 'It's just that I've been talking to this woman, a friend of a friend. An Englishwoman.' At the very last second I stop myself calling her by name. 'She was in the Samsonov household. Like you, she's been here, too, for ages. Since before 1930. Since 1916. I wondered if you knew her.'

Then I look him in the eyes. He is staring at me and he keeps staring for a long time.

His old wife stops chewing her plums and stares at her husband. One prize for living with someone for sixty years is that even a change of breath, a stiffening of sinew, alerts you to change, to possible threat.

MacIntyre touches his lips with the linen napkin. 'As you can imagine, Mrs. Ozanne, I know many English people who have been through Moscow through many years. Although now . . .' He glances at Charles, '. . . today there are so many it's difficult for an old man to keep track . . .'

I persist. 'But in 1938 would there be many English in Moscow, Mr. MacIntyre?'

'Why should I know this Samsonov house?'

'I just thought you might,' I say. I take a deep breath. 'Her name is Mary Martha Johnson. She called herself Marie Samsonov a.'

Charles is kicking me, hard, under the table, signalling me to desist. I can see I'm in for that speech about fools rushing in where angels fear to tread.

I do not desist. 'Mary Martha was an Englishwoman, brought here byt the Samsonovs before the Revolution. She said an Englishman offered to get her out, back to England, in 1938. He told her that these were not times for an Englishwoman to be here.'

'What makes you think I was that Englishman? The Englishman who talked to this woman?'

I look him full in the face. 'The man she described looks just like you. He looks like the man I see on that very fine portrait.' I bite my apple to break the tension of the moment, as though what I'm saying is some very ordinary thing.

His old hand with its crusty over-long nails raises itself to his cheek and runs the length of the long port wine stain.

He nods. 'Samsonova?'

'That's her Russian name. Marie Samsonova.'

'She was very brave,' he says harshly. 'But foolhardy. She should have gone.'

'Her friend was here.'

'I knew that.' He glances at one of the back clad women and she starts to gather plates. 'So she is still alive?'

'Yes. She lives like a Russian. Has done all these years.'

'Should be impossible,' murmurs Charles.

MacIntyre turns to Charles. 'There is much that would surprise even you here, Conrad. Old men and old women are the least of it.' He stands up, and we all get to our feet. He raises a hand, as though something has just struck him. 'Oh, there is one thing you might do for me, old boy. I have been editing my diaries. Nineteen-thirties and all that. Thought I might publish them, what? Would old Marchant be interested in them? Got his K now, I see. He's still the *gauleiter* of your outfit, I believe?'

I can feel rather than see Charles breathe a long sigh of satisfaction. Their general political chit-chat and now me as the eccentric bait must have done its trick. But Charles doesn't answer straight away. I'm sure his editor would be very interested in the diaries, but I admire Charles' noncommittal response.

'I would have to talk to Sir Ranulph, Mr. MacIntyre. So much coming out of Russia at the moment . . .'

Now I am forgotten. The men are walking out of the room. Mrs. MacIntyre takes my arm as we walk through the double doors. Her voice is in my ear. 'He will ask you to collaborate on the translation of the Vasnetsov stories,' she murmurs, her voice dry as old leaves. 'I would not bother if I were you, my dear. Not wise to get involved with him. That Mary Martha woman was very sensible, even then.'

I turn to her, puzzled. 'You knew her?'

She shakes her head. 'I knew nothing. I know nothing. It was always better that way.'

Later, as we put on our coats and gloves in the hallway Herbert MacIntyre broaches the subject of the translation. His wife is standing behind him, her face bereft of any expression. I protest that my lack of any grasp of Russian could be something of a stumbling block. He flicks a hand in that characteristic gesture. 'Translators are ten a penny.' he says. 'We can get a translator for you.'

'I know a very good translator.' I say cautiously. I'm assuming Volodya is *good*.

'Well now! Ten a penny, as I said.' He picks up a card from the outstretched paw of the great bear and puts it in my hand. 'Just tell me when you can block in a stretch of time, Mrs.Ozanne. I will be in touch.' His tone is patrician. Dismissive. As though refusal on my part is unthinkable. I glance at his wife but she is looking in the other direction.

The door is being held by one of the shadowy ones and there is no other way but out. MacIntyre is on his way back up the stairs before we are through the door. I wait until the last echo on the gate alarm has faded and we are speeding, or bumping, our way back to Moscow before I turn to Charles. 'So who does he think he is? Tolstoy? Bluebeard?'

Charles chuckles. 'Well he certainly isn't Karl Marx.' I decide that I like Charles. What fun if Caitlin did nail him even if he is a confirmed bachelor! 'You knew about his books, didn't you? You checked on my credentials and took me along as a decoy.'

'I'm a journalist, Olivia. I check things out. I set up contacts. I write. You were my secret weapon. I knew about the books. I didn't know about the connection between him and your old woman. That was a surprise. It certainly caught the old boy's fancy.'

'So you really do want his diaries?'

'Everyone wants his diaries. There'll be television programmes, everything. I'm putting together a package for various interests in England and America.' He has his notebook on his knee and is scribbling as he talks.

I put my hand on his. 'Stop scribbling a minute, will you, and tell me who the hell he is?'

'Nobody knows for sure. That's why the diaries will be dynamite. Roughly, he's a millionaire who came here, fell for the place and never left. Came here for good in the early Thirties, when he inherited his fortunes; kept his nose out of Russian internal politics apart from somehow obtaining Stalin's patronage. Perhaps Stalin liked to have his own pet millionaire. They all liked to have their tame Westerners to give them credibility. MacIntyre entertained the *apparatchiks* at his Bluebeard's castle and shut his eyes to the heinous things that were going on. Claimed to be apolitical but the act of shutting one's eyes is, of course, a political act. There are other murky things that are hinted but not said. Suggestions of brokerage in international affairs. He's a real *fixer*. A very deep mole for the West, some say. But I don't believe that. Too partisan for him. What I do believe is that he really is a kind of neutral man and that very neutrality has been of use to both sides from time to time.'

'He is not a nice man,' I say.

'Nice? *Nice* doesn't make good politics, Ozanne. Or good news.' He starts to scribble away again. 'Talking about *nice*, how did you spot him as your old lady's potential saviour?'

'He's English. His size. And the port-wine stain.'

Charles's pencil is poised above his pad. 'We must have your old woman. A good touch that. Nice contrast. Two antedeluvian survivors at both ends of the social scale. I'll talk to her tomorrow.'

'You will not. And you can't 'have' her, as you put it. Caitlin has instructed me that if she can't have her, you can't have her. Mary Martha's a human being. She's not to be *had*.'

'Ah, Olivia. You forget. I'm the archetypal, hard-nosed journalist. Beside me your daughter is a Persian cat. It is my job to 'get' people. A newspaper has a very eager mouth.'

'Well this time it can go hungry,' I scowl. Even so, all the way back into the city my mind is working overtime on ways of keeping Mary Martha safe from this piranha pair.

In Moscow, Charles comes up to the apartment with me to say hello to Caitlin. I leave them to their vodka-tonics and jump in the bath, exhausted physically and mentally by the day's events.

But also I need some peace and quiet to think very quickly what is to be my next step. Those two either know or will soon know where Volodya lives and from him, of course, it is only half a step to Mary Martha. There in the steam, with the rumble of voices in the next room I make up my mind.

In five minutes I am damp but fully dressed in jeans and a thick sweater. I am just blowing my hair dry when Caitlin pops her head round my door. She is slightly pink. I wonder what they have been up to in the sitting-room. 'Oh, you're dressed. I thought you would be resting after your hard day. Moscow can be

224

so tiring. A nice rest …'

'I'm fifty years old, not eighty, Caitlin.'

She frowns. 'No need to be sharp, Ma.' She pauses. 'Seems you made quite a hit with Charles.'

'He's a nice bloke. Not the twerp I thought he was in the first place.'

'Always so judgmental, so judgmental. People really have to prove themselves to you, don't they? I never dared bring anyone home when I was young. All you did was analyse them and tell me just what made them tick. They ended up like wingless butterflies.'

I raise my brows. This is news to me. I thought Caitlin didn't have any friends. Too busy being a genius. 'Writer's habit, darling,' I say lightly. Analysis.'

'Anyway, Charles is just writing his report on MacIntyre and faxing it to London. Then we are going to Janni's for some supper. We'll be very late I'm afraid. No need to stay up.'

'Righto. I've things to do myself. Don't worry about me.'

'Things?'

'Reading. And I have an idea for a new story from something I saw today.'

'Ooh.' she says vaguely. 'Good.' She never ever sees what I do as *work*. Never reads the books. Never comments on their progress. He weird Herbert

225

MaIntire know more about my writing that she does.

I lie on my bed and start to scribble some invented story based on one of the Vasnetsov pictures. Twenty minutes later Caitlin calls that they are going now.

I go into the narrow hallway in my thick socks.

'Bye, Charles,' I say. 'Good visit that, today. Thank you for the chance to meet old MacIntire.'

To my surprise – and I think to Caitlin's – he leans over and gives me a great smacking kiss on the cheek. 'It's a pleasure, Olivia. You're a trooper.'

I withdraw, blushing and wait for the click of the outside door and the whirr of the elevator. Then I throw a few things into my rucksack, topping them up with apples and tins of food from Caitlin's cupboard. Then I pull on my thick ski coat and Caitlin's fluffy rabbit-skin hat.

I peer out of the window and watch while Caitlin goes across to Piotr who is talking to the militiaman. Piotr jumps into his own Lada and drives away in it. Off duty now, I assume. Caitlin jumps into Charles's car and they roar off. The plan must be for them to come back here together, or to go back to Charles's flat together. Either way I hope he sleeps with her. One way or another, my darling Caitlin could do with a bit of naked passion..

TWELVE

Caitlin Ozanne caught the reflection of her face - a floating white oval punctuated by dramatic eyes and reddened lips - in the darkened window of Charles Conrad's car. Her hair, released from its usual severe French pleat, was loose about her face, dropping in dark filaments on the high military collar of her fine wool coat.

Though intellectual rather than physical vanity was her weakness, Caitlin was not displeased with her undeniably fine looks. She sat back with a sigh of satisfaction that emerged from the furthest reaches of her solar plexus.

Charles glanced at her. 'You look a wee bit like a Cheshire cat, darling.'

'Just nice to get away from the apartment, to have some fun.'

He raised a brow. 'Get away from. Olivia, you mean?'

She shrugged. 'Wherever she goes she gathers trouble in her wake.'

'Seems a game soul to me. You should have seen her with old MacIntyre.'

She chuckled. 'Game soul? She'd hit you with

her handbag and call you a patronising twerp if she heard you say that.'

'It really sounds as though you don't like her, your own mother.'

'Like? You don't *like* mothers, Charles. You're landed with them. You can do as much post-fact rationalisation on them as you like, but up close they still reduce you to some blubbering infant.'

'Blubbering infant? Not you, darling. I bet you were not a blubbering infant even when you were a . . . er . . . blubbering infant.'

'How about you? I suppose you and your mother are entirely civilised together. Very grown-up, I am quite sure.' She was enjoying a rare chance of getting personal with Charles. Up to now, their relationship had been an energetic occasionally sensual combination of the comradely and competitive, and it had quite suited her that way. She was conscious now of a lurch. An emotional change of gear.

'My mother? Never knew the woman, darling. My people were stationed in Malta when I was small and I was bunged off to school in England, of course. Holidays at Granny's in Exeter. Rum old bird she was, she had a stick as big as a chair leg and was not beyond lashing out with it if . . . when . . . I didn't toe the line. Then my father was killed under a tank during some war game, and my mother stayed out there to run some import company and married some Maltese importing chap.' He paused. 'Nice enough chap but not who you'd choose.' His voice was bleak.

She put her hand on his knee and left it there.

He coughed. 'Anyway, we're talking about your mother, not mine. I'm becoming interested in this old lady Olivia's been seeing. D'you know she might have hit on a connection between her and old MacIntyre? Bloody good counterpoint for my colour piece about the old goat.'

Caitlin snatched her hand away. 'The cow! She's given you Mary Martha. I'll kill her.'

He took her hand very firmly in his. 'Oh, there's no question of that. Your mother made it quite clear there was to be no 'giving' of anyone to anyone. She's protecting the old woman like a jealous lover.' He squeezed her hand. 'D'you know, I rather like your mother, Caitlin. She's a rum bird. I can see where you get your . . . er . . . *oomph,* if you know what I mean. I always knew you had hidden depths, Caitlin, but somehow, till now . . .'

As they sped through the darkened streets of Moscow in Charles Conrad's car, Caitlin reflected on the fact that her irritating, careless, meandering mother had made more progress with the uptight Charles

229

Conrad than she - intelligent, professional, beautiful as she knew she was - had made in eighteen months. She stretched out her legs and snuggled back into the seat. No point in looking a gift horse in the mouth, though, was there?

She didn't think about her mother again until five hours later when she was lying beside the gently breathing Charles in his king-size bed.

The party had been the usual – buzzing with shop talk, weighed down by embarrassingly fine food and decorated with some desultory dancing. To her surprise Charles did not leave her side all evening, even when Janni wanted 'a quick . . . er . . . 'private word' in his ear.'

Now she closed her eyes now and reflected on her own particular *coup*. It was a legend in their ex-pat community that Charlie Conrad did not get *involved*. This gave rise to an undercurrent of gossip that he was a deep-buried gay, which Caitlin had never believed. She stretched her legs down in the bed, reflecting on their balletic, rather surprising episode of love. At the core of the surprise was the fact that Charles was hesitant and rather shy in the run-up to the inevitable stroking and plunging finale.

Caitlin shot up in bed, waking Charles and making him mumble 'Wassit? What is it?'

'My mother! She's alone in the flat. I should—'

He reached over and ran the flat of his hand down her back. 'Do you know you have the most beautiful back? Just the right amount of flesh on your exquisite bones.' He pulled her round to face him. 'Ah, you're blushing. How can the intelligent, cool, experienced, sophisticated Miss Ozanne be blushing?' His eyes dropped from her face and slid downwards. 'All over.'

She grabbed a pillow and held it against herself. 'I have to go back to the flat. God knows what she's up to.'

He removed the pillow and ran a gentle finger from her throat right down between her breasts to her navel. 'She'll be fast asleep, darling. She's had a busy day. Now come here and we'll play this game I know called Lie Back and Think of England.'

'But—'

He closed her mouth with his and any thoughts of her mother were obliterated by her own coursing blood.

She pulled her lips away from his for one last second. 'She will be fast asleep, I suppose. I can explain to her later.'

'Ssh. Of course you can, darling.'

My eye lights on a young man and an older woman heaving bulky sacks and rucksacks off the train.

'Potatoes, Olivia,' says Volodya, catching my look. 'They grow them at their dachas and bring them into the city to sell them at the markets.'

The people streaming off the train thin to a trickle and we climb onto it, laden with our bags and cases. Mary Martha carries her own bag, but Nina, the Grey Auntie, stands helpless as a five-year-old, and has to be pulled onto the train.

There are no seats. Volodya wedges me into a corner and presses the Grey Auntie onto the heap made by our cases. As the train swings and jerks into its journey his body closes towards me and leans away in some kind of swaying dance. Such temptation. His eyes gleam mischievously. 'This will not work, you know, this running away. In the end you have to go back. To Caitlin. To London.'

I shrug, and then lurch into him as the train takes a sticky corner. He puts an arm around me and we sway together. His lips are in my hair. He says something which I cannot catch. 'What was that?' I say.

'We will get a seat soon, Olivia,' he enunciates hoarsely in my ear.

I could have sworn he said he loved me, but

perhaps I am mistaken. Wishful thinking you may say.

Herbert MacIntyre's dacha – that palatial country retreat - is, it seems, rather atypical. I find that Volodya's 'dacha' is not so much a country retreat as an allotment hut in a scrubby area pockmarked by other huts, some barely improvised from an assortment of old and new birch planks. The elaborately patterned brick path and the carving of the silvery splitting wood on the verandah rail bespeak a certain former miniaturised excellence. But the inside of Volodya's hut is neat, bare and very chilly. There is a stove in one corner, a high padlocked cupboard in the other, beds pushed against two walls. A pockmarked table stands in the centre with two chairs drawn up to it.

On one wall hangs a small icon, crudely executed in shades of green and the deepest vermilion.

Volodya sets about lighting the stove and Mary Martha, having lodged the Grey Auntie on one of the beds with a rug over her, takes a knobbly loaf of bread from her rucksack and places it at the centre of the table. She sits down and glances across at me. 'I wondered why we had to come here,' she says. 'There's no potatoes left to harvest and the summer fruits are gone, apart from the bottled plums in the back there. Are we running away, like?'

I empty the apples and tinned food from my knapsack and sit opposite her. 'I suppose we are, really.'

Her eyes flick round the room, as though some threatening apparition might leap from the wooden walls. 'We've broke no laws,' she says. 'We live unto ourselves.'

I shake my head. 'Nothing to really threaten you, but . . .'

I tell her then about meeting Herbert MacIntyre.

She raises her sparse brows. 'Still here? I'd have thought he'd a' gone long ago.'

'Well, the newspaper people, my daughter included, think your story and his story are interesting.'

She cocks her head. 'They'd write about me in their papers?'

'Oh yes, I think so,' I say carefully.

Her eyes narrow. 'My folks at home would see?'

'Oh yes,' I repeat. 'Sure to, it's a big story after all.' The room starts to fill with smoke as Volodya finally ignites the wood in the stove. Mary Martha coughs a little, watching me over her big knuckled hand. Then she says. 'What about you? Could you write my story?'

I shake my head. 'I'm not a journalist. I write

stories for children.'

She looks at me, a shrewd light in her eyes. 'You *could* write my story, Olivia. *Once upon a time there was a little girl called Mary Martha Johnson who lived in a little village in Durham* . . . Just put it down like I say it. Plain.'

'That would be a book, Mary Martha, not an article.' She has no idea of the scale of the thing she's asking me to do.

She ignores my uncertainty. 'That way you could take the book to my sister in Durham. She'll have family now of course. Children. Grandchildren. Take it to them. So they will know who I was.'

'Who you are,' I correct her.

'I've not got much time now. I'd rather you did it, Olivia, than one of those newspapermen.'

'There'll be no money, Mary Martha. Well, little money.'

'I'll survive,' she says dryly. 'I've survived all this stuff, haven't I?'

'Right,' I say. 'Right. If that's what you want.' I reach inside my other pack for the little voice-recorder.

Volodya sits back on his heels. 'Will you have enough power in there?' he says.

'The batteries are charged and I've brought the charger.'

'Here?' he laughs. 'No power here, dearest

Olivia. Wood stove, petrol lamps. That's it.'

I clap my hand to my forehead in mock drama. 'Oh my god, I'll have to write it down. Do you think I can cope?'

So that's how it we do it. We talk through the day and into the evening. Then the tape wears out and I write by the light of a petrol lamp. I write of Mary Martha's life – on the very edge of absolute poverty, yet illuminated by the relationship between the two women. I write of brave people they had known and lost and their late delight in the church and all its glories. I write of their terrible times during the Great Patriotic War when Mary Marth says that she finally, finally felt Russian.

Every now and then she returns to her childhood in Durham – the father who died in the shooting accident, the mother who washed clothes to make ends meet. The sister called Ellen Alice.

I scramble to get Mary Martha's terse phrases down in their entirety. I've not brought enough paper and have to use the backs of Volodya's translation sheets, brought out by him, only very slightly damp, from the cupboard in the corner.

Volodya is sitting on the floor beside the roaring stove, his long legs out before him, and his lids slipping down over his eyes as he too listens.

In the end the spaces between Mary Martha's stories become longer and longer and finally she is silent. She uses the edge of the table to haul herself upright, standing quite tall in the narrow space of the hut.. 'Will that do you, Olivia? Nowt else to say,' she murmurs. 'That's about it.'

I block the stack of sheets together neatly. 'I couldn't have written another sentence. My hand is nearly drop ping off.'

'I hope it makes some sense to you, like,' she says, doubt creeping into her voice.

'Of course it makes sense. It's truly amazing.

'Good.' she goes over and shakes the Grey Auntie awake and pulls her off the bed. 'I'll have to take her out to the lav,' she says, 'before we settle down. Can't have her wetting the bed.'

I watch the two old ladies hobble out of the door and think of the stories under my hand, of their youth and their dramatic middle age, their true passion for each other.

Volodya sits beside me and his hand comes up to wipe away my tears. 'I do love you, Olivia Ozanne.' He says the words clearly, distinctly.

I start to bawl then. 'Don't say that! Don't say it. How can I go back now? How can I leave her and you? I must stay. I've got to stay.'

He tries in vain to comfort me; my tears only stop when I hear the quiet voice of Mary Martha from the open doorway. 'What I would like, Olivia, is for you to do that story, write it down properly, like, and take it up North to Ellen Alice, or her family, or someone up there who knew us. So then I know we will survive. Me and Nina, we didn't die in this wilderness.' She leads her friend towards the bed and with neat precision starts to remove all her outer garments.

Volodya gives me a quick hug and sits away from me. 'There now,' he says briskly. 'You have your mission. You have to go back to complete this mission for the Brown Auntie.'

Now there's a cold draught in the big space in between us. 'The kettle on the stove is hot, so we will have coffee before we go to bed.'

I am disappointed when, apparently out of deference to the aunties, Volodya settles down to sleep on a rug on the floor and leaves me in the high bed on my own. I drift in and out of sleep, dreaming, as has been frequent in these last days, bits of Mary Martha's life as though they were my own.

I wake up suddenly in the smoky pitch darkness. A hand is pulling me from my bed. Volodya's voice in my ear. 'Shsh! We go on an adventure. Put all your clothes on.'

I scramble into my clothes, knickers, sweaters inside out. He plonks the fur hat on my head and I follow him. He takes his small torch in his teeth, flings a great folded blanket over his shoulder, takes my hand and drags me away. We go up into the trees behind the dacha, the light threading its way past dripping branches, the stillness broken by the occasional flurry of an up-shooting bird as our progress disturbs them. We have been walking for nearly ten minutes when he grunts with satisfaction as the trees open out a bit to make space for a low structure, like some animal hide supported with roughhewn planks. Carefully he spreads the blanket inside and lays his torch on the ground. Then he turns to me. 'In winter if we lay here we would freeze to death. Tonight we shall be a little cold and damp, but we shall be together. For the last time, I think.'

'No.' I am decisive. 'I shall stay here in Moscow. I must stay. I can't leave her or you.' I'm clutching at him like some lovesick schoolgirl, my protestations thin even in my own ears.

I can feel rather than see him shaking his head. 'No, you will go, Olivia. You don't have the papers to stay. And Mary Martha has given you a mission, is that not so? And me. I am just a ship passing in your night. Is that not what you say?' Then he picks me up as though I were a tiny fragile bird rather than a plump pigeon, and lies me gently on the ground and slides down beside me, pulling me to him. He laps the blanket around us both and then strokes my hair back from my face. 'It is too cold for me to do what I wished, dearest Olivia.' He draws my hand down so I can feel him soft, inert. 'Or perhaps, like Mary Martha, I know you as not a foreigner, as my countrywoman and now I cannot perform.' I can feel his body shake with laughter. 'Would that not be a strange thing?'

We've been dozing and snuggling and whispering for an hour when my foreignness started to have its effect and he was fumbling with the frustrating layers of my clothes and I with his. Gaggled up by clothes like this, we make love among the groaning pines to the sound of the susurring, scratching of bare branches moving and rubbing one against the other. My mind is clear and my body is like a trembling touch-paper. It seems that we go on for hours, regretting the lost time in the past, and anticipating the years when we will be apart.

One part of my mind is focusing on Mary Martha, innocent of lust such as this but passionate just the same. The noise of tractors and heavy machinery wakes us from our last sleep and I leap up, pulling down my skirt and buttoning up my coat. Volodya sets to straightening his clothes and folding the sopping blanket.

I peer through the trees behind the hide and blink at the sight of a great stone quarry where the working day is just starting. The figures down below are like matchstick men as they go about their day's work with their toytown machines.

'Volodya! Can you see that?' I squeak. 'Did you know we were on the edge of all that? They could have seen us.'

He shrugs and hefts the blanket onto his shoulder. 'They are too far away.'

'You know this place?'

'I was coming to the dacha since I was a child. The quarry then was a river valley where we fished and swam.' He put a hand on the creaking roof of the hide. 'The legend in my family was that I was conceived in this place.' He takes my hand in his and starts to pull me along the track. 'And last night I am born again.'

Caitlin's Volvo is waiting in the dirt road just outside the dacha. Piotr, lolling at the wheel, watches us with a grimly sardonic eye as we trail out of the trees and across the verandah. Mary Martha is sitting on one side of the table and Caitlin, ramrod straight in a bulky green ski-jacket, is sitting opposite. The smile she flashes at me is only barely triumphant; it hardens as it settles on Volodya, who stands quietly in the doorway, the dripping blanket over his shoulder. 'Mother, thank goodness. I thought the pair of you had run away. Didn't we, Mary Martha?'

'I told you your Ma'd be back any minute,' Mary Martha butted in determinedly.

I smile widely at them both. 'And so I am. How did you find me, Caitlin?'

'I left a note at my apartment,' Volodya chimed in from behind me. 'I knew they'd find where I lived through my employers. Then—'

I turned on him. 'You left her a note?'

He shrugged. 'You needed a little time. But then you had to go home. That was always the case.'

'Listen to Volodya, Mother. He is talking sense.'

Caitlin looked round. 'Now. Where're your things? We have to get you home, into the bath and onto the plane. We can't have you in bother for overstaying, can we?'

I am annoyed – with both patronising Caitlin and over-protective Volodya, but also with myself for allowing myself to be handled like this. So, later I take some satisfaction in insisting on the Aunties and

Volodya coming back into Moscow with us in the car. The discomfiture of Caitlin at close quarters with the four of us – bundled, damp and not very aromatic – is at least to be relished. She sits, eyes forward, beside Piotr, refusing to look at me squashed on the back seat with the Aunties,and Volodya on the floor, tangled up with our legs.

Caitlin's bristling annoyance does not trouble me a bit. I am enjoying the added bonus of Volodya rubbing the cold from my feet with tender fingers as the Volvo bumps its way back into central Moscow.

THIRTEEN

The drilling hum of the vacuum cleaner invaded both Joseph's ears and his body, as it vibrated in his hand. He started to compose a joke in his head about this man who thought a vacuum cleaner was a vibrator for larger men. But he lost the punch line as the nozzle of the vacuum caught onto the toe of Janey's tights and started to tussle with it like a wayward puppy. He turned the machine off at the plug and sat down on the floor to disentangle the mangled tights.

Janey popped her head round the door. 'What's up?' she said.

'Didn't hear you come back,' he said. 'The Hoover's eaten your tights.' He pushed the machine away from himself, scraping it along the wooden floor. 'I'm sick of this,' he said. 'Never was any good at it.'

Her eye flicked round the room. 'Done now anyway, lover. Just wind the thing up and put it in the cupboard. Then, as a special treat, you can help me unpack this shopping.' He followed her down the passage, vacuum in hand.

When he got into the kitchen she had tipped all the shopping onto the table. He picked up an apple.

'Apples? Peaches? South American coffee? Mint Imperials. What's this?'

She hauled two bottles of Friexenet out of the second bag. 'Something to celebrate,' she said. 'Olivia getting back from that hole of a place. I bet she's not had real coffee in a fortnight.'

He picked up the black bottle. 'Or artificial champagne?' he said, starting to twist the plump cork.

She put a hand on his. 'No, Joseph, not yet. It's her celebration, not ours.'

The cork popped - a hard powerful sound that thudded off every surface in the small kitchen. Joseph shook his head. 'The nicest thing about champagne, even artificial champagne, is that it doesn't keep. You have to drink it straight away, don't you?'

I am glad this plane has done its final taxi, its lurching with that surge of naked power into the clear air. Now I am flying high over Moscow. Peering downwards I am amazed at how dark the city is: so few lights. London at night is like a box of bright jewels.

I have just endured a tussle with an official in the customs hall. The official, a tall woman built like a gasometer, took a look in my briefcase and lighted on my Mary Martha notes. She happened to turn them over and see Volodya's Russian scrawl on the back.

245

Attention rippled through her and she called across to another official who strolled across and took a look at the papers. I kept saying that this was scrap paper. Someone had lent me scrap paper, I am writing a story. A story. You know? *Once upon a time?*

In the end I unzipped a side panel for my case and took out a copy of my book *Child of Cyrmra*, complete with a fuzzy photo of me on the back panel. She took it from me, turning it over, fanning the pages – looking, I presume, for secret messages, microfilm, stolen jewels. Whatever.

Then the gasometer grunted, shrugged her shoulders and handed it back. 'Eet matters little in these days,' she said. She waved away the other official and zipped my book back into its compartment. Then she beamed, showing crooked teeth. 'You like the writer Chekhov, Mrs.Ozanne?'

I nodded vigorously. 'Love him. A very wise writer. So wise about people.'

'Good. Happy journey!' She pushed back my cases and nodded, looking beyond me, eager for her next victim.

Sitting here on the plane I miss the wet streets and the menace of the city I have just left behind. I miss Mary Martha. I miss Volodya. My God, what's happening to me? I even miss Caitlin.

Back in England, the air is bright and soft, the messages shooting out at me from the buildings as they pass the windows of the car are clear. Bay windows, neat curtains. Shaved lawns. Fiestas and Micras twinned on concrete drives. The only differences between the houses marked by the slight variation in style: doors, windows; an occasional outrageous gesture in a colour deviating from the white, the racing green and the dark reds that are the current style.

The owners of the house on the corner of my *cul-de-sac*, who like to scream their non-conformity, have changed the elephant painted on their garage door for a tiger. I remember a conversation with Caitlin's maid Katya, trying to explain how ordinary people in England buy their own houses through a mortgage.

'A mortgage? What is this?' She even stopped drying the dishes to ask. 'How can ordinary people buy a house? How is it possible?'

I can't believe I've been away from England a mere two weeks. My own house stands out by virtue of – or should it be by *vice* of? – its peeling paint (once the prescribed racing green) and the long untended grass on its lawn. Janey's little mini is on my drive, nose to nose with Joseph's heavily manacled motorbike. A light is on. A welcome party. Well!

Inside the house Janey and Joseph are very much at home, sprawled over the sitting-room floor half dressed. They are fast asleep, with two empty bottles of bubbly beside them. I shake Janey and she opens a bleary eye. 'Crikey!' she says, sitting up. 'Where did you pop up from?' Then she slides back to the floor.

I poke at Joseph, who merely groans. 'Moscow,' I say. 'Didn't I tell you?'

In the end I haul them both to a sitting position and they stay propped there while I pour strong South American coffee down their throats to bring them back to the land of the living. It takes half an hour to gain their waking attention and fix them with a very stern eye.

I feel just like Caitlin. 'Now then, you two. What on earth have you been up to?'

I travel North in freezing style, on the back of Joseph's motorcycle, kitted up in his old leathers, which barely fit, and a helmet which makes me look like the an alien being from Doctor Who. This cheap transport is convenient, as the trip to Moscow has rendered me penniless for the time being. True, there will be a useful surge in December when the paperback of *Child of Cyrmra* limps onto the market.

Taking Joseph on the search for Martha Martha's sister is a good ploy, don't you think? To get the boy out of the rapacious clutches of my best friend. Give a friend a mission and you never know where it'll end. I don't advise it.

But then, I am on a mission myself, aren't I? And Heaven knows where that will end.

We stop at a Little Chef outside Darlington, and eat a sausage and chip platter. Joseph picks away at his food as I tell him of my plan is to track down the person or the descendants of Ellen Alice Johnson. Go to the library and look at the censuses for 1911 and 1921. Then church records for marriages and births, and then we'll be on our way. 'Just think, Joe, if we find her! How great to put them in touch after all these years!'

He pushes his plate away.

'Eat that!' I resent the peculiarly maternal note combining solicitude and rage which threads through my own voice. 'You've had nothing since breakfast.'

He is looking around restlessly, blind to the bright colours, the toddlers in designer bibs and the pre-teenagers showing their belly-buttons. Humbert Humbert would have a field day in a place like this.

249

'We should have gone to a pub,' Joseph says. 'Had a pub lunch.'

I shake my head. 'We're draining off the alcohol, not topping it up, Joe.' I reach over and spear some of his chips. I'm so much more comfortable with Joseph than with Caitlin. With him there is more warmth, less judgment. He is more vulnerable, gets into more scrapes . . . 'You didn't say why you've planted yourself in my house. I can't think it was with the intention of seducing my best friend—'

'Seducing? It was her. She—'

'You're twenty-six, Joe, supposedly in control of every- thing above as well as below that studded leather belt.'

He picks up the sausage with his fingers and starts to nibble it from the end. 'To tell you the truth, Ma, it was very mutual. I've always liked her, you know. And we're both over the age of consent. What harm is there . . . ?'

I groan at this. 'You don't see it, do you? You going out with older women bothers me not one jot. But your going out, however temporarily, with my best friend, that's the end of it for me. I've lost her.' It is only as I say the words I realise their truth. How things are changing.

He finishes the sausage in silence then makes a

final attack on the chips. 'Do you really want to know why I'm here?' He scrubs a tiny paper napkin across his greasy mouth. 'Do you really care, in the middle of how amazing Moscow was and your obsession with this fascinating woman who came from Darlington?'

My children press different but equally effective buttons when they deal with me. Caitlin presses the oh-mother-you-are-a-dizzy-fool button. Joseph presses the you-never-paid-me-any-attention-because-your-own-affairs-are-more- important button.

The buttons press on a ready bruise but I never show it. I smile now into my son's handsome, haggard face. 'Of course I care, idiot! But I knew you'd tell me in your own good time. So why are *you* here? Why didn't you tell me to get lost when I asked you to bring me up here on the bike? Why aren't you down there with your buddies, carving a furrow through your young life and preparing for your ;remature death?'

His head whips up at this.

'. . . Which is what you seem to be doing. And which for five years from when you were fourteen to nineteen I begged you not to do. Then, you must forgive me, I got bored with it, bored with you and bored with your whining father, who blamed me for you and you for me. So I handed you over to yourself and handed him over to the lovely Naomi. And then,

251

forgive me, I got on with my own life.'

'Mother, you don't need to . . .' he mutters, his chin on his chest.

'Oh, I'm sorry. I thought you wanted me to show how I care, to be up front with you.' To my consternation there are tears in my eyes.

'Here!' He sits up straight and pushes the tatty napkin across into my hand and watches me dab my eyes. Then he looks around. 'Do you think they'll charge for second coffees in here?'

In the next three days Joseph drinks gallons of coffee while we are combing records in the library and the county record office. Once I show him the method he's a meticulous research assistant. He never mentions the pub, or suggests the off-licence once. At night in our lodgings, tossing and turning in sheer longing for the touch, sound and smell of Volodya, I can hear Joseph through the thin wall muttering and shouting in his sleep. Or in his lack of sleep.

Then a loud scream rips through the air, curls along the landing. I reach for my dressing gown. I sit on his bed and shake him awake. 'What is it, Joseph?

'It's a dream, only a dream,' he mutters. He blinks up at me, and then smiles his weary smile. 'Yes. This horrible bird. Seems real at the time.' His eye trawls the narrow room. 'I could murder a drink.'

I put a hand on his cheek. 'Or be murdered by one?' I say sorrowfully. 'Will you tell me properly now why you're here, Joe?'

'The police have it in their heads that I am dealing. And I am not. But a girl took a pill and collapsed—'

'And it wasn't you?'

'No.'

'Then go and talk to them.'

He slips further down the bed and the blankets move as he shakes his head. 'I'll go when I'm ready. And I'm not ready yet.'

The next day we turn up a name and a present address. Ellen Mary Stobart, born in 1965 according to the records. Twenty-six years old. When she was born she lived in a village called Gainford, just outside Darlington.

I have now abandoned those ridiculous leathers and when I've taken off my helmet at what I hope is Ellen Mary Stobart's gate I imagine I look like a fairly normal, middle-aged woman in tailored trousers and suede jacket, clutching my briefcase packed with tapes and my Mary Martha notes.

I know this is the right house the minute she

opens the door. The bright squirrel-brown eyes, the heart-shaped face, the square-on, sturdy stance are very familiar. She looks at me, then beyond me at Joseph standing there behind me in his leathers. 'Yes?' she says.

She keeps us at the door as I stumble into an explanation which gets more and more preposterous as it succeeds. '. . . Look, perhaps we could sit down somewhere. I have some things to show you . . .'

She shakes her head. 'There've been people here, taking children, robbing houses. And those thieves seemed respectable. Not tearaways, according to the television.'

'I have my passport. I can show you my passport.'

She shakes her head. 'You would, wouldn't you?'

I look around. It is a very pretty village with rolling greens. I spy a seat. 'Look, come across there. We'll sit down where everyone can see us. That should be safe enough.'

She vanishes inside and re-emerges in a very pretty peach ski-jacket and a bunch of keys with which she proceeds to lock the door behind her.

On the village seat I show her the tapes and the papers and tell her the story of meeting Mary Martha and my astonishment at her survival. 'So she sent me here to look for Ellen Alice, her sister. I've been looking in the records and it seems—'

'Ellen Alice me great Grandma. Big Nana we call her, though she's right little now.'

'Now? She's still alive?' I glance across to the little cottage. Ellen Mary shakes her head. 'No, she's not here. She has her own place, a little council bungalow. Keeps it neat as a pin. Sharp as a needle. Very independent.' She shivers. 'Hey, it's turning right cold out here. Why don't we go in and get a cup of tea an' I'll ring Big Nana and tell her I'm coming to see her, with a very big surprise up my sleeve.' She laughs up at Joseph and he smiles back. In that uncomplicated laugh I see the young Mary Martha, laughing and talking with Nina, whom she was to love with all her heart.

We go to see the grandmother in Ellen's car, a battered Fiesta which nevertheless is spick and span inside and out. Joseph wheels his bike to the back of Ellen's cottage and takes a seat up front with her. Wordless communication is zinging between these two, so thick in the air you could slice it..

Ellen drives to the edge of the town to a sprawling council estate and parks up beside a neat row of bungalows fronted with battered communal grass. She lets herself into number seven with a key and, after a few minutes, comes back out and leads us in down a clean, bare passage.

The sitting room smells of air-freshener and cough medicine. It's sparsely furnished, as though cleared for a final exit; the furniture is teak, considered smart in the Sixties. One corner is dominated by a large television and a rack weighed down by dozens of videos. Dusty silk flowers flutter over a low table.

'Put the light on, Ellen. A person can hardly see in here.' On the couch, sitting very upright, is Mary Martha; or a new Mary Martha with a short haircut and a perm, crimplene cardigan and Marks and Spencer's moccasin shoes. She blinks up at me in the half light of the late afternoon. 'Our Ellen says you know our Mary Martha. But I told her that was rubbish.'

'Sit down, Mrs.Ozanne.' Ellen's hand is on my shoulder. I sit down, and Ellen sits beside her great-grandmother and takes hold of the claw-like hand.

I feel I am at some kind of tribunal. 'Yes. I have met her, Mrs.Stobart. I was in Russia recently—'

'That's where our Mary Martha, me big sister died. Russia. There was a letter to say she died.' The reedy voice is very insistent.

I shake my head. 'A mistake, I think. There was a lot of confusion in the Revolution.'

256

It is her turn to shake her head. 'It'll be a mistake. Somebody pretending . . .' she says stubbornly. I reach into my bag, take out my little machine, place it on the table and turn it on. Mary Martha's reedy voice comes forth. '. . . *and I used to play on the green with our Ellen Alice. Patty pans. Tins with mud which were, like, pretending to be food. We entertained each other to tea, like.*' In the background I can hear the sound of Moscow trams as they turn in the street below Caitlin's flat.

Mrs.Stobart lies back on the couch for a second then sits up straight. 'Well, I wouldn't'a believed it. Not in a million years'

'The voice sounds like you, Big Nana.' says Ellen. 'Like you only different.'

I laugh. 'Well Mary Martha has been talking Russian for seventy years.'

'In *Russian?*' The old lady is staring at me now. 'And how is she, our Mary Martha, then?'

'She's very well, considering.' What a world there is in those words.

'Says on the telly they're starving out there.'

I shake my head. 'Not quite. Not now.'

There is a long pause. I wonder what else there is to say. Finally I speak again. 'She asked if I would come to see you, Ellen Alice.' I look across at young

Ellen. 'To see who is in this family. And she asked me to write her story, from the tapes, and from my notes so that all of you would know about her. These tapes are copies made specially for you anyway.'

Old Mrs.Stobart is shaking Ellen's hand. 'You can sort out some photos, pet. Give them to this woman here. Of you and your Dad, and your Uncle Stephen and their lot. Give them to this lady here. You and me can write to our Mary Martha can't we? Write to her and tell her that we're all here, tell her about us.' She turns to me. 'Our Ellen's a good scholar you know. Degrees, certificates. Our Mary Martha had a good head on her. Everyone said that. Too good for service. We all said that.'

By the door, Joseph is moving restlessly from foot to foot. Ellen relinquishes her grandmother's hand. 'Maybe I should leave you and Mrs.Ozanne to it, Nana.' She looked up at Joseph. 'Me and Joseph could go to the pub. Leave you in peace for half an hour.'

Joseph frowns at her then looks at me. 'I can't go to the pub, Ellen. I'm what they call a recovering alcoholic, you see, and I'm trying very hard at present.'

How naughty of him. How hypocritical of me that I wish he hadn't said that.

Ellen is blushing. I don't know whether this was from the turn-down or the revelation. Then he gives her one of his beaming, heartbreaking smiles. 'But I'd like to take you for a ride on my bike, if you're game.'

She laughs then and leaps up to join him and they vanish through the door. I take her place on the sofa beside Mrs.Stobart. The old woman peers up at me. 'Do you know I'd not a' thought of it, save for today's happenings, but our Ellen is the very spit of our Mary Martha. The very spit.'

I think a lot these days about out tendency to make sense of things by making circles: of resemblances between one generation and another; of connections between one situation and another. We make then between one location and another. Ellen Stobart and Mary Martha make a circle. Joseph and young Ellen make a circle. Volodya and I make a circle. And he makes a circle with Mary Martha and Nina. And they make a circle with the young Mary Martha and the young Ellen Alice Johnson, soon to be Stobart. Religions, batty and benevolent, make use of the circle. I confess myself to being very much drawn to the Celtic circles: those precise tightly drawn rings; those snakes coiling back to nibble their own tail; those birds entwined with each other and then swooping around to form the ellipse.

And I know now that I am participating in the closure of various circles as I sit in this neat tidy room

259

listening while Ellen Alice Stobart slips from asking about Mary Martha, to telling me of her own life: life made hard when her railway-man husband died too early; of two bright sons and even brighter granddaughters. 'Teachers, nurses. One a solicitor even. And our Ellen's an engineer like her Dad. Tell our Mary Martha that.'

I put a hand on hers and have another flash of familiarity at its bird-bone feel. 'I'll tell her all you've said, Mrs.Stobart. You can be sure of this. Perhaps we can arrange for you to talk on the telephone .. Her hand turns in mine and she clasps me tight. 'Call us Ellen, pet. That's me name. Ellen Alice Johnson, sister to Martha.'

I'm forced to travel back south by coach by current poverty and the fact that Joseph has decided that Gainford suits his retreat mode and has adopted Ellen as his muse. Or she has adopted him as her project. He tells me he knows that the moment he saw her he knew she was the only person he wanted to be with. Seems he wants to paint a picture for her. Of the bird in the nightmare. He is a funny boy. I asked him about Janey and he said she would understand. I know he's right about that but I don't think me and Janey can be the same again.

Ellen cornered me last night and told me not to worry about him; she would take care of him. She'd make sure he went back and talked to the police. He had evidently told her why he was wandering around here like a lost soul. 'So don't you worry about him!'

'I don't. He's a grown man.'

She smiled then: a wonderful, wise Mary Martha smile. 'Of course you don't.' She leaned closer to me then, and whispered in my ear. 'I've taken to him, Olivia, really taken to him. And I really appreciate what you're doing for my Nana. I can't tell you how.'

I hugged her. 'He's a lucky man.' I hope he stays lucky. As lucky as Nina was through a lifetime. Another circle.

This bus station is cold and draughty. Ellen and Joseph stand with me in the queue, their breaths dancing on the air, keeping warm by stamping from foot to foot. The bus roars round the corner and we all relax, only to wait impatiently as the driver makes a great business about getting the luggage on board. And we all wave eagerly, relieved as the driver closes the doors, slides the bus into gear, and sets off.

I settle down in my seat. I have a table of my own, so can spread out my books and papers, place my recording machine just so, with its earphones beside it. I travel by bus because it is so cheap but I regret that it is so hard to write on buses. Your pen skitters all over the place. What I need is one of those little computers like Caitlin and Charles. I wonder if the bank would lend me the money to buy a little computer. But as I lay my head back on the newly laundered headrest I know that won't be necessary.

In those hours while I was talking with Ellen Stobart, looking at her family photographs and watching Joseph and young Ellen in their courting dance, the back of my mind was burrowing away at a new idea. Here on the bus it speaks itself into my mind. I hear the words as though I am speaking to someone else. Janey perhaps. What I will do is sell my house, store my stuff, and go back to Moscow. I will live there properly for a while.

I'll spend time with Mary Martha and write her story at the same time. I'll tell her about her sister and her wonderful family. I'll show her the photographs. I'll work with Volodya by day on old Herbert's fairy story book. And by night we will make love. I'll get Herbert to pull his old spy-strings to let me bring Mary Martha back here England, to see again the quiet green stretches of land, the small villages with their ancient churches: the place where she was born.

But first I must sleep. And what strange circles we find in sleep.

FOURTEEN

This time when the taxi drops me off at my house there are two cars on the drive: Janey's little mini and a very familiar chunky Mercedes of dubious vintage. This is the point where I regret for the hundredth time my tendency to hand out my keys to all and sundry.

My two guests are sitting in silence in my bare, immaculately polished sitting room. Janey's conscience must have driven her to great domestic heights. Janey herself is enthroned on the peacock chair turning the pages of a magazine and Lee Compton, owner of the Merc, is sitting with his briefcase on his knee making obscure coded marks on a fluttering spreadsheet.

The touch of ice in the air is very familiar. These two do not get on, of course.

This being in the middle of two distinct factions is a signal experience in my life. It happened in school. It happened in college. In the college where I taught, it happened again. One would-be friend, driven with frustration, bawled at me that I was too keen to see the other's point of view, who did I think I was – God? This accusation has embarrassed me a bit, but down the years I've concluded that though it might make people question your loyalty, and prevent you from being a member of many a cosy clique, seeing two sides of the coin is a heaven-sent faculty for a writer.

Lee leaps up now and enfolds me in his meaty embrace. His aftershave has always been loaded with too much perfume. 'Darling, where have you been? It's the second time I've been in town to find you gone.'

I pull away and stare up at him. He's looking much fitter since he went on his diet and acquired his personal trainer, but there is something quite wrecked about him. Something which comes from within. This was the element which first attracted me to him, that dangerous quality. But now my blood is not up, my skin is not tingling. 'Lee! You're looking marvellous,' I say.

He hugs me harder and I wrench myself away. 'Put me down, you great galoot.' I look past him to Janey. 'Good to see you, Janey.'

She puts down her magazine and stands up. 'Olivia I . . . shall I put the kettle on?'

'No.' I give Lee a small push. 'You make some coffee, love. I need a quick word with Janey.'

'OK.' He flushes, angry at his dismissal. 'Sure.'

I turn to Janey. 'Don't say anything about that other thing, Janey. I'm afraid I've left Joseph up

North.'

'Thank God for that.' She made a drama of wiping the sweat from her brow. 'I was wondering what the hell I would say to him if he was with you.'

'You would say it was an aberration.'

'An aberration? Hell, yes. That's what it was.' She shrugs herself into her short denim jacket. 'I'll go now, then. I've gone through the whole house . . .' a small smile sketches itself on her face, 'there's not a sign of anyone's misdeeds anywhere. I'm off.'

I don't protest. The circle has turned for Janey and me and we both know it. As I wave her away at the door I reflect on the fact that the circle has turned as well for Lee and me and I have now to consider how to let him down gently.

Lee Compton and I go back a long way. An ex-footballer from the minor leagues, he lectured in PE in the college where I taught. I was playing 'happy married woman' then. But one time I defended him at a faculty meeting and after that we still indulged in a little colleague-like flirting and innuendo. He left the college, to start a new career in sporting PR and seven years passed before we met again outside a pub in Fowey in Cornwall. I was there holed up in a small hotel, trying to meet a deadline for a book, and he was there for a series of meetings about a new sports manufacturing project. The upshot was this: I made too much love that week, and did a lot of writing – I met my deadline – but I got no sleep. When I reached home I slept round the clock to make up a twenty-four hour sleep debt.

Since then Lee and I have met many times on this kind of *ad hoc* basis, mostly to make love when he was travelling in my area. To be honest it was more of a meeting of bodies than a meeting of minds. In a surreal fashion it suited us both. Janey always considered Lee was a sexual opportunist with an outsize . . . er . . . libido. But, as I said to her, it takes two to tango.

'Has she gone?' Lee is balancing three of my best china mugs on a tray.

'Yeah,' I say, planting myself onto the peacock chair. 'She has things to do.'

He hands me the mug with the blue bird on it. 'Well now, isn't this nice? Just the two of us. Now then, tell me all about Moscow. Was it the dump they all say it is?'

I leap to the defence of Volodya's city. 'Dump? The whole thing was amazing, Lee. So foreign, and much more Eastern than I thought. Faces in the street from blond Scandinavian to Chinese. Buildings from Stalinist Gotham city to onion-top churches where they're ladling on the gold leaf again and the priests are coming out of the shadows—'

'Woah! Woah! I believe you, honey. I believe you!' He put a gentle hand on my arm.

I slow down. 'It's such a place, Lee!. The buildings, the people. What's happening there even now! It's amazing. On the brink. You want to get your company there, get a foothold. In five years' time . . . It is an intriguing place.' I glance around the sparse room. 'I'm going to sell all this, you know. And I'm going out there to live.'

He slops his coffee into his saucer. 'To live? You're crazy. I wouldn't trust that lot an inch. Reds. Spies. Butchers.'

'It's all changing, Lee. Not the Sixties now, you know. And it's not an Ian Fleming scenario.'

'If you believe that you want a brain transplant,' he says sulkily. He looked me up and down. 'You've met someone, Liv. Some Red who wants to marry you so he can get to the West. They're all at it. There was a story in the Telegraph—'

'I'm going there. He's not coming here.'

'Ha!' he says triumphantly. 'There is a *he*!'

'That's none of your business. You know that Lee.'

Now he does something very strange. He puts

his cup on the table beside him, comes across the room, hitches his immaculate pants and gets down on his knees before me. 'No need to do that, lover. Sell up if you want to. Get rid of this dreary place. And come and throw your hat in with me in the West Country. We'll see each other twice as often. Nice little cottage by the sea—'

I put my hand over his mouth. 'Stop it! Stop talking as though I am about to take the great leap into senility.'

He sits back on his heels. 'Senility! It's insanity to do what you're proposing to do. Crazy.' He shrugs. 'I don't want to lose you, Olivia.'

'You never had me, Lee. You have your wife and your three daughters and your two granddaughters. You don't have me. You never had.'

He stands up, brushes the knees of his trousers and pulls me to my feet. He draws me to him and I turn so that the kiss he aims for my lips lands on my cheek. 'Come on, Liv! Be a sport. Just one for the road? For old times' sake?' I twist out of his grasp.

'You cheeky . . . pup. There's no holding you, is there?' I stand back, fold my arms and start to laugh. 'We've had some laughs, some good times, Lee. But that's it. All it ever was. Now things are changing. I've changed. The wheel has turned. Go away.'

'Wheel, what wheel?' His voice is sulky but he is folding his spreadsheets and placing them carefully in his briefcase. Ever the realist. 'You never stop talking in riddles, Liv. Comes from writing those kids' books. Softens the brain. I always said that.'

'Just like playing all that football has softened your – well – all the other parts.'

He clutches his briefcase to him. 'Bitch!' he says mildly.

I smile broadly. 'Thank you,' I say, holding the door wide open. 'Bye, Lee!'

As I watch his car roar down the *cul-de-sac* I celebrate again a sense of release. And also wonder at the new-found certainty that, except for Volodya, I don't want any other man to touch me again. Not ever.

I've never felt that before. Even when I was first married to Kendrick. Nor with any man I've had relationships with since. I wonder briefly if it is a sign of getting old, or if it's a sign that I am finally getting out of my adolescence and into some kind of maturity. Heaven knows what that will do to my ability to write children's fiction. I can't count the people who have suggested that, when I grow up I might write an *adult* novel. They would be rubbing their hands at these changes. Now I can join their world.

That is as maybe. In the meantime, there is work to do. There is the house to put on the market, the conversion of the Moscow tapes and notes to some kind of draft account of Mary Martha's life, and – this month's task – the correction of printer's proofs for next year's novel called *The Grey Mantle*. This one is a time-slip novel which moves between the experiences of Tom, an abused child of the present day, and Uwe, a Jewish child in wartime Vienna.

It is three months since I finished the novel and I have the distance now, as I read it, to see that it is not half bad. A bit slick, somehow, here and there. I mark those parts for further really close attention and move on. As I read I experience the usual frisson of guilt for burrowing into pain to make my fiction, but it must strike a chord out there somewhere, from the letters I get from children and from adults remembering their childhood only too well. The books certainly sell – in modest amounts but they sell.

You might say I bought my ticket to write about childish pain many years ago, sitting miserably in a tight dark cupboard for hours, or in marginally greater comfort in my own small bedroom for an afternoon, a day, a whole weekend: contained by my mother's icy disapproval of some small misdemeanour; fed at long intervals by food congealed and stiffened for a

270

prescribed period in the icebox. Hot food, apparently, was too good for such an evil child. I never eat cold food now. Salads are an anathema. No wonder I can't slim.

There was a letter waiting for me when I got back, from the home where my mother now resides. It seems she is refusing all hot food now. Funny, that.

The estate agent, a spotty version of Joseph in an unlikely suit, visits the house and tells me that despite the difficulty of the market at this time – negative equity and all that – he felt sure he could move it in a month or so. He hoped I would give sole agency . . .

'Months?'

'Three to six months and you'll be lucky at that. As I say, the market is very sluggish.'

This casts me into gloom which I alleviate by writing a short, passionate, moderately pornographic letter to Volodya, a letter to Mary Martha with the first exciting news about her sister Ellen Alice, and a longer, windier one to Caitlin, eulogising my time in Moscow and telling her of my current plans to sell up and move there. I will need her to sponsor me, of course, but she is not to worry, I won't move in with her as I will live with Volodya. I have the Herbert MacIntyre fairy-tale project to complete, and I can write my own stories there as well as anywhere. After all, they are mainly spun out of my own head.

In the package I enclose a letter to Charles Conrad, asking him to send on another letter, also enclosed, to Herbert MacIntyre. In that letter I inform the old man that I will be happy to work on the fairy-tales and would he dispatch a copy to Mr. Charles Conrad, who will get the book to my chosen translator. I ask Charles to make sure Volodya gets the copy.

The job on *The Grey Mantle* finished, I dispatch it with some relief to my publisher. The difficulty of this moment of dispatch never gets easier. Twice I retrieve it from its parcel to make final-final amemdments.

Then I set about the complicated task of transcribing the Mary Martha tapes and putting them into some kind of narrative and publishable order. I give myself a two-month deadline for this task, by which time it will be Christmas and with luck the house will be sold. Then I can go back to Moscow, show Mary Martha – and Volodya – the completed manuscript, sell it for her, and we can all get on with our lives.

I try to talk to my agent Sally Courtauld about the Mary Martha book, but she is Welsh and given to self-regarding tears and too much drink. I catch her on a bad morning. Her voice is slurred. 'What? You must be mad, darling. Waste of time. No market for things like that. Localised self-publishing, yes. You won't get a tickle in the real market.'

I put the phone down on her, reflecting on the fact that she hasn't really done a thing for me. I sold my first book myself and took her on as agent, on the advice of my editor. Since then the books have sold themselves on continuance and she has juggled creatively with her ten per cent of my admittedly modest royalties.

I must get rid of her.

Letters start to arrive. There is one from Caitlin in sheer rage at my craziness, urging me to stop the insanity. But she will sponsor me again if I insist. And a letter from Charles tells me that old Herbert is delighted with my decision – and it looks as though he is biting in regard to his memoirs.

He goes on. 'And your lovely daughter is on top form as ever, Olivia, having made a contact in the circle of the son of a general who looks as though he is a coming man in the new set-up. And the tom-toms tell me you're thinking of decamping here. Well, well! Brave heart!'

And there are rather stiff little letters from Volodya, vowing great affection but chillingly distant. A stumbling letter from Mary Martha tells me her amazement and delight at my discovery.

Volodya's letters warm up when he gets the book of fairy tales and starts to translate them, sending them to me in single stories, efficiently translated but with a rigidity which robs them of their childlike essence. It will be my job to retell them, investing the dense simplicity of childhood into the lines.

I become involved with these tasks. I only go out for food. I have the phone off the hook and the post is piling up unopened. That is, apart from post from Russia and one letter from Joseph hoping I am all right and saying that he has a job on the lines in Ellen's factory and he has found the secret of life: to live on love, not drink or those other little things that help you chase the stars. *'And Ellen has cleared out her garden hut for me to paint, built me a drawing board and bought me paint and paper.'* Such a girl! And he hopes I am all right.

I write back to say I am all right but in retreat with a big writing job so not to bother me unless it's life or death. I do understand that in his case it may be life or death, of course.

I am cocooned in the house, only emerging

from my chrysalis now and then, to show potential buyers round the house.

I like these quiet phases, when I do some of my best work. I have always created such cut-off times, to complete the odd article or conference paper. I have used them to burrow back into my childhood and invent fictions to draw off its poisons; to make characters who are me yet not me, and whizz them into the future and deep into the past. I construct realities which give me some kind of control: it goes some way to heal that child still sitting there inside me like the smallest figure in a Russian babushka doll.

As these days flow quietly one into another, I am disentangling the delicate understated life of Mary Martha, counterbalanced by the statuesque poetry of Russian myth. I am truly enjoying myself.

I knew it was too good to last. The bell is jangling and someone is banging on the front door. I lift the curtain to be confronted by the sight of Kendrick's highly polished Rover. In the back is the lovely Naomi with one wriggling child on her knee and another beside her.

I open the door. Kendrick is standing on the slatted wooden doormat, stamping his feet against the cold.

'Hello, Olivia.' His voice is brisk, the sharp points on his handsome face pink with the cold.

I open it wider. 'Come in.' I peer past him. 'Is that Naomi? You can't leave her out in the cold. Bring her in.' This is very big of me. We have never actually met, of course.

He raises a brow. 'You're sure?'

'Course I'm sure.'

We hustle them from the car and into the house. It just takes a few minutes to get them established with milk and biscuits, tele-cartoons for the children and coffee and magazines for the mother. I have to admit to a fleeting curiosity as I look at these children who are half-brothers to Caitlin and Joseph.

Kendrick sweeps me into the dining-room and clicks the door shut behind us. He looks around at the bare room, the bleak space only broken by the computer and the piles of paper on the dining table . 'How can you live like this?' He puts a hand on the unopened mail. Then he smashes the telephone back onto its hook. 'I have been trying to telephone you.'

'I live very well like this, thank you. I love it. I am working. I do not want to see anyone, to read anyone's letters, to talk to anyone.'

That's when he breaks into an angry tirade about me selling even this hovel and going native in Russia without so much as a by-your-leave. Caitlin must have been blabbing.

'And whose by-your-leave am I supposed to ask? Yours?'

'That is not the point, Olivia. It is embarrassing, undignified . . .'

I reach up and put my hand on his lips, stopping him full flow. 'Kendrick! Nothing, not one bit of any of this, is your business.'

'No. Yes. It is. Olivia, we were married for nearly twenty years—'

I laugh out loud at this. 'Marriage? Twenty years of deception, farce.'

'Not really. Not all of it. Not at first. You changed. You have changed more since.'

I can't help laughing. 'No. Now at last I am me. All those years I was another person. I married you to get out . . . away from my mother. Trouble is I didn't quite realise she would come with me,' my hand goes to my head. 'In here.'

He is distracted a moment. 'Did you see your mother when you were up there? Joseph says you were up there in the North.'

'You've talked to him?'

'On the phone.'

'What did he want?'

'What does he ever want? Money.'

'There is a girl up there. Perhaps he—'

'You didn't answer my question . . . about your mother. Did you see her? How was she?'

The chill is starting. I shiver. I thought I had got out of that. 'No. To be honest it didn't cross my mind to go to see her.'

He shrugged. 'Never were much of a daughter to her, were you?'

'She wouldn't know me. She doesn't recognise anybody.'

'Still, deep down—'

'She doesn't know anybody,' I repeat. I swallow thw words I want to say.

The challenge I've not yet met with my mother, this person I've loved fiercely, feared greatly, and hated roundly in an attempt to survive, is the challenge of feeling sorry for that babbling loose mouth, the wavering hands, and the sad shrunken body. All I've managed to feel so far is pleasure, the joy of my final escape; revenge for that hard cold childhood which was so threaded with fear like the name of a seaside town through rock.

That's why I don't go to see her. In case I laugh. Such pleasure and joy is entirely inappropriate and I'm afraid it will show on my face. The nurses will disapprove.

That's why my mind would not even acknowledge that when I visited Ellen Alice Stobart I was within fifteen miles of my unknowing, unknown mother.

Now I open my dining-room door and allow the gale of childish chatter to invade this bare space. 'Now, Kendrick, if you could take your family and get on with your life and just let me get on with mine?'

Naomi, very sweet in a short-jacketed suit with a Peter Pan collar, is standing up, one child held in front of her like a shield. I smile at her, my best teacher's smile, right into the eyes. 'No need to keep you, Naomi. I must say you're doing a very good job with those children. And what a lovely suit that is. Kendrick always did like leather.'

I watch them as they trail out. Kendrick shoots me a glance, half appeal, half hate, but I shake my head very vigorously. 'Bye, Kendrick. And you will tell Caitlin not to send you on errands like this in the future, won't you?'

An hour later I jump at the razor-edge ringing of the telephone and remember Kendrick smashing the receiver back into place. I hesitate, then pick it up, to hear the lilting, sober Welsh tones of Sally Courtauld. 'Olivia! Dear! Have you seen it in The

Nation? Is that what you were talking about? Old MacIntyre? That old man all those rumours were about? And there is mention of this woman, a woman there since the revolution. Is this your old woman? And there's something here about buried treasure. Incredible.'

The Nation is Charles Conrad's paper. I have not seen a newspaper in weeks.

'Listen. I'll read it to you—'

'Stop. I'll go out and get the paper. Then I'll call you.' I put down the phone carefully, and then begin to run.

I read the paper as I walk back and it flaps in the wind. The story is under Charles Conrad's byline. It does mention Herbert MacIntyre and the forthcoming publication of his diaries in this newspaper. But the brunt of the story is the death from pneumonia of a woman called Nina Samsonov a, lifetime companion to an Englishwoman Mary Martha Johnson, who once, before the war, was offered escape from the Soviet Union by Herbert MacIntyre. There is some mention of her hiding jewels beneath the corners of the house.

The paper proposes to campaign to restore Miss Johnson's English passport so that she can visit again her homeland left more than seventy years before.

With some difficulty I fold the paper and put it

under my arm. My brain is racing as I slowly walk home. Mary Martha must be missing the Grey Auntie, no matter how much she once protested that her Nina was not there inside that fragile old shell. Somehow I must get there, be with her before Charles, Caitlin - and their entire breed - extinguish Mary Martha altogether, with the heat of their all-devouring attention.

I must go there. I must go there now.

SIXTEEN

Volodya is more amused than dismayed at my frantic efforts to clean his room and put some kind of gloss on it for the benefit of the photographer tomorrow. I straighten pictures and put books and papers in order. I shake covers and cushions, trying them this way and that way on the day-bed to get the most artistic effect. Volodya's French clock and his intriguing artefacts are dusted, placed and replaced, in a colourful, contrived still life.

After an hour he takes both my busy hands in his and says, 'Enough, Olivia. Enough! It is presentable. Presentable. I know what you do. You watch the Auntie's back. But you have done enough. We will eat.'

He has placed a low stool by the chair, on it a tray set with wooden platters bearing bread, some kind of sliced meat and china beakers of red wine. I am suddenly so hungry I could devour the wooden platters themselves without much trouble. We eat in silence; I do not stop until I have eaten all my food and half of his, and he has poured me a second beaker of wine. He stretches his long legs out in front of him.

282

'Now where were we before your lovely daughter came in and created her whirlwind?'

I watch him over the rim of my beaker. 'I was trying to get out of you why I am as welcome here as a storm in winter. You looked at me as though I were something the cat had brought in.'

He smiled slightly at this. 'The cat? Your expressions, Olivia—'

'Well?'

He hesitated. 'I have another job, Olivia. As well as the nursery tales. This American academic, an expert in Pushkin, she—'

'She?' I am hit in the solar plexus. 'Oh. I see . . . Another foreign woman.'

He shrugs, his eyes veiled. 'I tell you, Olivia. This is what I like.'

How ridiculous. I am fifty. Grown up. Not a floundering teenager slavering over some crush. But I have moved too fast, taken too much for granted, broken my rule of lending too much of myself to another person. I suppose, looking at it practically, the worst casualty here is my dignity. I'd better watch myself.

'Well,' I say brightly, 'who you work with, and for, is none of my business, is it Volodya?'

He is slipping away from me already. His hand

with its long tapered fingers is that of a stranger. I look wildly around the crowded room. The day-bed is looming ridiculously large. My eye settles on my bags, still tucked behind the door. I march across and grab them, 'I should go to Caitlin's.'

He peels my fingers from the handles. 'No. No. You stay here, in my room. I will take the Grey Auntie's room. There is a day-bed in there.'

I remember the aunties used to sleep in Mary Martha's room, and use Nina's room as a sitting-room. I stand there a second, hands hanging loose, then go and sit on a chair. I look up at him and smile brightly. 'Is it interesting, this Pushkin work?'

He shrugs. 'It is work. For me, there is little one can say new, about Pushkin. But there are people who will discover him for the first time. Especially now.'

The mirage of the Pushkin woman arises in the silence between us now. She is tall, and oh so slender in that disciplined American fashion. A sweep of thick, beautifully cut straight hair. She is not young, but she is young enough.

No competition. I am no competition.

I am suddenly dropping, muddled with exhaustion. I look longingly at the day-bed. 'Volodya. I am so tired.'

'Yes, yes, you must rest.' His natural solicitude is

like sandpaper on my skin. 'Such a long day for you, my dear girl.'

The door clicks behind him. I resist the desire to fall there and then onto the bed, and change slowly, deliberately, into my long nightgown and wrap. Then I take my wash-bag to the little washroom so I can clean my teeth, and wash as far down and as far up as I can, as I did once long ago when I stayed with my grandmother, my father's mother, whose house also lacked a bathroom. I went there for the last time when I was five, after my father died, and have a vivid memory of being dragged away by my mother who was screaming at the top of her voice that the house was too hot and too filthy. She couldn't breathe, couldn't breathe.

I peep in at Mary Martha on my way back to Volodya's room. Her tiny figure lies still and straight under an unruffled woven coverlet. She sleeps in only half the bed. The space beside her is smooth and empty.

I wake up in the deep dark to find myself tucked into Volodya's day-bed. I cannot remember pulling up the coverlet or turning off the light. The room is black but I know someone is there in the shadows by the door. 'Volodya?'

My ears pick up a rustle which is essentially female, the scent of gardenias. I squeeze my eyes closed and open them again. A woman is standing there with a wing of black hair and a blouse with a ruffled red collar. I close my eyes again and she is gone.

'Volodya!' my call is long and plaintive.

The first person to get to me, to put an arm around me, is Mary Martha, bundled up, her coat over her nightie, a pixie-hood on her head. 'What is it, pet?' she says in her soft voice. 'What's wrong?'

Now Volodya's anxious face looms above hers. 'What happened, Olivia?'

'There was a woman. Just there by the door. They both peer behind them into the empty space. '. . . Then she vanished.'

'What did she look like?' says Mary Martha. 'This woman?'

'Dark.' I touch the side of my face. 'She had a wing of dark hair coming down here. And a kind of red ruffled blouse.'

Now Mary Martha strokes the tumbled hair away from my face. 'Don't you worry about that, pet. I told her not to bother you, but she said she wanted a look. Didn't I tell you she was together again, body and soul? My Nina.' She squeezes my hand.

'I could smell gardenias.'

'That's right, pet. But it's many a year since she could get hold of that scent. Many a year.' She takes a step backwards and puts my hand in Volodya's. 'You sit with her a bit, Volya. The lass is in need of company.' Then she floated out of the room, not much more than a ghost herself.

I sit up straighter and Volodya edges onto the bed. He is wearing tracksuit bottoms; his body glows white in the semi darkness. I am still shaking and do not resist as he pulls me to him, stroking my hair and whispering in my ear words in Russian which I do not understand. Around us the air is replete with feeling, trembling in the air, a shadow of the passion that has kept Nina so close to Mary Martha even after death.

And he is with me under the covers stroking his flat palms down my arms and legs, calming me as though I were a bolting horse.

And of course we make love with the power of a dam breaking and he is whispering in my ear that he loves me, in Russian and in English.

And I know it must be true because I cannot feel like this into a vacuum. He has called this emotion up in me: scoured the base of my feeling, forced me to show my hand, to recognise depths within myself that I did not know existed.

Ellen was holding the motorbike helmet in front of her like a shield. 'You have to go, Joseph,' she said. 'Go back to London.'

A gust of cold north-east wind touched the back of his neck. He put his hand behind her and pushed the door of the shed to. 'Come in. It's freezing in here.' He tipped up his drawing board. 'Now then, what do you think of this? I think I've snared that bad old bird for once and for all.'

The bird was there, of course. But this time he was in the company of four others, exactly like him. The five birds were woven with wonderful, intricate elaboration into a self-perpetuating hoop, the long jewelled beak of one folded into the wing or tangled into the feet of the next one. 'Got them all chasing after each other. Closed off. Neat, eh?'

Ellen closed her eyes, and peered at the picture through the fringe of her lashes. Now the colours merged into an abstract kaleidoscope of pulsing colour. This still page seemed to move and ripple under her gaze. 'It's really . . . well . . . amazing.'

'See what it's called?' He held it up, nearer to her eyes, his finger pointing to a small part of the design in the left corner. Webbed there, in curlicues of feather and flowers she could make out the word *Imagine*. 'It's

288

for you,' he said.

'But you could sell it. You need to sell them. The money.'

'I'll paint more, now. But this one's for you.'

She put down the helmet on the bench and took the picture from him. 'Thank you,' she said. 'I'll treasure it.'

He picked up the helmet. 'So why must I go back to London?'

'You frighten me. You being here has been truly marvellous, but I am starting to get frightened.'

He frowned. 'We need never do all that again, Ellen. The epiphany. Honest. That was just to share . . . so that you would know—'

She shook her head. 'That night was perfect, Joseph. I'd never have done that with anyone else. No other person could make me feel like you did then. It was very . . . generous. But what you do, how you are, it's different to me. I like what I do, organising people and materials so the right number of tools comes off the production line at the end of the day. It's exciting. Important.'

'You can still do that. I can paint—' He grabbed her arm and shook it.

She wriggled out of his grasp. 'I can't compete with . . . all those epiphanies, Joseph. And I can't join you out in that world because my world is too important to me. It's solid and it lasts. To you my world'll become more and more boring. I know it. And the thing about that girl, the one who nearly died, is grinding at the back of me. You should go and sort that with the police.'

He stood back from her, flicked his hair and confined it with a thick elastic band. 'I thought—'

'That I would join you in all that craziness? Be pulled in?' She shook her head. 'You're lovely Joseph. Bloody marvellous in fact. And I'll miss you. But you've got to go.'

He put a single finger on the picture. 'What about this? Will you throw that out too?'

Her grip tightened on the still damp board. 'I'll treasure it, like I said,' she said. 'Treasure it for all time.'

Volodya has slipped out of my bed in the middle of the night and when we meet in the morning he is distant again, and it is as though those night-time hours are a figment of my imagination.

The surprise of the day is that Charles Conrad and the leather-coated Russian photographer bring Herbert MacIntyre with ~~him.~~ them.

I peer behind them, looking for Caitlin but she

290

is not with them.

The three men fill the little flat, darkening the sombre winter light. The rest of us are like flies squashed against the wall, which rather spoils the work Mary Martha and I have done: putting on our best clothes, fluffing out our hair just so, and filling old vases with flowers from the stall at the metro station.

Herbert MacIntyre sweeps off his tall fur cap and bows deeply, first to me and then to Mary Martha, to whom he speaks in rapid Russian. She nods and talks back, gesturing vivaciously, like a much younger woman.

Charles murmurs in my ear. 'They talk of the time before the war. Seems the old boy fell for Nina and she tried to get him to get Mary Martha out, but Mary Martha turned the offer down. Wouldn't go without Nina, and MacIntyre wouldn't let Nina go. Intriguing version of the old triangle, what?'

The rattling talk fades away, and Mary Martha turns to me, her brown eyes shining. 'Just fancy, Olivia! I never thought I'd see anyone again, who knew my Nina at her best. Like she really was.'

Herbert MacIntyre turns his turtle gaze on me. 'Those first Vasnetsov stories are looking very fine, Mrs.Ozanne. Such crisp expression. Yet dense, like poetry. I look forward to seeing them in their entirety.'

I smile, gratified despite myself. 'Thank you. I must say I am so dependent on Volodya here, the original translation is his.'

I introduce the two men. They shake hands cordially enough, but I sense a wariness on the part of Volodya, who can probably smell the not-always-savoury smell of old power that attaches itself to this ancient Englishman. 'Fine work, sir,' says MacIntyre gruffly. 'Fine work.' Those two drop back into Russian and again I am the onlooker.

Then, total confusion reigns as Charles produces a bottle of fine vodka and the photographer embarks on his work. With the exception of Charles, who is directing operations, there are photographs of us all, in every combination: MacIntyre and Mary Martha; MacIntyre and Mary Martha holding an early portrait of Nina; Mary Martha on her own with the portrait of Nina; MacIntyre with an early portrait of Nina. Then Volodya and I are added to the mix. Then Mary Martha poses with the early postcards she sent to her mother. Then close-ups of just the postcards, of Nina's scanty jewellery box, of the icon I first saw in the little blue church. It is all quite exhausting and after two hours of this Mary Martha has lost her sparkle and is showing her age. She drifts off to lie down and I shoo them all away, glad to see the back of them.

292

Volodya, when I return from the door, is back at his table, head down over his papers. I stand slightly behind him, watching his racing pen. 'Is that the Pushkin?' I say, surprised at my own timidity.

He pushes his glasses back on his head and looks up at me in the daytime gloom. 'No,' he says. 'It is the last of the fairy-tales.'

The French clock ticks away a good thirty seconds. 'Good. I can work on them while I'm here and leave them for MacIntyre.' My voice is shrill, over-controlled. He is clearing the last of me, out into the wings. The Pushkin woman, with her wand-like figure and her fall of thick hair is centre stage.

'Good.' He nods, his glasses fall onto his nose and he bends once more over his work.

'Volodya, I—' But the telephone rings. He answers it then nods across at me. 'Your daughter,' he

I feel a rare gratitude to Caitlin. 'Ma?' Her voice is clear and sweet down the line. Someone is with her. She is performing.

'Hello, darling.' Now I am being over-hearty. I have an audience too.

'Charles was just saying you were a real trooper this afternoon.'

'You make me feel as though I should be riding for the Queen.'

293

'Now, now. We were just wondering whether you would like to come out with us tonight. Charles still needs a few words of wisdom from you for his article. And he has a message from old MacIntyre. There is a party. Er . . . Volodya could come as well.'

The light from the lamp is making a silver halo round the top of his bent head. 'A party? Volodya is very busy,' I say briskly. 'He has a deadline to meet. But for myself, I would love to come.'

He looks up at me now, the faintest of smiles on his face. 'You must go, Olivia. It will be good for you,' he says quietly.

I cough to clear my throat. 'When? When will you call?' 'About nine.'

'Yes. Right.' I crash the phone back into its old-fashioned cradle and flee the room.

Mary Martha is sitting up on her bed, looking yet again through the photo album. 'Can I really go and see them all? Can I go with you?'

I sit beside her and take her hand. 'You most certainly can. You most certainly will.'

Joseph's leathers creaked as he adjusted his shoulders for the shot. The bar was dirty and much too hot. He wished he had turned down the challenge of the pool game. But the lads in the bar had pricked up their ears at his accent, jeering about *bliddy* cockneys, and he had thought that winning the game would be the best way to keep them quiet. As it was, this was the fifth game he had won and the wadge of notes in his top pocket made up for the discomfort of the jacket.

He certainly needed the money.

There was, of course, the option of removing the jacket, but it would be nicked in a second in a place like this.

He had packed his hold-all and come into Darlington, getting away from Ellen to decide exactly what to do. The thought of going down to sort out the business of the dead girl buzzed around in his head. Maybe then . . .

He bent down and potted the last ball. A murmur of appreciation fluttered through the crowd that was gathering round the table. Five in a row. Amid fairly respectful bantering, he turned down another challenge and went to sit in a corner with his pint.

Two men, one with short red hair and one with an over- barbered beard, strolled over from the door. Red Hair spoke. 'Good win, son. New round here, aren't yer?'

He nodded, heart sinking. All they needed was the big black boots to declare their police identity. He took a long drink of his beer. A trembling quiet settled on the bar as the drinkers turned slightly to get the policemen out of their eye line.

'Here on business are yer?' Beard had a surprisingly light voice.

Joseph shook his head. 'Just passing through, actually.'

'Actually?' They exchanged glances. 'Your bike outside, is it? *Actually*, like?'

'Mmm.' Joseph downed the last of his pint with great care.

The policeman kicked his holdall, still there under the seat. 'This your bag?'

'Yep.'

'What say we take a look inside?'

His head went up. 'You've got no right—'

'Ah, but actually we have, son. Wrong face in the wrong place gives cause for suspicion.' Red Hair was grinning.

Joseph stood up. 'I say I haven't done anything.'

'We believe yer, son. But I tell you what, we can go down the police station and you'll get a really good chance to prove it. Can't do fairer than that, can we?' He picked up Joseph's hold-all.

The drinkers watched with detached interest as he walked out of the pub, a policeman fore and aft.

Outside the pub the three of them stood staring at the bike. 'What's this?' Red Hair kicked the box. 'This looks special. Could you open it for us? *Actually* I'd quite like to see what's inside.'

Joseph hauled out his keys and unlocked the box and opened it to reveal the chainsaw. Beard policeman 'Bingo!'

Red Hair pursed his lips in a very long whistle then said: '*Actually*, sir, it seems like it's our lucky night,' he purred, fishing out his mobile phone.

The apartment of our host, Leo Crabtree, the very young Moscow Bureau Chief of a very heavy newspaper, is on an entirely different scale to Caitlin's modest apartment. This is in a much older building. Tall rooms; wide spaces. Beautiful wooden doors and floors; turn of the century mouldings. The scale rather engulfs the modern Finnish furniture, making it look smaller than it really is.

Leo is obviously used to the reaction of space-starved visitors. He smiles kindly at my astonishment, telling me how the apartment was acquired for the paper in the Fifties with the aid of the spy Kim Philby, who was visiting Moscow as a British diplomat at the time. Friends in high places indeed.

To my surprise the conversation is not difficult

to follow. Apart from Janni the Dutchman, the faces are new. Among the journalists at the party is only one Russian, a young man who was an expert in the English metaphysical poets. He's as much of an outsider as I am, really. Caitlin has a few words with him, but after that no one addresses him directly. The flow of conversation is all, yet again, about the implications of the recetn *coup*. I am stunned by the naïve authority of statements like, 'Where Gorbachev went wrong . . .'

I have nothing to offer here and, like the metaphysical poet, am seen to have nothing to offer. So I can slip back again into my own thoughts, back to my meal at TrenMos with Caitlin and Charles.

Caitlin called for me at Volodya's apartment on the stroke of nine. She merely raised her eyebrows when I presented her with my packed case, saying if it was all right with her I'll stay with her for the rest of the time, until we were sorted to get Mary Martha out to England. She glanced across at Volodya who, head down, was working at his table.

'There is so little room here,' I went on hurriedly.

'Yes, of course. No problem, Ma.'

In the car she did venture a comment. 'Lover's tiff?'

'Don't be ridiculous.' My voice was not as crisp as I would have liked.

In that peculiar middle-class fashion, we were to eat out before the party. We made our way to TrenMos, where Charles had gone on ahead and secured a table. He waved and stood up, and I felt rather than saw Caitlin's tremor of pleasure at the sight of him.

I hope it will be all right for those two. I look at them side by side, here on Leo Crabtree's sofa bandying political insights back and forth as though they are playing for some kind of hard currency. I bless now Kendrick's genes which have made Caitlin so beautiful. Perhaps it is post- or even anti-feminist to gloat over offspring who combine the unfair advantage of beauty with the equally unfair advantage of brains. The rest of us just scramble up that mountain.

A funny thing occurs to me. I started out life being frightened of my mother and will end it, most probably, being frightened of my daughter. Yet another entwining circle.

They have moved on now to Charles' literary *coup* with the MacIntire diaries. 'In truth it was Olivia here who did the trick.' He says. They all look across at me. Bright intelligent faces. Well fed. Glossy hair.

Charles smiles at me. 'I was saying, Olivia, about old MacIntyre. How you wormed your way into Bluebeard's lair through your fairy stories.'

Leo Crabtree giggles. 'Have we Sheherezade in our midst, perhaps?'

I smile sweetly at him. 'Mixing your myths, Leo? From your writing I had the impression that you were a stickler for accuracy.'

'Well,' Caitlin butts in hurriedly. 'Myth or fairy story, MacIntyre's coughing up for Charles. Memoirs, everything.'

'Yes, great,' says Leo. 'Great.' His eyes swept around the company. 'Now, drinks! Your glass is empty Olivia?'

I hold out my glass, and then sink back into my chair, cradling it in my hand. I am forgotten again now, in some new discussion about the political scene at home. I can't get into politics seriously these days. They stumble and bumble so, and politicians tend to be strangers to the truth.

My thoughts go back the earlier part of the evening when the three of us had dinner at TrenMos. Charles and I had a good conversation: he wormed things out of me about my childhood in the North, my dabbling with student politics: my time in teaching, my theories about literature in and on the lives of children. Exposed to Charles's smiling, forthright attention it was impossible not to reveal more than one ever would in an ordinary conversation. His is clearly a good journalist.

Some stories I told him, about my time in teaching, about children I've worked with, surprised even Caitlin, whose novel, unambiguously keen interest fuelled even further the confidences that spilled forth. It dawned on me then – probably at the moment it dawned on her – that she might just be proud of me, in a weird kind of way.

Charles told me that Herbert MacIntyre was keen to take me somewhere, to show me something. 'He would not tell me where. Said it was private. Said he would collect you tomorrow at two.'

'Well,' I say, trying to keep the misery out of my voice. 'You'd better tell him to collect me at Oktoberskaya, at Caitlin's. I'm there now.'

Caitlin and he exchanged glances but he didn't comment.

Then I changed my mind. 'No. I'll go across to Volodya's in the morning. I need to talk to Mary Martha. She'll think I've deserted her.'

Now, here at Leo Crabtree's elegant apartment, the party is breaking up, with much shaking hands and air-kissing. Caitlin and I stamp our feet to keep warm while Janni stands talking in the doorway for ages with Charles. I am struck again by the fact that with all these people, work persists, one way or other, through every waking hour.

Even my very pleasant conversation with Charles over dinner was, to one degree or other, *copy*. I am under no illusion about that.

The next day I am welcomed with almost open arms by both Volodya and Mary Martha. Volodya fusses over me, taking my coat and hat, and the bag of groceries I've picked up at the Irish supermarket and then settling me on the chair. But even with this attention I know that a distance is being maintained. There is now a line over which I must not step. So my smiling face is just a little stiff with the misery I'm holding down inside.

In my deepest soul I know that I will never fall for anyone again. What I feel now will go on forever. After this anything will seem trivial. It's ironic that this thing with Volodya has finished nearly before it started.

Now he makes Mary Martha camomile tea and settles her on the day-bed opposite me.

'By,' she says looking at me very directly, 'I thought for a minute you'd deserted us, Olivia. And there was I sorting my things out so my case'll not be too heavy.'

I shake my head. 'No, no. I thought I would like to spend a bit of time with my daughter while I'm here.

She smiles wistfully. 'Daughter! Now me, I would have liked a daughter.' She sighs. 'But it wasn't to be.' She frowns at me. 'So, your own ma? Is it a long time since she died?'

I shake my head again 'My mother's not dead, Mary Martha. It's a year or so since I've seen her, to be honest. But it makes no difference. She's very . . . she doesn't know anyone . . . it's as though she's not there.'

'Like Nina, you mean?'

This makes me even more guilty. 'Well, yes, but worse, really, I—' I am protesting too much.

Her turn to shake her head. 'Not much of a mother, was she?'

'Well, she was difficult.' Then I blurt out. 'I'm not much of a mother myself, to be honest.'

She sighs . 'Poor lass,' she says, tenderly.

And I don't know whether the *lass* she's referring to is my mother, or me, or Caitlin. It could apply to us all.

At two o'clock Volodya, calls us over to the window. I stand in front of him. I can feel the heat of his body, his breath on my neck. 'Here is your caller,' he says softly in my ear. Down below in the street, already surrounded by appreciative onlookers, is MacIntyre's gleaming Rolls Royce. I turn to Volodya. 'Should I come back here, or . . . ?'

He shrugs, but does not look at me directly. 'Of course, if you wish. Mary Martha will wish to see you. I'm afraid I will be away. I have an appointment at the Institute with the Pushkin scholar.'

I brush past him and bolt down the steep stairs, wishing Pushkin and his descendants to the seven fires of Hell.

Herbert MacIntyre is sitting in the back seat of his car, a fur-lined rug tucked around his knees. The chauffeur waits for me to sit and drapes another rug across my knees. The old man nods. 'Good to see you again Mrs.Ozanne.'

'It's very kind of you . . . although I have been wondering about just where we're going. Quite a mystery.'

'You will know very soon.' He sits, perched

forward like a bird, resting his gnarled hands on his silver-topped cane.

'I was interested that you knew Nina Samsonova and Mary Martha in the Thirties,' I venture. I am genuinely curious.

'Samsonova had a rare beauty.' His voice is rusty, like a little used wheel. 'Rare.'

'And you offered to get Mary Martha out?'

'She refused. She would not go without Samsonova.'

'Could you have got Samsonova out?'

The old eyes peer into mine. 'It is history now. I was in my prime. As was she. A great beauty as I say. Yes I could have got them both out. But I wanted Samsonova to stay. For Russia. For me. I had . . . have no understanding of the devotion between these two women.'

'And afterwards? They lived in penury. Starved.'

The great shoulders moved in a skeletal shrug. 'Samsonova chose that. The price was so little, so slight, she would not pay it.'

I am beyond rage. The man is, and was, no more than a barbarian, incapable of an altruistic action. Even the offer of escape for Mary Martha was to get rid of a rival. We are silent for the next ten minutes as the car glides through the streets, gathering appreciative

305

glances as it goes. One man raised his hat high at the sight of it.

Finally we sweep round a corner, past yet another dusty high-rise block, and purr to a stop beside an immaculate white-painted house, with painted wooden door and window frames, and a long carved wood verandah.

'Who lives here?' I am suddenly suspicious. The joke about Bluebeard is wearing a little thin. MacIntyre waits until the chauffeur has handed us both out, before he makes his announcement. 'The ghost of a man lives here,' he says. 'It is a national monument: the house of Viktor Vasnetsov, whose pictures will adorn those fine stories you are writing. He was something akin to William Morris. Built this house himself, held court here for visiting artists and craftsmen, for his brothers and sons, children and grandchildren. I came here myself many times.'

The keepers give us felt overshoes to protect the beautifully polished floors, and then we wander through the inside of the house, which smells of cedar-wood maintained as a shrine. We linger in the great studio on the first floor, which has tall windows on three sides, and ladders which Vasnetsov used to reach the monumental canvasses that are ranged around the room. The images are detailed and painstaking but I find myself disliking them, thinking of the quicksilver, curlicued drawings that Joseph makes of dragons and spiky heroes focusin on just such themes as these. But Joseph's work has a passion and magic which is absent from these great canvasses.

'Fine, don't you think?' MacIntyre's tone is complacent, almost patronising.

'Vasnetsov was allowed to paint as he wished? All his life?'

A short bark spurts from those narrow lips. 'Sensible chap, old Vasnetsov, not like those self-important nihilists who called themselves writers and artists. He looked back to an ideal age, towards the history of the people, looked to myth and fairy-tale for his inspiration. His choice of subject matter was ideologically pure and above reproach.' MacIntyre had obviously rehearsed this many times; his tone crackled with honeyed approval. 'So what do you think, Mrs.Ozanne?'

I am suddenly very tired. I rub my palms across my eyes. 'The house is a work of art in itself, Mr. MacIntyre. And the paintings are very craftsman-like. I can see that from the books. But something has been nagging me. And now I know what it is. These pictures have no soul. How can they, if the man himself sold his soul to enjoy an easy life here, surrounded by his children and grandchildren, always above reproach?'

MacIntyre's lip folds into a thin line but he is not as angry as I had thought he would be. His claw-like hand touches my forearm. 'Ah, Mrs.Ozanne. From the outside it is always so difficult to understand, so easy to condemn. And what about souls in the West shackled by washing machines and winning the pools? The idolatry of footballers and film star glamour?'

'I . . . I must go. I'm feeling . . .' I race from him, through the rooms, scramble into my outdoor shoes and wait for him in the car. In that time I make up my mind that I will not allow my stories to be used for this project. I have signed no contract.

But MacIntyre pre-empts me as he gets in the car. 'Now, Mrs.Ozanne, I believe we are to try to get Samsonova's little friend out again? And this time she will go? I would be happy to help you in this.' And he puts one bony hand on my knee. The old goat. Ever the horse trader! I wonder how many shabby deals, half-agreement, half-blackmail, that he's entered into down the decades. Vasnetsov is not the only one who may have sold his soul to the devil.

SEVENTEEN

'So, dear Caitlin, what's happened about Sir Volodya and your mother? I thought there was something rather sweet there. They seemed really smitten.' Charles Conrad was sitting on Caitlin's desk, swinging his legs. Through the closed door they could hear the chatter of Elizabeth and the deeper tones of young Roger Slett-Smith, asking questions as always.

'Keeping tabs on her, are you?' Caitlin asked.

He shrugged. 'I have been round to his apartment to see the old lady now and then.' His piece on Mary Martha and MacIntyre, entitled *Staying On*, had been a great success. A nice taster for the serialisation of old MacIntyre's memoirs which would come later in the year. Sir Ranulph had sent Charles a personal note of congratulation on his coup.

Of course there was money for Mary Martha, and Charles felt driven to show Mary Martha – and Olivia Ozanne – that he had not exploited her, not really. He called round at the flat to give Mary Martha the spare picture proofs, and continued to call, with sweets and groceries and other trinkets that might amuse her.

Her favourite thing was a Polaroid camera with

which she took photographs of things in the flat and the house and the street. 'I'll take these photos home when I go. To show our Ellen Alice where I've lived all these years,' her voice crackled with satisfaction and anticipation.

'Your mother's often there,' he said now to Caitlin. 'Those two are great friends. But Volodya rarely. They must have fallen out.'

Caitlin was leafing through her 1985 Soviet Gazetteer, checking some information for a piece she was writing. She was not unhappy with Charles's presence. He had taken to dropping in after he'd completed his round of going to meetings, talking to contacts.

Often he had *buckshee* tickets for the Bolshoi, or some such bait, to tempt her to a night out. The two of them were definitely now regarded as an item in the group of diplomats and journalists they counted as their friends. Caitlin had had many quite flashy affairs in her time but had never experienced such a close, almost dogged, courtship. It was very intriguing.

'Volodya and my mother?' she shrugged. 'Seems as though it's cooled, and that's no bad thing. For a while I was worried that she'd end up here, drawing her pension, barefoot in a bread queue.'

'Wouldn't you do that, for the man you . . . er . .

310

. fell for?' He was making a pattern on her desk pad with a red marker. She made a note, and then closed the Gazetteer. 'Of course I would,' she said, smiling sweetly. 'But then that's hardly likely, is it?'

'Don't you want your mother to be happy?'

'Perhaps Volodya's found someone else to flash those big blue eyes at,' said Caitlin, surprised at her own bitterness on her mother's behalf. In these last days Olivia had been a rather sombre presence in the flat, working away at the fairy stories and the Mary Martha tapes with professional assiduity. Her lightness, her gaiety, her sheer mischief seemed very much on the back-burner. Caitlin stood up and pulled on her fine wool jacket. 'Well then, kind sir. Where to tonight?'

He straightened up and grinned at her. 'Jazz. I think tonight is a perfect night for fine Georgian wine and a good serving of sub-American jazz. A trumpeter as sweet as Bird. A discovery of mine. You will love him.'

*

It was not the first time in his life that Joseph had spent in a cell, tieless and without his shoelaces, but it was the worst. The other times had been for unsubstantiated suspicion of possession, for being drunk in the street, for climbing a church tower, stoked up on speed, in search of a Higher Being he had glimpsed in the bell tower.

This time it was deadly serious. His name was in the system and they had discovere his connection with the party where the girl had taken the bad drugs. The policemen were treating him with chilling courtesy, not the jocular disdain with which they greeted his earlier exploits. He had been questioned once at length, in the presence of the solicitor found for him by his father.

The central question being asked, time and time again, was, of course, whether his presence at the party was merely as a guest. And whether he had given the girl the tablet. If he was not dealing, if he had not given Tracy Moran the E that did such damage, why then had he run away? Gone undercover like some skulking rat? And why did he carry a chainsaw? Had he been watching videos for inspiration or something?

They asked the questions again and again. Stubbornly he responded with the same thing, again and again. It was a crap party, a crap experience and he wanted to get out, away. He wasn't a dealer but there were plenty of dealers there. He saw the girl collapse and it frightened him. So he ran. Once he was away it was hard to get back. And the chainsaw was for work. He chopped down trees for money.

'Not enough money for drugs, surely?'

'I don't do drugs now. Bit of booze, yes. But no drugs, not for a year now.'

Back in the cell, contemplating his boots, he thought how the removal of the laces emasculated them, somehow. They were like fat old ladies without their corsets.

In the end he was bailed into his father's custody for a week, pending further enquiries. His father's handsome face, as he sat in the back of the court, might have been chipped out of granite. There was no reading his thoughts as he nodded slightly to the magistrate. After growling to Joseph that he was losing a morning's work over this, he was silent as he drove home. He dumped Joseph on the drive and drove off again, leaving Naomi to show Joseph to their guest room, which was nicely done out in Ikea floral.

So Joseph settled down to a week of miserable contemplation of his fate, lightened only by the possibility of building Lego aeroplanes with his half-brothers and teasing his stepmother.

He wrote a card to Ellen, telling her London was lousy and wishing she was here and asking if she'd check on his motorbike which had been impounded by the Darlington police. And he loved her, by the way.

There can be no darker place in the world than the embarkation hall at Moscow airport. The lowering black ceiling exactly fits my mood as Mary Martha and I shuffle forward in our queue. Mary Martha looks elegant in her new clothes and her little diamond earrings, the present from Nina, swinging from ears fragile as tissue paper shells.

Charles Conrad is riding shotgun on us, primed, ready to explain Mary Martha's complicated papers to the Russian at the barrier. We are all tense and surprised as we are waved through with little trouble. The claw-like hand of Herbert MacIntyre has clearly done its work even in this dark place. Suddenly we are through, too quickly even to give Charles a hug or turn round to wave at Caitlin who is at a further barrier. We are channeled and funnelled through, examined very carefully with two young men with machine-guns before we board finally onto the plane,.

It has been a month of hard work. I have finished the fairy- tales and delivered them to MacIntyre at a bizarre lunch at his dacha. I have transcribed most of the Mary Martha tapes and started to check facts with her. Christmas has come and gone without us noticing. Volodya has been remarkable by his absences and his quiet restrained presence. I wait for the pain to fade but it grows, becomes more intense as I try to resign myself to this final parting. He was even absent from the flat this morning when Charles came to collect us.

I am lighthearted enough with Mary Martha, participating in her excitement. But inside I wonder whether this misery will ever end. Our tickets place us halfway down the plane. There is a small man with owl-like glasses in the seat beside the window. I put Mary Martha between him and me and take the aisle seat myself. I strap her in and hold her hand tightly as the jet fills its belly with power and creeps, then races across the tarmac before bumping to a lift and moving into the air over Moscow. I wish I was in the window seat, could see now this marvellous city that I won't, ever, see again.

I travelled here a few months ago and was one person. I go away quite another.

Mary Martha unclasps her hand from mine and wriggles in her seat. 'There,' she says, quite composed, 'we're on our way now pet.' Then she does this extraordinary thing. She turns and speaks to the little man beside her: a perfect stranger. 'I'm going home you know, back to England.'

The man grins, showing small, well kept, very white teeth. 'Really? D'you enjoy your visit to

315

Moscow?' He says Mosc*ow* in that American way.

'Yes, no. Parts of it. You see I was in Moscow for a long time.'

'Me too. I've been there a month. How long were you there?'

She pulls down the cuffs of her snowy white blouse. She knows exactly what she's doing. 'Ooh. Seventy years, just about.'

His head literally jumps at this. 'Oh, really? Now how might that be?'

'Well . . .' and she tells him her tale, very briefly. He is really impressed, nodding and urging her on for more details.

Then she sits back - I have to say it - oozing complacency. 'And what were you doing in Moscow?' she says innocently.

'Well, ma'am,' he says respectfully. 'I'm a scholar specialising in Pushkin, I am writing a book on him. And my university, thank the dear Lord, saw fit to send me to Moscow to work at the Institute. The book is to be published both in Russian and English. A kind of academic joint venture. Fashionable in Moscow these days.'

I lean across Mary Martha. 'Do you work on this book alone, Mr...? ?'

'Doctor, ma'am. Doctor Harvey Walkin. No,

ma'am. I do not work on my own. I've been working with this charming Russian guy. Volodya, he's called. Volodya Seitsev. . . . Marvellous man.'

Mary Martha claps her hands. 'We know him. He is our friend.;

'Guy has remarkable linguistic comprehension. Knows Pushkin inside out. Remarkable. Clever man. Not that you'd know him, of course.'

'Oh, we would, Dr. Walkin. We most definitely would.' At last I am smiling.

Caitlin caught sight of Volodya just as she and Charles, arm in arm, made their way out of the airport. The Russian was standing in front of a column, hands deep in the pockets of his heavy coat, looking straight ahead. Tears were coursing down his cheeks, which were flushed and shiny with withtears.

They walked across and Caitlin put a hand on his arm. 'Volodya, what is it?' she said.

He blinked, then took out a silk handkerchief and blotted the whole of his face. He re-emerged and sniffed. 'Olivia has gone, and with her my life. My life is ended.'

Caitlin frowned. 'But you have left her, neglected her, Voloday. She's been walking around in misery. What have you done, you silly man?'

'It had to be so. She had to think it was ended. Otherwise she would stay and share this miserable life and it would be no good for her.' He lifted his hands in a gesture of helplessness. 'I love her too much.'

'Oh, you . . . you *galoot.*' She glanced up at Charles then put her arm through Volodya's. 'Come on, we'll all go somewhere nice, and cry into our beer together.'

The three of them drew glances as they walked, arm in arm, out of the airport. They were quite a picture, the glamorous Western couple and the distinguished man, obviously Russian, at their side.

Kendrick Kerslake surveyed the sturdy figure before him. Small and rather square; heart-shaped face, bright brown eyes. This girl wasn't Joseph's usual hippy fare. He opened the door wider. 'Come in. I'll see if he's awake. You might think at two o'clock on a Saturday afternoon . . .' he raised his glance to the top of the stairs. 'Ah, Joseph, a friend of yours, I believe.'

'Thanks Dad,' Joseph winked at Ellen. 'Come on up.'

Kendrick coughed. 'Joseph, I don't think ..'

Joseph shook his head. 'You don't want us sitting over you while you watch the football, Dad.'

Kendrick shrugged. 'Well perhaps you'd bring er

. . . Ellen in to meet Naomi later.' The sitting-room door – rag- rolled in an effective shade of blue – clicked behind him.

Ellen looked up at the rumpled figure at the top of the stairs. 'How are you Joseph?'

'Bearing up. Out of the nick, waiting for a proper arrest as far as I can see.'

'How's the girl?'

'Still poorly. But still alive.'

She noted the rings under his eyes, 'That's something, I suppose.' She made her way up the stairs, but eluded him at the top when he tried to grab her. 'No! I came to see you as a . . . friend. I was concerned about you, getting that card from you.'

He opened the door of the tiny bedroom and bowed her in. 'If you squeeze sideways you can sit on the bed. I'll sit on the floor here to preserve your . . . integrity. Dad'll have his glass to the wall listening for the bumps and grinds.'

'I checked about your bike for you. The police say you – or your agent – can collect it any time, seeing as it's not stolen or reported as being involved in any nefarious happenings.'

'Good. Good.'

They sat staring at each other for a long while, then both spoke together. 'Joseph, I—'

'You've got to listen to me.' 'You first.'

'No you first.'

'Right. Miss Ellen Stobart. I promise you. If this mess gets cleared up – which it may not – but if it does, I'll come up there and camp out in your garden. Pursue you till you give in. I am not, repeat, not giving you up that easy.'

She blushed and laughed. 'I came to say, if - when - you get this mess cleared up I want you back up there. I missed you before you got to the end of the road. You went off too fast.'

He reached out across the narrow space and took her hand, turned it over and kissed the palm.

An hour later they did go down, frustratingly demure and unruffled, to meet Naomi who was delighted to see them, glad of new company. She dragged Ellen into the kitchen to help her make the tea and questioned her closely about how she came to meet Joseph.

Later, over tea, Ellen turned to Joseph. 'Oh, I forgot to tell you. My Nana had a message from your mother. Apparently my old auntie has her papers now, and should be coming home any time now. Big Nana is so excited, can't wait to see our Mary Martha.'

'I don't know what Olivia wants, dragging some poor old woman over from Russia,' grumbled

Kendrick. 'Up to her tricks again.'

Naomi flounced to her feet. 'Kendrick I'm sick-sick-sick of you picking holes in people. Never a good word for anyone. God knows what you say about me behind your back. If you think I'm gonna stand twenty years of this you've got another think coming.' She barged out of the sitting-room.

Joseph clicked his teeth and winked at his father. 'Well, Dad, looks like you're gonna have to turn on the sweet talk to get out of that!'

Kendrick's face was red, but, meeting Ellen's shrewd gaze, he shrugged. 'Time of the month, I'm afraid,' he said smoothly. 'You ladies become so unpredictable. Do you suffer in that way, my dear?'

Joseph's fist connected very swiftly with his father's jaw and he dropped like a felled pine.

Ellen knelt down and started to pat Kendrick's unconscious face. 'Now what have you done, you idiot?'

Joseph shrugged. 'Hardly touched him. Probably fainted at being defied twice within the space of an hour.'

'Well, you'd better be very contrite now, else if he kicks you out of here you'll be back in the cells, you silly lad.'

EIGHTEEN

Mary Martha and I stayed overnight in my house which was as sparse and bleak as ever but served as a roof over our heads for one night. Among the pile of post on the mat was a letter from the estate agent saying, regretfully, that the sale had fallen through. On the bright side he had another purchaser in mind and he was pursuing that.

My guest was very impressed with the house, enthusing over the large windows, the space and light and the fitted kitchen. That made me look at it with a fresh eye, I suppose. I had always despised it, thought it a cross between a rabbit hutch and the foyer of a very small seaside hotel.

I talked to Joseph on the phone; he had an extraordinary story about being arrested. But that is now reduced to a kind of house arrest with Kendrick and the doll-wife. Ellen is with him, so that's something. I should do something for him, but I don't know what.

We drove north in Janey's car. 'Five days? Take it, Olivia, take it! I'll use the bus.' Janey, sentimental at heart, was entranced by Mary Martha's story. Anyway she was still feeling the need to exorcise her residual guilt at allowing herself to be seduced by Joseph.

The journey north has taken longer than it should have, because I thought the motorways would be too much of a shock for Mary Martha. I thought as well she'd prefer to see the towns and villages, even with their tangled-up centres. Perhaps this would be a better re-introduction to England after seventy years than the miles of cones and the hold-ups on the A1 North.

She kept her eyes glued to the window, drinking in the trees and hedges, the farmhouses and market towns, the cars and lorries with equal wonder.

In York I parked the car in the big car park by the Ouse and we walked over the bridge and found a tea-room whose crisp white curtains exhaled more promise than the dank interior. Obsolete, battered postcards of the minster and the walls offered themselves from an ancient clip holder in front of the till.

Mary Martha sat looking around her, munching her ham and chips, nodding with approval at the tables crowded with ladies of a certain age who were killing time over tea,. She gazed with open admiration at the pretty mini-skirted waitress. The vibrancy of her naked interest spread through the room, breaking down the natural reserve, that veiled oblique interest which characterises the English café.

By the time I got back from the counter with the second pot of tea she was deep in conversation with the woman from the next table. 'I'm going to see my sister in Gainford, to tell you the truth. Seventy years since I saw her, you know.'

Other heads turned in frank interest. Now again I noticed the cadences in her voice which marked her out as a foreigner.

'Been in Australia, have you?' said the woman. 'There was something in the paper about them sending children from the orphanages.'

'No, no, no,' Mary Martha shook her head quite vigorously, sounding quite cross. 'I sent myself, and I was no orphan. I went to Russia. Been in Russia more than seventy years.'

A hot gust of approving curiosity swept through the room. The women looked openly now, nodding a kind of benevolent interest in this stranger.

With her belted Russian coat and her hair smooth under her round hat, Mary Martha was out of place here. Here the ladies of her age looked all alike: their white hair, fluffy and permed, and pastel anoraks engender a uniformity that made strangers look like sisters.

I drove on again on automatic pilot, waiting patiently at junctions for the queues of cars to clear, Mary Martha, snorting and snuffling, beside me.

Then with her safely asleep my concern for her and my imaginary scenarios about her meeting Ellen Alice in an hour or so's time, could go onto the back burner. I could let my mind drift back again to Volodya and his extraordinary deception about the Pushkin scholar. What an elaborate strategy to get rid of me! How very humiliating. But even in this humiliation, I was pleased to bury the mirage of the long lean American woman . . .

Mary Martha's head flicked back up again and she coughed. 'Your mother, Olivia! Didn't you tell me she lived up here somewhere, near my sister?'

'No. Not near at all. A good twenty miles away.'

'That must be no distance. Not in a nice car like this. We can go there first,' she said in a composed fashion, brooking no argument. 'You will want to see your mother.'

'But you must be tired, Mary Martha . . . Your sister . . .'

Even as I protested weakly I knew she would get her own way with me. Kendrick and Caitlin, even Joseph could never make me do what they wanted.

325

And here was this five-foot-nothing scrap of frail old woman dictating, making me do something against which my soul revolted.

'Tired? How can a person be tired, Olivia? This lovely comfortable car. This warm day. And our Ellen Alice can wait another hour, seeing she has waited seventy years.' Tucked inside her bag were two letters from her sister that she had read a dozen times at least on the plane.

So it is Mary Martha's fault that I'm here in Gathermore Hall visiting my mother. Why can she make me do this? I don't want to do it. This is not my idea. Yet here I am in this spuriously clean, Dettol-scented house with it dusty portraits and soiled carpets, to see my mother who, to put it mildly, I dislike intensely.

A wheelchair in the square hallway is standing slightly skewed. The clumsy gaffer-tape mend on its back shines like a healing wound against the faded leatherette. The place smells of vinegar and kippers, Johnson's powder and burnt coffee.

'Here we are, dear.' The attendant who leads us down the corridor has a plump wobbling bottom and elastic bandages on her calves. In the little room she leans over the bed. 'Now, Serena, love. Look who we have here! It's your daughter and a friend of hers.' She turns a bland face to us. 'I'll leave you to it then. So nice for her to have visitors for once. It can make such a difference.'

I don't want to look at my mother; to see her hard tight face so slack; don't want to battle again with this desire to laugh and cry at the same time.

'Don't she look peaceful?' Mary Martha murmurs. She is right. The face on the pillow is serene. It is pale, pared back white as a sheep bone you would find on the moors here; her generous hair is brushed out, fanned across her pillow in gleaming strands.

Her eyes snap open and I jump back. She turns towards me and her face is illuminated by a wide smile. I realise now that it is not Kendrick from whom Caitlin gets her great beauty; it is my mother. I never knew that. How could I not have known that?

She holds out a white, blue-veined hand. 'Olivia, darling! Did you bring it?'

Marty Martha pokes me in the back and I take a step forward and clasp the hand which lies passively in my grip. 'Did I bring what, Mummy?' My voice, in my own ears, sounds ridiculously young.

She snatches her hand away, making me step back. 'The spade, idiot girl! The spade. The lupins need splitting. Lifting and splitting.' The voice becomes cracked and ugly. 'Tiresome, tiresome, why must you always be so tiresome?' Her hand starts to beat on the counterpane. 'Why, why am I so cursed with such a child?'

Mary Martha takes her hand and strokes it.

My mother frowns, and then nods. 'Beatrice! You came.'

Mary Martha shakes her head. 'Not Beatrice dear. I am a stranger to you, but still I'm pleased to see you. You make me think of my dear sister Nina. I came here with my friend Olivia. We have come a long way to see you.'

My mother clutches her hand tighter. 'She beat me, you know.' Her tone drops to a whining confidentiality. 'Beat me black and blue. But clever, she was.'

'Who is this then?' Mary Martha whispers back.

'That woman my father married. Not my own mother. D'you know she used to beat me with a garden cane? I had to walk right down to the end of the garden to get it for her. And sometimes she would send me back to get a thicker one. Called me *shy*, she did.'

Mary Martha places a hand down the side of my mother's face and strokes it. 'Poor little thing,' she says. 'Nobody could say that was fair, could they?' Her eyes lift to me where I stand frozen three feet away. 'Now that wasn't fair was it, Olivia?'

My mother flips a malevolent glance towards me. 'Who's that woman?' she barks at Mary Martha. 'Is she your daughter?'

Mary Martha nods, smiling slightly. 'In a manner of speaking, yes. She's all the daughter I'll ever have.'

My mother's eyes go dull again, light receding behind a blank opacity, deeply inward. 'And she was clever, that woman my father married.'

Mary Martha hitched her bottom onto the bed. 'So how was she clever, then?'

'She only ever hit me on my back and bottom. Always where it wouldn't show. My goodness, she was sweet when my father was there. Sweet Sal. He called her that. Sweet Sal. Bitch.' Spittle starts to bead up on the puckered corners of her mouth and her free hand drums the candlewick counterpane. 'I tried to show my father, you know. What she'd been doing. And she said I was rude. Dirty. Lifting my skirt for him like that.'

Mary Martha glances back at me, to where I am standing, ready for flight.. 'Poor little thing. Don't you think so, Olivia?'

'Yes,' I whisper. 'Poor little thing.'

Then my mother starts to laugh, a loud cackling

exhalation more like the neighing of a horse. I am prickling with ice. I remember the laugh; how crisply it defined, punctuated, those years when we were incarcerated together in the house of my childhood: that wild, despairing laugh which echoed through the house as she exulted over 'getting something sorted'. That something might be me, it might be the Electricity Board, the Council, one of her ever-shrinking band of friends . . .

'That was bad, bad,' mutters Mary Martha. 'What a thing to do to a little child.'

Now my mother grabs the front of Mary Martha's coat and pulls her too close. She whispers even more conspiratorially. 'But I can get my own back, do you see? I locked her away, that little girl. Stopped her eating devil's food. She searched out the heat, the devil's flames. And she got it too, where it didn't show. Like for like, you know.'

Circles. Oh these tragic circles. Old as she is, she's pulling me to her, winding me in to her pain like a fisherman winding in a wriggling, helpless fish.

I stand behind Mary Martha and touch her shoulder. 'Me. She did that to me, Mary Martha. When I was little,' I whisper into her ear.

'But that wasn't you, Serena. Your own little girl, that was.' Mary Martha frowns into my mother's face.

330

'You did that to Olivia.' She is pulling back, trying to loosen the choking grasp. My mother clasps her closer. For a second they forget me, these two old women, rocking together in the pearly gloom of the dark afternoon.

My mother scowls at her. 'My own?'

'I bet you're that sorry, aren't you, for hitting your own little girl like that? For hitting Olivia?'

'Mmm.' My mother's glance slips sideways to the window which is slimy with condensation. 'It's such a problem with the lupins, don't you see? They'll have to be split or there will be hell to pay.' Her hand slips from Mary Martha's coat and her eyes close. 'Hell to pay.'

And now she is fast asleep.

Mary Martha raises herself stiffly to her feet and crosses herself four times and mutters a prayer in Russian. Then she looks at me, 'Poor soul,' she says, 'You'll want to set off again now, Olivia. We've been here long enough, I think.'

She takes my arm and we make our way slowly out of the building. And now I am thinking of Caitlin. How afraid of her I was when she was born. How I gave her to Kendrick when she cried, frightened of what I might do to her. How I kept my distance from her when she was a child, tearing and rending the circle, that bad circle, for once and for all.

It was then that I set about remaking myself, inventing a person who took things lightly, who told lies, who was a bad mother and a bad wife so that she wouldn't be there to beat her children where it did not show.

Mary Martha sits in silence till we are crossing the river at Croft. Then she says. 'Who's this Beatrice, then?'

I have to laugh quite crazily at this. 'She was my mother's cousin. Her best friend. The perfect cliché. She ran away to America with my father when I was five.'

'I thought somehow that your Da'd died.'

'My mother always told me that he'd died of multiple sclerosis. She was very active in that charity. She told me all about it one night when I had offended her. Can't remember what I had done. It was the night before I sat my final examination at college. Claimed I was neglectful. Like him. I always tell people he died, myself.'

Mary Martha puts her small bony hand on my knee. 'Poor lass,' she says. 'But there's no need to take on now, is there? It's all in the past. All of it. Leave it, Olivia.'

I want to rage at her, that this is all platitudes.

Platitudes. The raw truth is that I was useless as a daughter, as a wife, and as a mother. I am only any good with people beyond that magic circle. Abstractions like Lee Compton.

And look at Volodya, I want to say. Here am I, madly immersed, totally in love with a man so removed from my world he might be on Mars. But when I try to pursue this wonderful thing, to celebrate it – as soon as I get under the wire, he is backing off, making elaborate ploys to escape.

So I am useless at this too.

When Charles opened the door he was wearing Nike shorts and his chest was bare. Not for the first time Caitlin noticed that, for a bulky man, he carried very little fat. He opened the door wide. 'Come in! Come in!'

From the living room television came the intermittent *thuck* of ball and clap of hands that indicated some sport or another.

Caitlin handed Charles the champagne and walked past him, taking off her gloves. 'Needed some company, I hope you—' She stopped inside the living-room door.

The Dutchman Janni was sprawled across the chrome and leather lounger. He was wearing a skimpy tee-shirt and shorts. His feet were bare. He flashed her a brilliant smile which only the paranoid would have called triumphant, and turned off the video. 'Caitlin, my dear lady,' he leapt to his feet and kissed her hand. 'You catch us *in flagrante.*'

'What?' Caitlin shot a glance at Charles who was reaching for crystal glasses from the black lacquered cabinet.

He smiled easily. 'Janni, stop teasing,' he said. 'The boring truth is, darling, that Janni and I have been playing badminton at the embassy and I am now attempting – and failing – to induct him into the delights of Test Match cricket. I can't tell you what a relief it is to see you.'

A pout suggested itself on the narrow countenance of the Dutchman. 'It is a very *boring* game. So English in the exaggerated restraint it demands on the players and the watchers. Like the way you see sex. Is that not so?'

'You do talk a load of guff at times, Janni.' Charles was pouring the champagne, letting it gurgle and bubble over the edge of the flutes onto the glass surface of the table. He handed them each a glass. 'Now then, dear friends, we will drink to the elegance of the English game, then Janni and I will make ourselves decent. Then, Janni, you will go to your meeting at the Interior Ministry, and Caitlin and I will make important decisions about what we shall do with our evening.'

Balancing her glass carefully Caitlin lowered herself onto the chrome and leather chair which still retained the heat of Janni's body. 'You boys go and change. I am perfectly happy here.'

She lay back in her chair and closed her eyes. The bickering and laughter of the men in the next room pricked her consciousness but did not penetrate it. Something had been bugging her all day: the hollow emptiness of her own flat. You couldn't count Katya, gliding around the flat in her own industrious bubble. The flat had never seemed empty before. But after she had watched the Olivia's shepherding Mary Martha like a mother hen past the customs, through the barriers, she had missed her. Missed her for the first time in a long time. She could not remember ever missing her mother. Not since that first time Olivia went to Paris. Something to do with work, that was. She and Joseph had had such a good time with Dad, who was better, somehow, when Olivia was away.

And Volodya had been sweet, really sweet as they came away from the airport. He was genuine in his grief at seeing Olivia go. Caitlin was disturbed - even amazed - that anyone should feel at that level for another human being. She had come here wanting to talk to Charles about this. In her businesslike way she wanted to see where their own relationship, which was going quite well now, stood in comparison with that between Volodya and Olivia. She didn't quite know how she was going to do it, but she would find the words. She usually did.

She opened her eyes to see Janni, elegant in his Armani suit, standing before her. He smiled beguilingly. 'You are so beautiful, Caitlin, and so very clever.'

She smiled her easy acknowledgement of his compliment.

He half knelt beside her. 'I wonder if I could give you some advice?'

She stretched her legs before her. 'Why not, Janni.'

His lips were invasively close to her ear. 'You are very beautiful and very clever, but, perhaps a little vulnerable to flattery, perhaps? It would be wise to . . . er . . . take flattery with a pinch of salt, do you think?' And with that he scooped up his sports bag and strode towards the door. 'Sometimes it can make you look rather silly, you know.' The door clicked behind him.

She leapt up and banged on the closed door. 'Bitch!' she said. 'Bitch!'

Charles emerged from the bedroom, tucking his shirt into his immaculately cut trousers. 'Caitlin, you're as red as a bowl of *borscht*. What was that about?'

She told him what Janni had said. Charles whistled. 'Rude boy.'

'I couldn't answer him. Anything I said would seem like protesting too much.'

'Take no notice, darling. He's cross at being sent away.'

'Jealous?'

He shrugged. 'He's a good friend.' 'Is he in love with you?'

He laughed. 'Be direct, why don't you?'

'Well?'

'He's got a kind of crush. Like a schoolboy. He'll grow out of it.'

'And you?'

He reached for her and kissed her nose. 'He is a good friend; I am very fond of him. If you are asking is he my lover . . .' he paused. 'The answer is that he would wish to be but he is not.'

And she had to be satisfied with that. But that evening there was a constraint between them which made both of them feel curiously tired with little cause. So, having drunk the champagne and listened to a new Traviata CD, Caitlin pre-empted rejection by yawning and saying she really must go. Charles did not protest too much. He went down in the lift with her and walked her to the car, shivering in the cold night air.

He stood beside her. His cheek felt cold to her lips as she kissed it. 'Your friend Janni has a poisonous tongue, you know. I really don't care for him at all.'

He swept her up in a big bear hug. 'Don't you worry about Janni, darling. He will be reprimanded. Now go home and get some sleep. I'll talk to you tomorrow.'

He watched as she reversed and made her way out of the parking lot and into the square. As her headlights flashed over his face for a second time she considered how very fragile relationships were. Charles was obviously fond of Janni. In what way Caitlin was not quite sure. If Janni had been a girl it would have been easier to object strongly, to talk about 'me or her!' in the good old street fashion.

But the elegant Janni was a different kettle of fish. His comment had made her feel obvious and pushy, vain and shallow; she was mortified at the thought of him and Charles talking, chuckling about her in their oblique male fashion. The delicate structure that had been this special friendship between her and Charles was buckling under Janni's delicate assault.

This sent her mind back to Volodya and her mother. Now if there was justice in the world, that relationship should survive. Caitlin hated to admit it, but they were very sweet together, those two.

Kendrick showed the policeman into the lounge and asked if he would like tea or coffee.

The policeman shook his head. 'Just a word with Mr. Joseph Kerslake, sir.'.'

'I'll leave you to it, then,' said Kendrick grimly.

Joseph, feeling his father's wooden discomfiture, was not sure whether Kendrick was afraid that the policeman would, or wouldn't, take him back to prison.

'I'll stay with you,' said Ellen, linking her arm through his.

'If you want.' He didn't ask permission of the policeman, who seemed to fill the room with his black uniform and silver buttons. Unreasonably, he hated the man for this. Hated him for his avuncular politeness; hated him for doing it all by the book; hated the fact that he could come here, to Kendrick's house as though it were his own.

The room was getting suffocatingly hot. Joseph put his head on one side the better to hear the beating of wings. If he half closed his eyes he could see the diamond gleam of the talons.

'Now, then, Mr. Kerslake,' said the policeman politely. 'Seems like we've some very good news for you.'

Joseph drove his fist further into his pocket. 'I can't tell you how much I'm dying to hear that.'

'Young Tracy has recovered consciousness.'

He stopped sweating; the whirring sound of winds was silenced. 'Thank God for that.'

'That's not to say there'll be no damage. The docs say there could be permanent damage. But she'll not be a vegetable.'

Joseph winced, fighting the desire to laugh. A cabbage. A cauliflower. An aubergine. He could see the vegetables layered in tight lines against each other, welded together to make Tracy's bold child-woman face. 'Can she talk?'

The policemen glanced round the room, taking in the neat colour co-ordination, the shining surfaces. 'Well, Mr. Kerslake, luckily for you, she can.'

'What's she sayin'?'

'She's saying sorry to her parents. She's saying she'll never do it again. She's saying thank God she's alive.' He paused. 'And she's saying she got the Es from a lad from her school who buys for a group of

340

them. Niall. What kind of name is that? Niall!'

'So I'm off the hook?'

Ellen was squeezing his hand.

'We know now that it wasn't you. We have no call on you.'

'So where do I go from here?'

'You go where you like, son. We've no call at all on you now. Just keep your nose clean and watch the company you keep.'

'Well, thank you for that advice. I'll try to keep it in mind.' It was not entirely possible to keep the sarcasm out of his voice. He wished the man would go, that his black suit and silver buttons would dematerialise and his body would float through the window like a great pink tadpole.

Ellen went to open the door. 'Thank you for telling us this. We won't keep you.'

The policeman looked her up and down and stayed put. 'This your boyfriend, love?'

She glanced at Joseph . 'Yes, he is.'

He moved towards the door at last. 'You look like a nice girl. Wouldn't trust him as far as I could throw him, if I were you, love.'

*

Ellen Alice fusses on about her granddaughter, who is missing. 'Gone off to see that lad. That son of yours.' She frowns up at me. 'They telephoned for her from her works, to see how she was.'

I don't know why I expected her and Mary Martha to fall into each other's arms but I did. They didn't do this, and I was nonplussed. Disappointed.

Now, the two sisters prowl around each other like a pair of slightly mangy old cats. Nervously I fill embarrassing stretches of silence by suggesting to Mary Martha that she should tell her sister this or that bit of her own story, then telling it myself.

In the end, Ellen Alice breaks into this chatter, shutting me up altogether. 'I expect you're tired, our Mary Martha.' She uses her stick, shiny as a new conker, to help her up onto her feet. 'I'll show you the bedroom, shall I? I got the spare bed ready. Don't normally keep bedding on that. Not since he died.'

Ellen Alice looks at me steadily. 'I expect you want to get on, Mrs Ozanne, ' she says. The she smiles. With her gap-toothed smile she is so very like her sister. 'Thank you for bringing her all this way. She is all right now.'

Now I am confused. 'I'll get Mary Martha's bags from the car,' I mumble.

When I return the sisters are standing surveying

the neat twin beds with pink Bri-Nylon covers. There is contentment in the room.

'This is very nice,' says Mary Martha. 'Isn't it nice, Olivia?'

'I always sleep in the one by the window,' says Ellen Alice. 'And I've left you three drawers in the dressing table Mary Martha.'

'It's all very nice,' says Mary Martha. She puts a hand on my arm. 'Suddenly I am tired, pet. Thank you for this, for getting me here.'

I nod and place her overnight bag on the bed. 'Right,' I say. And I make my way out, duly dismissed.

I drive for a while, not quite knowing whether to laugh or cry. In the last week I have been ditched by the love of my life. My daughter has got rid of me with a sigh of relief. My son seems to be on the verge of prison. And, despite the fact that I have singlehandedly changed the direction, quality and location of Mary Martha's life, I have just been dismissed at the door like a cold caller.

The sparse beauty of countryside only partially alleviates my misery. I finally park beside a country cottage with a *Bed and Breakfast* sign creaking over its door. The brisk young woman in jeans welcomes me despite the lateness of the hour. I accept the offer of an instant cup of tea and ask to use the telephone.

My agent Sally Courtauld is in her office and is sober. 'Darling! I've been trying to reach you. We have a buyer for the Mary Martha story, although the contract for that might be a bit tricky with you going in double harness with the old woman. And they're selling your children's book to France and Germany and Israel, and . . .'

I let her chattering voice flow over me. For once it is balm, honey, pouring over me, healing hurts and sweetening sour corners. I need this today. How I need it.

NINETEEN

The Azeri rug, hanging on the wall in a lifestyle store called Marcon, finally forced on me the decision to take my house off the market once and for all. The shop was more like an aeroplane hangar than a place of business. The rug, hanging there on its bright brass hooks, was woven in reds, purples, ochres and greens which glowed with luminous density in the bright spotlight. It was a dead ringer for the one in Volodya's apartment.

'That rug, I've got to have it,' I said to Janey, who had come with me to choose paint.

'You're mad. We're here for paint, remember? To tart up your utility room so that the house will sell? And we have to be cheerful, that's what you said.' Her voice has an edge to it. We were still not back to what we were, Janey and I.

I stroked a hand down the carpet. 'I've changed my mind,' I said, hardly believing the words emerging from my own mouth. I had been suffering a resounding silence from Moscow. No doubt Volodya was onto bigger and better things. It made sense of course. All those years deciding that compromise, even in love, was the ticket to survival. Why should he cling to the idea of a heavyweight storyteller like me?

That was the rational side of my brain. The other side of my brain still kept me really busy, of course. I kept seeing him in mirrors standing behind me; feeling his hand on me as I lay in the bath; dreaming that we were making love in my sparse bedroom, and waking up to find myself alone.

It was after the most vivid of these dreams that I decided that that was *it* as far as men were concerned. How could I feel like that again? Impossible. To go through that whole thing would make me weary and old. That was when that I cooked up this plan of buying a cottage in the country near Mary Martha. And near my mother, come to think of it. This would, of course, still mean selling the house.

Now in the shop, charged up with money in the bank from the foreign royalties, I faced Janey across the hanging carpet. 'I'm not selling the house. I am buying this carpet to put in it.' I sent Janey for a shop assistant and a trolley and stood with my hand on the carpet, terrified now that someone would come and steal my treasure from under my nose.

The next half-hour was quite insane. We charged around the whole store, up and down the cluttered alleyways, loading item after item on top of the folded rug: copper vases, bright-coloured pottery jugs, swathes of mulberry velvet, carpet cushions, and ersatz oil lamps. After registering her surprise, Janey joined in the fun, holding up items like an auctioneer, to be accepted or rejected by me with my newly emerged intuition for what was *right*. On one stand I pounced on a china clock, made in Taiwan, but bearing a passing resemblance to the mid-nineteenth century French style of Volodya's clock.

A peculiar thing happened to me as the objects piled up on the trolley like items from an Indian bazaar. The chilly, heavy feeling, which had put leaden heels on all my actions since I returned from Moscow, seemed all at once to lighten. The dense colours of the carpet, the glitter of the brass reached out to me in this echoing shop hangar and warmed me. I began to feel so light that I had to cling to the handle of the trolley to stop myself flowing up through the air like Mary Poppins.

Then, as the items were called and clicked through by the checkout girl, who peered through the long curl of hair which fell down the side of her face, I felt in my bag for my purse. It was not there. 'Janey!' I touched her arm. 'I hope you've got your credit card.'

She sighed and reached into her bag. 'How on earth you cope on those escapades of yours, I can't imagine. Moscow? Huh!'

Later, as she helped to heave the rug through the door of my house she said, 'So you're really staying?'

'So it seems.' I wanted her to go now.

She lingered to help me lift the chairs to spread the rug. She tried the ornaments on the shelves and fireplace, snipped price labels off the goods and put them in the waste bin. She looked round the room, now cluttered and colourful. 'This is really marvellous, Olivia, but is it you? It is so different.'

'It's me that's different.'

She hesitated expectantly but I could not confide in her as I would have done once. 'Well, I have to be off,' she said. 'I have phone calls to make and a Yoga class at six.'

'Yes, yes. Well, thanks for the help.' In the old days, after such a jaunt, she would have slobbed out here with me. We would have had a bottle of wine and a Chinese takeaway and have spent the evening making the usual jokes about men and life and confided yet again about the further fringes of our childhood.

I scrambled in the sideboard and found my cheque book. 'How much was it, that bill?' I scribbled the amount and scrawled my signature on it. 'Great of you to leap to the rescue, Janey.' She smiled rather sadly and drifted away.

Now I am sitting here alone in this strange, cosy, cluttered room. At least that cheque won't bounce. Things are looking up a bit again. A writer's money is designed in ebbs and

348

flows. It seems at last there is a bit of a flow. I've had the cheque from Herbert MacIntyre for the fairy stories, with it the promise of a couple of complimentary copies of the book. And there is my half of the contract advance for the Mary Martha book. And there have been unexpected trickles from the Foreign rights for the last children's book.

I could have lived very well in Moscow on all this. And now I have my Azeri rug and my Taiwan French clock. But I will not be going back to Moscow.

The doorbell goes and I leap up, determined to make Janey stay on and have a drink. I've been very ungracious. At this rate I'll end up entirely alone.

But it's not Janey, it's Joseph, his battered helmet in his hand. Behind him his big bike, pulled up onto my drive, is shining in the beam of light from the door. Joseph's face, less gaunt now and somehow less attractive, is grave. He puts a hand on my shoulder.

'What is it?' I say. Of course, it is trouble. I know it is trouble.

'Come and sit down.' He half pushes me into the sitting room. He looks round. 'Blimey! What have you been up to?'

'Do you like it?' I'm trying to keep calm about the trouble. Perhaps the police are on to him again; he is in yet another scrape. But I thought he'd be safe up there now with Ellen. You wouldn't think there was scope up there for anything really bad.

He touches the mulberry velvet, which I have thrown across the sofa. 'Cool. Very retro. Very different.' A small smile flits across his lips. 'The last time I was in here—'

'You were rolling around in here with Janey. I know.' I sit down on the couch and pat the ruffled velvet beside me. 'Now sit down and tell me.'

He sits down and takes my hand in his; his long blunt fingers are stained with nicotine. 'I'm sorry, Ma, but she died. Ellen said I must come and tell you. It wasn't really expected, they said she had been really well but—'

I clutch at him. 'No. No. She just got here; she has to enjoy her time up there. Live the life she couldn't before. Get to know Ellen Alice and young Ellen—'

He is shaking my hand, his grip painfully tight. 'No, it's not the Russian Auntie, Ma. Not Mary Martha. It's Grandma. She died in hospital. Ellen Alice and Mary Martha have been going to see her, you know. Ellen's been driving them across there.'

I disentangle my hand from his, and slide back down on the couch, closing my eyes. My head, my body, my very fingernails seem to be vibrating with relief: relief that it isn't Mary Martha. I feel relief, shaming relief, that Serena Ozanne, that architect of my childish sorrow, that unmitigated tyrant, is dead. I keep my eyes closed tight to veil this shaming relief. Now I hear again her reedy voice telling the story of her own stepmother and how she, the little girl Serena, had been made to go down the garden for the punitive garden sticks.

And for the first time I feel pity for Serena Ozanne - a pity that makes my face swell somehow in its own skin, that melts the lump in my throat and sends relieving floods of tears to my eyes, a torrent drumming in my ears.

Joseph's leather jacket creaks as he puts his arms around me and rocks me backwards and forwards. 'Let it all out, love,' he murmurs in my ear. 'Let it all out.'

This makes me think of Volodya murmuring in my ear and I sob even louder.

'Do you know what I have been thinking about all the way down?' His voice sounds rational, ordinary. So very young.

Muffled by his shoulder I shake my head.

'That scrambled egg she used to make. Terrible watery stuff. Made the toast soggy enough to float off the plate.'

I sniff. 'I didn't know that,' I say, pulling away. 'That the toast was soggy? That she made scrambled egg for you.'

'You didn't know very much those days, Ma. Off on a cloud of your own you were. One minute you were lovely, the next you were not there. You were not there a lot, really.

351

I've been thinking about it lately. Thinking how young you were when you were floundering round then, not quite managing us, and not quite managing Dad, not quite managing Grandma, not quite managing the house. You were not much older than I am now. How would I manage all that? .I'd be into the nearest boozer, at a guess, for consultations.'

I stop crying then, and grab some tissues to scrub every last trace of wet from my face. Joseph relaxes a little, his arms dropping from me. He sits back on the couch. 'Do you know, Ma, this room is very nice. Now I know where I get my artistic streak from. I thought I was a throwback of some kind. Like twins.'

I push my hair back off my face. 'How is the drawing going, then?'

'Churning 'em out, Ma. Not much else to do up there. I've brought a folio, a whole collection of them, down here. Thought I might go into town and hawk them. Might make some dosh. You never know.'

'And how is Ellen?'

He shrugs. 'She's just there. Made me some peaceful space. Got me going again.'

'Do you love her?'

He shrugs again. 'She's good for me, but I don't know that I'm good for her.' He paused. 'Will you go North?'

352

I shake my head. 'My mother can come down here. She lived here the best part of her life. I suppose I can take care of her now that she won't shout me down. Not from the grave.'

Black has never been my colour, so I spend the two days before the funeral making this kind of caftan from the mulberry velvet. It is quite ridiculous but it suits my mood. On the morning of the funeral, it swishes round my calves as I go to the door to receive yet another wreath from the patient florist. There's even one from '*Kendrick, Naomi and Family*'. Fancy that.

The death of Serena Ozanne was in the paper, of course, and since then it seems as though the phone has not stopped ringing. All those people whom she alienated, drove away, have talked to me about their memories of Serena in her finest hour, when she was single-handedly running the MS charity, raising amazing sums for others 'like her husband' who suffered from this dreadful affliction. 'That was of course before she had her . . . illness . . . and buried herself up North.'

The illness made her paranoid, turned her into a hermit. Eventually she fled North to escape those whom she saw as invading her inner space.

Caitlin, to my surprise, sounded devastated on the phone and said she was coming home. I protested that really it wouldn't be expected . . .

Joseph has been wonderful, never away from my side except for one rather fruitful visit to an agent in Covent Garden with his paintings. On three nights he makes me huge pasta meals which he forces me to eat. Each evening we share a bottle of wine and become maudlin together as he tells me more things about his Grandma which I never knew.

I don't tell him about the tyrant, the domestic terrorist, who expiated her own pain on me when I was too young to understand. I understand now but it is too late. Too late for me and for Serena.

The hearse is late. Outside, the light rain damps up the spring shrubs. Janey catches me looking at my watch. 'Don't worry, honey,' she says. 'Any minute now.'

She and Joseph are surprisingly relaxed. Even so, every time I go to the kitchen to rearrange yet again the table of drinks and the trays of food, one of them follows me there, to avoid being alone with the other.

Now suddenly the hall is awash with men wearing black suits and long faces, lifting the wreaths with practised care. I climb into the back car, only taking in the hearse, with its strange burden, with the side of my eye.

To my surprise, there are people outside the church. Ellen runs up to Joseph and hugs him, then turns to me. 'I am so sorry, Olivia. This is sad for you.'

I frown at her. 'Thank you for arranging . . . you know . . . getting her here.'

Behind her are two little old ladies with identical permed hair and identical dark poplin raincoats. It is a second before I recognise Mary Martha, who comes and puts her hands in mine. 'How are you, Olivia?'

I long to ask her why she has cut her beautiful hair and what is wrong with her nice Russian coat, but I merely nod. 'I am fine.'

'These times are hard, I know, love.'

'I am managing, thank you.'

The service is full of the good things Serena Ozanne did for her community, for her church, for her charity organisations. The vicar actually refers to her as a good mother and a good grandmother, guiding her grandchildren down the Way called Straight. I wonder briefly who has told him all this guff, then I realise it was me, talking to this intense young man with his big brown eyes which bled bracing, sufficient sympathy. I did what I can do best. I wove him a tale of the good mother, to keep him happy and satisfied.

Mary Martha and her sister travel with Ellen and

Joseph and me to the cemetery. Ellen Alice comments approvingly on the service and Mary Martha holds my hand. I am surprised at my own disappointment that Caitlin has not managed to get here. She must have taken my admonitions to heart. Sensible really. But I am so disappointed I could cry. But I am utterly frozen as I watch my mother's coffin being lowered into a deep hole made pretty with artificial grass. I look hard in my heart to find the smallest scrap of real grief, a minute crystal of forgiveness. But the corners are dark and there is no feeling there. A sharp squeal of breaks cuts into the sombre words of the vicar, who is talking about Serena Ozanne being made of earth. '. . . and earth she will become!'

He pauses.

I can feel cold air as the people behind me and Joseph make a space. Then Caitlin's gloved hand feels its way along my arm and clutches my hand. Beyond Caitlin looms the bulk of Charles Conrad, his arm close around her. I breathe out, somehow satisfied.

The vicar begins again.

Suddenly I am thanking God, in whom I don't believe, that my son and my daughter are with me, holding me in a loving fashion, sharing, exchanging feeling. Serena's circle is at lsat broken. The pain, at least, is not perpetuated unto this generation. The price of that, of keeping what some people

356

would call an un-motherly distance from my children, has been hard. And it has had an impact on them, making them, for good or ill, the people they are.

At last the business of burial is finished, and there is a palpable relaxation of tension. The formal lines break down and people drift away to a discreet distance, then stop, as though not wanting in the end to leave this woman whom they had all known. Soon they would be saying things about Serena having a good innings, how she had been a tireless worker for charity . . .

Caitlin, her eyes streaming, takes me into her arms. 'I had to come, Ma. I had to. I don't know what's the matter with me. I've been crying my eyes out since I heard. Yet we weren't close. You know we weren't close.'

Joseph puts an arm on her shoulder.

Dry-eyed, I stroke her face. 'You did the right thing, Caitlin.'

I turn to shake Charles's hand. He closes it in both his. 'I am sorry about this, Olivia. I hope I don't intrude. Caitlin'd been in such a state. I had to be in the UK anyway.'

'He's going to Washington,' sniffs Caitlin. 'Prime posting, that is.'

I glance from one to the other. 'I'm trying to get her to come with me,' says Charles ruefully. 'But . . . she's her mother's daughter. Career woman to her fingertips.'

The vicar comes across to shake my hand and smile knowingly as I thank him for an excellent service. I introduce him to Caitlin and Charles, and he shakes their hands too vigorously, saying that he knew them in print. Knew them very well.

At last, with a flap of his black cloak he strides off. Charles takes me by the shoulders and turns me round, away from him. 'And I'm afraid we've brought you another intruder. He was very desperate to come.'

And there he is at the edge of the crowd, a very familiar figure standing between two ancient ladies - this time not the Brown Auntie and the Grey Auntie, but Mary Martha and her sister Ellen Alice.

Mary Martha is clinging to his arm, smiling her gap-toothed grin and gesturing me to come. 'Volodya! Olivia,' she callss. 'Here is our Volodya!'

His hair has been cut, but it still lifts in the wind. He is wearing the old-fashioned suit he wore that night we dined at TrenMos. And his bright eyes, that deep sea blue, are beaming into mine. He holds his hands out to me and I start to run, dodging piles of earth and temporary headstones, fielding the glances of surprise and disapproval. I leap into his arms. We kiss and inside me my blood stops surging. This is right. This is so right. Serena has relented in the end, and brought me something that will melt the ice and warm me now and always.

So there you are. The funeral guests have been - swooped on the food and drink with appropriate appetite, toasted Serena - and gone. Joseph has taken Ellen to stay at his father's house; Caitlin and Charles have gone back up to town to dine and hopefully to sleep together, before he goes on to Washington tomorrow. (I don't know whether that relationship has a future, but its present looks quite satisfactory, thank you very much . . .) Mary Martha and Ellen Alice are tucked up in exhausted sleep in my spare bedroom.

And here I am, sitting on the Azeri rug beside the fire in my cluttered sitting-room now lit by seven candles. I can hear Volodya's feet padding down the stairs, and he comes in, his white skin gleaming in the candlelight. He sits down beside me and pulls me quite roughly into his arms. His lips touch my ear. 'And here we are again, Olivia Ozanne. Making love by candle-light with two venerable ladies sleeping innocently just a few feet away.' His fingers trace the contours of my face. 'But this time for all time. No ending. No finishing.'

'No lies about beautiful Americans wom4n? ' I turn and kiss him, reminding myself of those grape-soft lips.

We relax then and lean against the sofa. 'This room,' he says. 'It is very nice. But it is not what I thought.'

'You know where this room started?' I say. I feel him shake his head.

'This room started one day outside the Oktoberskaya Metro Station. On the flower stall. When you decided to advise me about the roses.'

Ends

ABOUT THE AUTHOR

A story teller from childhood and after writing and publishing while relishing and surviving academic life Wendy Robertson became a full-time writer. She has published twenty-four novels (both historical and contemporary), two short story collections and she continues to write occasional articles on issues close to her heart. And she loves writing her blog *A Life Twice Tasted*.

She lives in historic South Durham, in a Victorian house that has played a role in more than one of her novels. She was for five years on and off Writer in Residence at HMP Low Newton – a life-changing experience where she encouraged a wide range of women to raise their self-esteem and realise their potential through original writing.

She says: 'The past-in-the-present dominates my mind, my imagination and my writing. I always *'see'* individuals, unique characters in their times whether in history or the contemporary world. And I tell their stories. My novels are mostly set in some crosspiece of time and place. The unique, sometimes quirky lives of my characters reflect the wide range of people I've come to know very well in my life.

She goes on, 'I have been a compulsive writer since I was eight and have lived through interesting times. *Anais Nin* once said that writers taste life twice, once when they experience it and secondly when they write it. This so very much reflected my own writing experience that I actually named my blog *Life Twice Tasted...*'

www.lifetwicetasted.blogspot.co.uk

OTHER BOOKS BY WENDY ROBERTSON:

The Romancer:

A Practical Guide to Writing Fiction

Dreamers, optimists, visionaries, enthusiasts, escapists.'
Wendy Robertson declares that all writers are 'Romancers'.

'(This book*) gives a rare glimpse of what it's like to be inside
the process of writing - the exact moment when the events of a
writer's life become the fabric of fiction.'*
Kathleen Jones

*'A moving and compelling exploration of the links between a
writer's life and her work. The Romancer should appeal to
readers and writers alike.* 'Pat Barker

*'More than just a memoir, this is a masterclass on the writing
process.'* Sharon Griffiths.

This book explores the way memory and dreaming - alongside
conscious and unconscious memory - have flourished at the
roots of Wendy Robertson's fiction.

In these pages aspiring and experienced writers will find
writing processes and practical approaches – including
Wendy's *Forty Day Plan* for writing a novel – to re-imagine
their own lives, inspire their fiction and develop their writing
to the point of success.

Paulie's Web

Inspired by Wendy Robertson's experience in prison,, *Paulie's Web* distils the tragedies, comedies and ironies of women's lives not just behind bars but out in society. The charismatic Paulie Smith - rebel, ex-teacher and emerging writer - comes out of prison after serving six years. . In the next few days she relished her freedom but struggles to readjust to the scary realities of life 'on the out'.

Important for her readjustment are Paulie's reflections on her life in prison. Her mind goes back to her first few weeks inside when she lived alongside the four very different women whom she first met in the white van on their way to their first prison.

Paulie's thoughts move from Queenie, the old bag- lady who sees giants and angels, to Maritza who has disguised her pain with an ultra-conventional life, to Lilah, the spoiled apple of her mother's eye, to the tragedy of Christine - the one with the real scars out and inside.

And then there is Paulie herself, serving the longest sentence despite having done no more wrong than being her own woman.

The unique stories of these women, past and present, mingle as Paulie - free now after six years - goes looking for Queenie, Maritza, Lilah and Christine, who have now been 'on the out' for some years and are - Paulie hopes - remaking their lives.

364

Cruelty Games

Rachel, an idealistic young teacher, tries to make changes in the lives of her tough pupils. The school – tough as it is – is a haven for Rachel's pupil Ian Sobell, whose mother neglects him and whose grandmother abuses him.

One of Rachel's adventurous projects leads her class to a place where, hundreds of years before, a boy hung for days in a gibbet until he died in agony: a punishment for the murder of his employers children.

Events on this day have a disastrous impact on the lives of both Rachel and Ian: a shock which lasts nearly two decades before they both move on to some kind of resolution, triggered by Rachel meeting Ian again after sixteen years.

'This novel was inspired by my experience teaching in schools where i worked with pupils like Ian who soldiered on under great difficulty, walking the line between violence and normalcy every day. i also know that their desperation and stress is often mirrored in the plight of good, sensitive teachers who have to deal with the ambiguity of children who may be seen as evil.'

Wendy Robertson

365